HAPPY TALK

A NOVEL BY RICHARD MELO

RED LEMONADE
A CURSOR PUBLISHING COMMUNITY
BROOKLYN, NY

Copyright © 2013 by Richard Melo.

Book Design by Luke Gerwe
Cover by Goodloe Byron
Copyediting by Nora Nussbaum

Printed in the United States of America

Red Lemonade
a Cursor publishing community
Brooklyn, New York

www.redlemona.de

ISBN 978-1-935869-17-7

Distributed by Publishers Group West

Library of Congress Control Number: 2012930690

10 9 8 7 6 5 4 3 2 1

For Les Paul, whose 'Lover (When You're Near Me)' inspired the novel's many moods.

Tonite

Dry ice fog rolls in from the wings of the stage, accompanied by a piano jazz vamp and murmurs of the backstage chorus ready to take places. Down in the pit, side players fill in the slinky, thumping rhythm. A follow spot hits the stage front and center. From behind a dark curtain, a man steps out 'in one.' He's tuxedo'd in a top hat and black Inverness cape, smiling like a pleasant rogue and conjuring a dark Peter Pan atmosphere.

He taps the floor with his white-tipped cane, then tosses it in the air where it disappears into a blaze of flash powder. Two plastic bouquets suddenly appear in his opposite glov'd hand. He glides to the foot of the lights and hands the flowers to ladies seated in the front row orchestra. Their eyes turning back to the stage, the spectators see he now has a new cane in his hand. He tips his hat and proclaims:

—Gentlemen and Ladies, tonite we present you Haiti, the New World island nation early Spanish explorers mistook for Japan, the West Indies Isle of Wonder where the marvelous is as commonplace as mountaintops. The democratic state where riderless horses gallop alongside your jeep, where donkey trains stretch for miles around the hairpin twists of peaks that rise to great heights directly from the sea, where a ghostly regatta of boats with colorful sails swelling in the wind lines the horizon. A state where you open your eyes to see a human skeleton crouched in a giant birdcage left in the shade of a tall palm, and nobody but nobody is saying a word about it. Where the sounds of cocks crowing and ringing church bells fill the air, and at dawn, when all becomes silence, you can still hear the voudoun drumming.

Haiti is a country of illusions, false perceptions, hallucinations, and exaggerations, where marble statues open their eyes and turtles fall off the top bunk and onto your bed. Haiti is a land of five hundred salt shakers and not one that works. Tonite, we bring you a school of young nurses and glamorous beaches; a ghostly drumbeat and the good folk it reaches; a film crew of playwrights, lechers, and leeches; hair-raising zombis and so-pleased-to-meet-cha's; a diplomat corps fraying its breeches; Chiqui' bananas and Caroline peaches, all presented to you amid the pastoral settings of the Nord Department.

Raise the curtain now, bons amis, on tonite's play!

Fast Is My Name
(1955, -53)

Over and over, the top sheets hover in a billowing arc above the two neat lines of dormitory beds. Forty young Nightingales, our girls in white, yank at them; yet it's as if the sheets would rather hang in the air than fall. A nursing student named Samantha Sound pounds her fist into the center of a sheet's bulging dome, and it begins to fall slowly like bread dough. Others follow suit, and the falling sheets create a light wind with a taste of bleach and quicklime. For those who have been at this a while, it's the scent of a well tended sickroom, airy and clean, two qualities rare to Haiti but as common as day and night at the St. Marc American School for Nurses.

—I don't know whether you heard, Culprit Clutch is coming back.

 —I sure as heck don't remember anyone with a name like that.

 —Culprit Clutch, that has to be the by-Goddest name I ever heard.

 —Name like that makes him sound like a tough in a moody western.

 —Sounds more like a vaudeville villain.

 —For my own tastes, I like the type of names they use in musical theatre. Why can't he be called Curly Cupid, for instance.

 —Sure, and why can't we all be Rockettes?

 —I have to wonder what ol' Culprit's up to. I thought he was through with us last time.

 —I wish it wasn't true.

 —He's coming back, and hearts will break all over the place, that's what the cards say, though not mine.

 —I didn't know you practice fortune-telling.

 —I do.

—How about astrology?

—My sign is Gemini.

—Jiminy Crickets!

—No.

—Shhh.

—Who needs men.

Miss Penny from Texarkana, the only student the others call miss, once spent a restless night dreaming through the motions of making beds. She dreamed over and over of the sheet falling listless and flat across the bed top until the one time when the sheet fell over the bulky form of someone sleeping. She peeked underneath to find no one there. It was just her imagination.

—I'm not sure what's more dull, making my bed or spending every night in it alone, says Cynthia who's notorious because of the leopard-print silk brassiere she wears beneath her nurse's smock.

—I like my sheets tucked in so tight it takes two people to pull them back, the way hotel maids make them back home.

—Beds are made to be seen and not slept in. I wish there were a way to sleep under the covers without disturbing them. (That's Ruthie for you, always adding her two cents without making any sense. You can tell by that look on her face, almost like she's going to sneeze, that here comes another canny insight.) —Not to mention, it's bad luck to watch someone sleeping.

—We're the only ones who ever get to see our beds, since company is not allowed to set foot in here.

—Company is fine. It's the opposite sex that's forbidden.

—That's the rule.

—To hell with rules. Rules are for the birds.

—No one is here to penalize us for breaking them. The head nurse has run off again.

—How many is that now?

—Miss Beatriz? I was awful fond of her.

—Beatriz is gone, and again, we are left to our own devices not to mention our vices.

—Why don't we ransack the secret wine cellar?

—There's still wine down there?

—There's wine?

—St. Marc's used to be a seminary. There seems to be an endless supply of wine in the cellar. Then again, it's only drunk after we chase off another head nurse.

—That's only half the time.

—No one tells me anything.

—We'll keep it a secret, just between us.

—Cat's out of the bag. Everybody knows!

—Except for our company, and we never have company.

—We'd have company if people knew about the wine.

—If men were allowed to set foot in here.

—The moody Culprit Clutch, hero of the High Sierra, is on his high horse coming back, tell me, what do you all think about that?

—Ask me again after I polish off my first glass!

Nadine is so tall that many of the girls would swear they only come up to her knees. Lucky for her, St. Marc's has high ceilings and doorjambs that fit her just right. Nadine has naturally curling hair she wears pulled back tight. If she should ever let it down, it would poof in all directions and take all the space in the room, and there would be nowhere for anyone to sit. Her hair is blonde indoors and red in the sun, and the humidity brings out the curls, and in Haiti, it's humid all the time. She has freckles so dark you'd swear they were painted on. She's so good at everything and the kind of person, all told, you'd believe she can do anything she sets her mind to.

She pours her heart into playing guitar and singing her own soft-spoken versions of the hit parade. When she sings, it sounds like crying, her voice hitting the notes at the top of her register at once, full breath'd yet light, and this is supposed to be such a bouncy tune! Nadine can be so darn tough when she wants to be, and so tall, but her voice breaks your heart, gives you goosebumps. Like the humidity, it curls your hair, though never quite like hers.

> Pacific island blue
> With sand set all aglow
> Let's see what waves are like
> Off tiny Bikin' Atoll
> Until next time, let's make nice
> Until next time, kiss me in peace.
>
> You won't know 'til you try
> To go and find the orange lagoon
> It's not there no more
> Been blast up to the moon
> Until next time, please stay you
> Until next time, what will we do?

The song winds down with an arpeggio and comes to rest with a lone chord played slowly until fading. You know she's finished not because she's stopped playing, but rather from an abracadabra wave of her hand. It cuts through the air and breaks us out of our trance. The murmur of the spectators gives way to applause and bravoes, we like your singing so much, Nadine; we're so very lucky to have you here with us; more, more!

—I'd like to sing like that, but I can't hit a note.

—When I hear her, I cry. I can't help myself.

—Thank you, Nadine, for the song.

JILL

There we all were, half us girls plastered and crying our hearts out at her beautiful voice and the sober girls never did figure out why this was, and what do you know? Some of them were

crying, too. Nadine's voice is just like that, uplifting, you
know, in a way that brings out the tears.

—Is he a doctor?

—Who, Culprit Clutch? No.

—At least not a doctor in the way you'd ordinarily think of a doctor.

—A shrink?

—Not even close.

—A witch doctor. (No, I'm kidding!)

—A doctor of divinity?

—Bite your tonugue.

—A priest?

—Mcrry Christmas, guess again.

—I know. He's Santy Claus.

—She's pulling your leg. She's pulling all your legs. Culprit Clutch was
a patient here.

—We don't take patients.

—I thought of him rather as an *impatient*.

—He was an *impatient*, because he couldn't wait to get the girls taking
off their heels. That's a figure of speech, since no one actually brought heels
to Haiti.

—Cynthia brought rollers.

—That's different.

—As for what Culprit was, he was nothing.

—That's not a very nice thing to say.

—He was gallant, I always thought. He saw himself a modern-day Don
Juan. While he might have had half the girls fooled, the other half wanted
him murdered.

—Don Juan, my eye. He had all the charm of a buzzard.

—Girls seemed to like him, sure beats me why.

—I thought he looked like Flat Top in Dick Tracy comics.

—He had bad skin, deep pockmarks from childhood acne.

—He was Peter Lorre in platform shoes.

—He had a lumpy head his hair couldn't hide.

—He was a Cro-Magnon Man, though not as hairy.

—He's still so far away that his face is a blur.

—That's so funny. I'm just the opposite. Since he's not here, I can see him perfectly.

—The last time he was here, did anyone think to take his picture?

—If I had a camera, I could have found better pictures to take. A photograph of my thumb would be ten times as darling.

—Who needed pictures of Culprit Clutch? I thought he'd never leave!

—Even if we had foreseen him leaving so suddenly, no one could have foreseen him coming back, now, so out of the blue. My fortune-telling cards didn't say one damn thing about that!

—Belinda Ballard, do you know what I've been drinking tonight? Wine!

—I was wondering why everyone's lips were red. Jill's lips are so red they're purple.

—Oh, gee.

—Now you know. It's from red wine. Let's pour you a glass.

—You need a glass more than anyone else.

—Where did the wine come from?

—There's plenty more in the secret cellar.

—The school was a seminary, before the Vatican made it a gift to President Roosevelt.

—The old Jesuits left the wine.

—Bless their hearts.

—It's not all they left.

—Do we know if this is vesper wine?

—What do you mean?

—Was it blessed?

—What difference does it make? I'm not Catholic.

—If it's blessed, it's not wine. It's the Blood of Christ. Before getting tipsy, I'd like to know.

—Would you like to place a person-to-person call to the Pope?

—No.

Later that evening, they drag their weary selves to their beds in neat rows on the second floor of the dormitory hall, more ready than ever for the Land of Nod, only to discover their beds recently slept in, not by them.

—Who's been sleeping here?

—We were all downstairs.

—Not only are the beds still warm, they have been hastily remade, and not the way we like to make them, tight.

—You let your imagination run away with you.

—No one's slept in your bed.

—But it's warm to the touch.

—It's a warm night.

—There's a bowl-shaped indentation on the pillow.

—It's always been there. That's from you sleeping with your head there every night.

—The sheets and blanket have come untucked.

—Do you know who did that?

—Who?

—Time did that, Ruthie says.

—What?

—Time. Think of Rome and all those marble monuments lying in ruins. Time did that. Time causes everything to fall apart. Time causes beds to come unmade.

—Gee, I only made it this morning, we all made ours this morning, and nothing like this has ever happened before. I just know I won't sleep a wink tonight.

The summer nights are so hot and humid that for the Nightingales, it hardly feels like sleep. They toss and turn and awaken with their white sheets stained yellow-brown where their bodies had lain. If they look more closely, they find mosquito carcasses embedded between the weaves of the linens. They can wash their sheets until the cows come home and not get rid of the dead mosquitoes unless they pluck them with tweezers. Girls like Jill and Nora do just that.

—It's bad enough that they won't send us home, but at least they could send new linen.

JILL

My uncle heard voices, and finally they sent him to the tee-hee farm. I thought it might run in the family, so I have been reluctant to tell anyone I see people who aren't there. Three people walk into the room, and I see four. Moments pass before I realize that there is a silent being no one else can see, the one not speaking, the one who's slightly see through. I don't feel like I've lost my mind. The others don't need to know about this. With the night jasmine as pungent as it is, and my hay fever so bad that my wheezing keeps the girls awake, it doesn't seem out of the ordinary that I keep checking the window, to make sure that it's shut. The real reason is to see if anyone is out there, real or imaginary. I half expect to see Culprit Clutch, since he's coming back; it's all anyone can talk about. My heart stops when I see Miss Penny, who is supposed to be asleep two beds over from me. Learn something every day: Miss Penny is a sleepwalker. Seeing her out in the yard like that scared the bejesus out of me.

NORA

Jill peeks out the window so often that I picked up the habit. She seems to see more than the rest of us. She's smarter than the rest of us. Mostly I was curious to look for whatever it is she sees. Last night, the citrus trees were in covered in white blossoms. This morning, it rained heavily and shook the blossoms loose. It looks like it's snowed. The snow outside takes me somewhere else, it takes me home. It's Christmastime, Central Park. I know it's not, but I will let myself have the illusion for as long as I can before letting common sense take over. Too late.

The Nightingales gather the next morning at the breakfast table.

—Was it the clap that brought Culprit Clutch around here the last time?

—It would make sense, a man like that.

—He fell into a tree.

—You mean, he fell out of a tree?

—No, silly! He fell into a tree. What he fell out of was an airplane.

—Are you sure about that? That would have finished him off!

—His parachute caught up in the branches.

—The reason he came here, or rather the reason we brought him here, on a stretcher, mind you, was so he could recoup from all his bad breaks.

—The human body has 206 bones. That's how many Culprit had before he fell. After getting caught in the tree, then falling the rest of the way to the ground without his parachute, he might have had twice that many.

—Oh, my!

—Don't worry about Culprit Clutch. He healed in the blink of an eye.

—If you ask me, he was a malingerer who liked the attention of all the pretty girls. He was a pest who wore out his welcome. He might have fallen from that tree on purpose.

—The only reason he stuck around as long as he did was because there weren't any doctors around to tell us when to take off his casts and bandages.

—That doesn't sound like it was his fault.

—There was a faction of girls who wanted to keep him bound in plaster for as long as they could, God knows why.

—I always thought he had his heart in the right place. If he truly was a malingerer, he'd still be here, don't you think, hey Janet?

—Nope.

—Can we talk about something else?

They pause while considering what next to say.

—It's changed so much in my two years here, Dinah says.

—Like they say, these are the good old days.

—It used to be back in 1953, you'd hardly ever hear planes in the sky; nowadays, you hear Piper Cubs buzzing about every afternoon. It used to be if you heard a plane, you'd think the Americans are invading again and hope they don't drop their bombs on us.

—The nerve of Washington, sending in Marines without telling us first, without evacuating us first.

—My most powerful memory of Culprit's skywriting is all the girls craning their necks, watching his plane, not daring to take their eyes off it for a second.

—I wasn't watching the plane. When the sky is blue, I am always looking up. I like the blue sky.

—Me, I was dying from suspense, wondering what that little plane would write. The letters take so long to form. I can remember now everything else that happened except what the message was.

—SURRENDER DOROTHY.

—That's from *Wizard of Oz*, you silly girl!

—It was something about *Cat on a Hot Tin Roof* playing at the American cinema.

—Nah, that's an advertisement you've seen posted on trees.

—Culprit wrote the words, LOOK DOWN.

—I'm glad you were able to read it. It looked like Japanese to me.

—Are you sure it wasn't, LOOK OUT BELOW? Since he was about to fall out.

—Yes, I remember very well what he wrote because it was so very strange.

—LOOK DOWN. What does that mean?

—I wonder if it's because when a skywriter is in the air, the tendency for everyone is to look up. It's natural for the skywriter's slogan to be LOOK DOWN to balance everything out.

—So what happened to him?

—He crashed his plane because he was drunk off Canopus 13.

—He didn't really crash. The plane flew out to sea without him on automatic pilot.

—How do you know so much about skywriting?

—My daddy's a flyer, and even now he does skywriting every year in Peoria just before the Fourth of July parade.

—I heard the winds got to him. Getting caught in a cross wind is enough to rattle even flying aces, and Haiti has some of the worst winds in the world.

—How do you know that?

—Climb with me up to the Citadelle, and you'll see for yourself, and bring a kite.

BELINDA BALLARD

Culprit won't have to look far. I didn't want to say anything around the other girls, but I have been under these types of circumstances before. When push comes to shove, I know just what to do to win over a man's heart. During my time at college, the boys all thought I was a knock-out, and grown men used to fall all over themselves to say hello to me. There was even a time when an old professor told me that I was bewitching, and isn't that the strangest compliment you ever heard! Especially when you consider it was coming from a married man. Sigh. If your Culprit Clutch is anything like that old professor of mine, all the rest of those girls may as well call it a day.

•

1953. P.F.C. B.J. Roper-Melo is the lone, lost Marine from the 1st
Guadalcanal Division, a self-exiled holdover from a bygone American invasion
of Haiti, maintaining his post, casting a watchful eye, mindful of any danger to
American interests inflicted in the Haitian theatre.

There is a saying among Haitians that all Americans look alike, and
here in the Nord Department, Roper-Melo is the only American many of
the outskirt characters have ever seen. Yet in the eyes of other Americans, the
P.F.C. bears little resemblance to the Modern American Man. Roper-Melo's
style of mustache, a throwback to the days of the War Between the States,
gives him the look of a Scottish Terrier. He casts the air of the type of younger
man who seems like an older man, while it is just as possible that he is the type
of older man who seems like a younger man who seems old.

His vigilant surveillance of the sky over Cap Haitien leads him to witness
firsthand the skywriter's distress.

Following the parachute as it plunges from the sky, Roper-Melo high
steps over uneven ground, leaping across short crevasses and dry stream beds,
climbing piles of jagged rock, and throwing himself down the other side, all in
the name of rescuing the fallen flying ace.

Culprit Clutch's parachute catches in a tall tree. The unconscious and
remarkably unbroken pilot dangles by his shoulders from the parachute's
cords. The P.F.C. unsheathes his machete and scales the tree.

In perhaps not the best of rescue plans, he begins to hack away at the
cords keeping Culprit Clutch from falling to the rocky ground like a heavy
sack of bones.

The angels are ringing their little bells. Behind a white, semi-transparent
curtain, they circle his bed, ghostly apparitions, more like convent sisters clad
in white than small-town American girls in Haiti learning to become nurses.
Angels or not, it is all the same to him. He cannot feel his body, but he feels his

heartbeat, his heart pushing to maintain blood flow through so many swollen extremities. The beat itself is loud enough to wake the dead in the next room over, if only there were dead in the next room over.

A switch is thrown and a lamp casts its scorching light down on him; it is so bright that he can see the skin pores on his arms, his hair follicles, blotches from the sun, blotches of unknown origin. It is stage lighting, although these were the physical traits you would never want to show off on stage.

With scissors, the Nightingales snip away at the last of his trousers, his undershirt, careful not to cut him, fat chance he would feel it anyway. They photograph him without clothes, hands propping his broken body in various positions to get the shots they need. They poke their fingers under his ribs, feeling for cancer, not that they know what cancer feels like any more than what a kidney feels like, but figuring that as long as they have him here, they should check him for cancer.

All the while, one student nurse holds his hand. They are wearing masks and hats and look the same to him. He can neither tell whose hands are whose nor whose hand is holding his. He thinks it is that one there, but then again, it couldn't be, because she walks away, and the hand is still holding his.

They find a blotch and cut off a piece of mottled skin. (—We ought to have that checked.) They snip a fragment of muscle. (—Let's get that checked, too; we can send it out with the other samples and film.) There is one last bodily sample they need. They roll him over, and a Nightingale sticks a long needle into the base of his spine and draws the milky fluid out. (—If there is anything wrong with you, anything, we'll find out what it is.)

—You've come all the way to Haiti, and you still get the best medical care in the world, the same exact care you'd get back home in the U.S.A. We've run a battery of tests on you, and we'll send your samples back to Washington, and when they write back and tell us what's wrong with you, we'll know how to treat you.

—In the meantime, we'll set your bones in a plaster cast. It looks like you broke a few.

He's unable to reply, nod, or even open his eyes. They can't be sure he's listening.

—Samantha Sound says you have 400 bones when 206 are all you need.

—Which bones does Samantha say are broken?

—I think it's fair to say they all are, or pretty close.

—Let's set even the unbroken ones for good measure.

—Poor thing, let's at least give him morphine.

—Shhh.

—Why? I know the protocol is only to administer morphine to dying soldiers in the field of battle, but since we are at peace, and he probably feels like he's dying, it's fair to give him a few cc's.

—We're out of morphine.

—How can we be out of morphine?

—This is a nursing school, not a dispensary. Who do you think we are? We never practice on live patients.

—What do we have here then? Chopped liver?

—Opal, what happened to the morphine?

—I get a headache every month, and morphine is the only way to kill the pain.

—But we had so much.

—Sometimes, the headaches come more than once a month.

—What should we tell our friend here?

—Tell him I'm not the only girl around here who gets a headache.

—Why don't you explain it to him yourself.

—Consider yourself lucky you're not a woman, mister.

—Miss Penny has gone to get doctors Millidieu and Bast. They'll know what to do.

Every two hours a pair of Nightingales come to check on Culprit Clutch. At daybreak, they bring him a bowl of cereal, spoon feed him, and wipe his chin. The cereal is too hot; she blows across the top to cool it down. Her breath smells like cinnamon. It might be the cereal.

They scooch him one way, then the other, changing his sheets without moving him out of bed. They brush against him, lean into him. He loves them all, and even more since he can't tell them apart. Even their voices sound the same, as do the things they say. Take any one of them, and before long you'll see only her flaws. Take them all, and you have the perfect woman.

Over time, they come to check in on him less often. His vital signs are always the same. They leave him alone at night, knowing his bedpan can wait for morning, and that as long as the windows are closed, flies won't come in the room.

SAMANTHA SOUND

These are the good old days, now that Culprit is here, and I sleep so much better knowing there is a man in the house, even if it's a man in such condition.

PEGGY JEAN

A fine figure of a man he makes, encased in full-body plaster across all but his eyes and mouth, his arms and legs elevated and dangling from straps. He looks like he's bouncing off his bottom like a rubber ball.

—What is that expression Sally had for him?
—Comically infirm.
—Comic is always better than chronic.

The doctors, Bast, Millidieu, and Hockey, come to see him once he's patched up.
—Serves you right, Ace, taking a plane up without learning how to fly ahead of time, says Doctor Millidieu.

—I think Mr. Clutch did an admirable job of flying. He even wrote words in broad pen strokes across the sky, Samantha Sound says. —His penmanship is very neat.

—Better than his flying, that's for sure, Doctor Hockey says.

—That's nothing. Let's see him try skywriting in the creyol, I bet he can't spell anything in the creyol, Doctor Millidieu says.

—The pain must be killing him, says Gwen whose sense of Culprit's pain is due to the orange aura surrounding him that only she can see. (—If I can take his pain on myself, she says under her breath, —I would do so, which is more than these other so-called Nightingales can say.)

—He actually feels much better than you or me right now, Doctor Hockey says.

—Even with all those cracked up bones?

—Morphine is good medicine and will take care of him fine for the next few days until the worst of the swelling goes down. (Doctor Hockey leans in over Culprit and adds, —You're lucky to be getting morphine. Protocol says you need to be dying.)

The bat-wing doors of the examination room are swinging. The three doctors are gone, back to sipping cocktails by the swimming pool at their swanky hotel in Le Cap.

—You didn't tell them.

—Tell them what?

—That there is no morphine.

—Of course not, do you think I'm stupid?

—What's the worst that can happen if the doctors find out? They send you home. Isn't that what we all want?

—They could send me to Diego Garcia.

—Sounds more exotic than this place.

—It's an atomic graveyard.

—What was in the shot they gave him?

—Simple sugar syrup.

—Poor Culprit! You'll have to tough it out for a few more days, my love, she shouts to him, patting him on the chest and acting as if the wires keeping his jaw shut affect his hearing.

Down the stairs and to the left, through an open door and long hallway, Sonia finds a small gathering of Nightingales in the Great Room just as they hear knocking at the door. It is a strong rat-a-tat-tat-tat, a pause, and then another.

They pull the door open to find a man standing there. He is dressed all in black with a white shirt, a tuxedo it turns out, with a tail and a cane and his hat is in his hand pressed against his chest.

—He must be hungry.

(This is how they talk, as if he wasn't there.)

—He looks hungry something awful.

—What are we having tonight, what is Henry Greathead preparing for us?

—Chicken and rice pilaf.

They take his hand and guide him through their school toward the dining room where they seat him and tie a napkin around his neck.

—Bring him a drumstick and thigh.

—Henry Greathead is a wonderful cook.

—What is Henry supposed to be anyway?

—He's our butler.

—That doesn't make any sense. We're not rich, and this is not an estate or plantation.

—He can't be our butler because we never receive visitors.

—He's our pastry chef.

—Don't you wish!

—He prepares our meals. That's good enough for me.

—I'm glad he's here.

—I didn't say I wasn't.

—You must really meet Henry Greathead, Samantha Sound says to the stranger. —I think the two of you will get along famously.

—I'll tell you what Henry Greathead is if you promise to keep a secret, Hedy whispers to their Haitian visitor. —He's a spy.

—You think everyone is a spy.

—Henry Greathead really is a spy, no lie!

—That's the most ridiculous thing I ever heard.

—Who's he spying on? Us?

—Them! She points at the wall as to indicate she means the people who live on the other side of the wall. For a moment, it's as if the wall turns transparent, and she can see right through it, the dense thicket, the glowing eyes of small nocturnal creatures stacked on top of each other.

—There's nobody out there.

—When it looks like nobody is out there, the Communists are out there. That's why they are so dangerous.

—If Henry Greathead was sent to spy on Communists, why is he always here?

—He's not here now.

—That doesn't make him a spy.

Upstairs, the Nightingales on the evening shift do rounds, meaning they pay Culprit a visit and leave just in time to pay him another visit. They bring him aspirin and change his bedpan. They smell their supper downstairs and decide to call it a day.

—Do you want your light on or off?

He gives no indication. His jaw is wired shut, and his extremities are encased in plaster.

—Off it goes then.

Once the light goes off, it sends the message to others that he's sleeping, and sleep is what's best for him, don't you dare turn on a light and wake him up. We should all go downstairs and let him sleep.

—Help me.

No one hears him.

—Help me.

No one hears him.

1955. There goes Miss Penny again, asleep, eyelids bandying about like Peter Cottontail. Now awake, she squeals as she speaks, telling everyone about her dream of finding a bed with the sheets and blankets missing. In the dream, she looks around and finds the bedding crumpled on the floor with a squirming beast beneath it. She can't tell by its form whether the animal is a turtle or a pig, but it turns out to be a hen, or rather hens, because there are two of them, or four, or more. There are so many hens under the covers fallen by the side of the bed that when she lifts the sheet, feathers fly everywhere.

—I'm not surprised Culprit Clutch is coming back.

—Neither am I, really.

—You would think that foolish man would be long forgotten by now.

—His name never comes up.

—I dreamed about him a few nights ago, that he was here, but then I forgot, until the murmurs began.

—You're lucky. I never remember my dreams. I wonder if he's been in mine, too.

—I've also been thinking I've seen him around, people who look like him.

—Who? The doctors?

—I'm not sure.

—Tourists? Diplomats?

—I don't know.

—There's no one else here but us chickens.

—Maybe you're thinking of those bums who live at that filthy camp and sleep in a supply truck. At least they are American.

—One is a Swede.

—What's their game, does anyone know?

—They're a bunch of Useless Bums.

—That's not a nice thing to say.

—It's what they call themselves, it's their name!

—I never!

—They have nothing to do. They were sent here by the United Nations as a movie crew. They have a supply truck filled with raw film stock and motion picture projection equipment, just no camera or movie reels to show.

—That band of rats? I thought they were deserters from the French Foreign Legion. A movie crew, you say? They'll let just about anyone make a movie these days.

—I think you'll find this interesting: Culprit Clutch has been appointed as the man in charge of the moviemaker squad.

—I stopped eating eggs after cracking one open and finding a chick very dead inside, Ruthie says. —It made me into one of those people without a taste for meat.

—I have some questions for the new head nurse, Miss What's-Her-Name.

—Miss Beatriz?

—Where have you been?

—Good luck finding her. That dame didn't last two days.

—What happened this time?

—Upstart Annette waved a gun in her face and told her to scram.

—She never even had a chance to unpack!

—Where on earth did Annette get a gun?

—It's just a cap gun left on the beach by some Italian kid.

—I personally think Annette was there on the beach, waiting until that kid wasn't looking, so she could swipe it.

—Why would Annette want a gun in the first place?

—Upstart Annette, she was a regular gunslinger back home, comes from Denver.

—Have you never fired a gun? There's nothing quite like it.

—Why would Annette go through all that trouble to steal a toy gun?

—Drawing a gun is a way to get people to listen to what you have to say.

—Who doesn't listen to Annette?

—The doctors.

—The doctors are a piece of work.

—You would think they would care about other people more than themselves, but not our men.

—There's something in Haiti that makes doctors go that way.

NORA

With neither doctors nor full nurses around last time he was here, we were responsible for Culprit's care, and we had no idea what to do. All's we've learned about nursing so far is that we don't need an understanding of the human body as much as we need to know how to follow orders and make a bed. There's no one here giving us orders to follow, and no one's bed to make but our own.

We were the ones who had saved Culprit. We were the ones who found him crumpled on the ground and who carried him back to the St. Marc school on an improvised stretcher made from a bed-sheet. We were the ones who set his broken and unbroken bones in plaster. We were the ones who spoon-fed him applesauce and held the glass for him while he sipped milkshakes from a straw. We were the ones who changed his bedpan, which comes with the territory though it was not what we expected when we signed up for this. We kept his morphine drip flowing, which would have been more effective if only morphine were dripping from it, but we didn't know then that someone had replaced the infirmary's morphine supply with sugarcane water.

The only order the doctors gave us was to wire his jaw shut, and they left it at that.

1953. They bring him a vase of flowers, hibiscus. They open his window to let in air and sunlight. They come in six at a time to lift him, while a seventh pulls off his bed sheet and fits a fresh one across the top of his mattress. He burps occasionally, and the student nurses, who for all their endless studying of the Chicago nursing manual from 1939 had never cared for a live patient before, reach in unison to wipe his mouth.

They show him kindness, and he is in love with one of them. The problem is he can't tell them apart.

Not everything is Caroline peaches. There comes a look in their eyes that spells out disaster. While they seem sweet, these girls conceal the balled up energy of the mighty atom. Pushing their buttons would bring about doomsday. A born dissenter, Culprit recognizes this look though doesn't have a name for it. *Unrest* is the best he can come up with.

Nothing hurts more than when he laughs. His jaw crudely wired shut, his laughing causes the apparatus to dig into his cheek. So he stifles his laughter. He isn't laughing at the unrest lurking inside the Nightingales' character. He appreciates them for it. The one he loves, he loves even more for it. What makes him laugh is that unrest is not the top quality you want from a nurse-in-training. Unrest doesn't nurse a sick patient back to health. His laughter is because no one had told them that. Tears stream down his eyes and his laughter doesn't last long because the pain is excruciating.

Good rest will heal you best.

Healing best takes good rest.

Their last patient was dead when he arrived, a cadaver sent to St. Marc's from the medical school at the University of Florida in Gainesville. The body had belonged to a middle-aged man, a heavy smoker, overweight, as profoundly unappealing in death as he had been in life. As ugly as he was on the outside, his insides were worse. In particular, the soot lining his lungs.

—I'll have to remember this the next time I want a cigarette.

—Remember, just as God is inside of us, cleanliness should be, too.

—This man reminds me of the pictures of the poor Japanese souls burned by the atomic bomb, only this is what the outside of their bodies looked like.

It is a scene that had repeated countless times in the history of medicine. There are the squeamish who faint, the ones who let tears fall, and the ones who can't wait to sink their hands into an open cut and pull something out of the belly, a heap of spaghetti, and who would swear it's steaming though the body has long gone cold.

—Try to guess what this is.

Two buffalo head nickels glued together.

—Guess again, it's a joy buzzer. It still works (as she demonstrates).

—How did that end up in this man's internal cavity?

—My scientific opinion is that he was an amateur magician, and this was part of a trick.

—Either that or someone who didn't like the joke stuffed it down his throat.

—My, what an odd thing to find inside someone!

—Do you think the joy buzzer was the cause of death?

—There is white makeup behind his ear.

—This man was a clown.

—You would think they would give a corpse a really good cleaning before sending him out to students, I swear.

—What do you think they should do, boil him?

—I think a sponge bath would be fine.

—I just saw his arm move.

—Impossible!

—You mean like this?

—Yes.

—That was me.

—You know, after all the lectures, the textbooks, and the slideshows preparing us to see the inside of a human body, it's still not what I expected. It all goes back to when I was a little girl and the bad dreams I had, probably from growing up with two brothers, but this is not what I expected to see. I was terrified when Hedy made that first cut down the length of the man's chest that all my childhood fears were coming true.

—What were you expecting?

—I'm so embarassed, please don't make me say.

—What were you expecting?

—Spiders, Miss Penny sighs.

Samantha Sound and Dinah pay Culprit a visit in his room.

—Watch his eyes, they follow my every move, Samantha Sound says.

—I can see that, says Dinah, while taking Culprit's pulse.

—It's the uniform, he's curious about my uniform.

—I'm not so sure it's the uniform he's looking at, dear.

—He is, look at him.

—He's a man, silly! Men don't concern themselves with the odds and ends of a nurse's uniform. Men concern themselves with the odds and ends of young girls.

—It's like they say back home: What can be more restful and pleasing to a patient than the sight of a nurse dressed in white? Samantha asks. She then spins herself around to give Culprit a full view of the uniform, the twirl of her skirt barely coming up off her knees. She then addresses Culprit with a formal air, —The crisp white uniform and cap are symbols of nursing the world over. White is very becoming to most women and altogether a comfortable and pleasing attire.

—Culprit Clutch, I know you can hear me in there! Dinah says, knocking on the plaster casing covering the patient's ear. —You stop looking at that girl like that!

Samantha is not wearing an apron but pantomimes the motion of tying one around her waist. —When a nurse performs a duty that might quickly soil her uniform, it is proper to wear a white coverall apron. I'm not wearing one now because we are only here to check your vital signs. If I were changing your bedpan, that's a different story. It's important to keep the uniform clean and fresh at all times. You can see my uniform is made of Indianhead, butcher's linen, and muslin.

—We are done here, Samantha. You can finish Culprit's lesson another time.

—You just shush, Culprit wants to hear this. Now where was I? The sleeves of my uniform are long and have turnover cuffs. There is also a little turnover collar, only slightly starched. Some girls prefer a stiff, linen collar, but it's uncomfortable and you'll never catch me in one of those.

Dinah gently pulls Samantha by the arm, in an attempt to drag her out of the room, but Samantha shakes her arm loose and steps beside Culprit.

—The correct and most becoming way to wear the cap is far back on the head, with the sides pinned to the hair, if necessary, underneath the ends of the turnover brim, she says. —That is so darling, the way he looks at me!

—Let's leave Culprit be, so he can get some sleep.

—If it's chilly, I wear a sack coat made of white duck with a waistcoat to match, and a negligee shirt underneath is cozy.

—Turn out the light when you leave, please, Dinah says as she leaves the room.

—We're not supposed to wear lipstick, though that doesn't stop some of us girls. I just don't know what I would do if I couldn't keep my lips on. Earrings, necklaces, and ornaments of every kind should be avoided. You can see the holes where my ears were pierced have healed right up. Looks like I won't be wearing earrings until I go home. Dinah!

The other nurse reappears at the door, startled by Samantha's cry.

—Something funny is going on, Samantha says.

Culprit is experiencing rapid, shallow breathing.

Methodically, Dinah opens a drawer and pulls out a paper sack. She puts her fist inside the sack to open it, then places it over Culprit's mouth and nose. Moments later, Culprit's breathing returns to normal. Lights are turned off and he is left alone for the night.

—Did you hear, Samantha Sound performed a burlesque number for Culprit?

—She did no such thing. She was explaining the practicality of the uniform.

—Samantha is a sweet, little country gal, wholesome as milk.

—Her act nearly gave Culprit a heart attack.

—Samantha is not the reason why Culprit lost his breath.

—What are you saying happened?

—Samantha said there was a frog jumping under Culprit's sheets.

—Did she see the frog?

—No she just saw the bouncing under the sheet.

—I hate to say this. That was no frog.

—Culprit's arms and legs are in traction. What else could it have been?

—If it was a frog, then why didn't Samantha pull the sheet back and shoo him away? I will tell you why. She was afraid of what she might see.

This is why the Nightingales are here, this is why they are Nightingales, to learn about the human body, to learn the nursing profession, to detach themselves from any ties that become personal, and lastly, to treat with utter indifference any matter that becomes, God forbid, sexual, tamp it down, tamp it right down.

Lying on a blanket on the courtyard lawn kept so neat and trim by M. Budé, a few of the girls chew their pencils while trying to think about how to describe it in their composition books, how to explain what happens to Culprit Clutch beneath his sheet.

—It's a phenomenon, one of them writes.

The next day, it is happening again, the phenomenon, and Cynthia goes so far as to pull back the sheet and gown to show everyone exactly what it is poking up from the area of Culprit's lap.

—Don't touch it!

—Don't be such a prude, Cynthia snaps back.

—We haven't read the chapters yet about venereal disease. Don't touch it.

—Venerical chimerical.

—You'll want to wash your hand after touching that.

—Of course, I'll wash my hand. I'll even use an antiseptic.

—If you touch it when it's like that, I don't think you can call yourself a virgin anymore.

—Don't be silly, Cynthia replies, drawing nervous laughter from the others. —That all depends on whether I'm the one touching it, or if it's the one touching me. She then raises her voice so she can be heard over the shrieks of laughter, —Sweetie, it's been a long time now since I thought of myself as a virgin.

—Don't worry, Culprit, Samantha Sound whispers in his ear. I won't let her handle sharp instruments while she's inspecting you that way.

Bold as can be, Cynthia reaches forth and finds instantly that her grip has too much traction to get a feel adequate to satisfy her scientific curiosity. She dabs her fingers in a jar of petroleum jelly, then smears it over the phenomenon. It's cold and it causes a contraction that runs throughout Culprit's lower body. The Nightingales all look down and take note of it in their composition books.

She rubs it in, the petroleum jelly allows her to feel the phenomenon more deeply. She bends it, tugs it, jerks it from side to side, while her classmates look on, many in horror, others rapt, pausing only to write down what they are seeing and in some cases, make sketches. She lets it fall and sees it settle to one side. She has experimented enough to answer a burning question she had always had on the nature of the erect male penis.

—There's not a bone in it, after all.

The crowd releases a sigh. Some are glad she's finished, and others are glad because they were just now wondering the same thing.

—You could have just read the chapter to find that out.

—Is there cartilage?

—Shark cartilage, says Ruthie. She doesn't know why she said that but it makes all the other girls laugh.

—There might be cartilage, Cynthia says, but she's done for today and not about to reach across him for a second time in front of all the girls. —The answer to that question will have to wait for another time.

It will not happen again, but the way that the Nightingales and Culprit Clutch relate to each other is never the same.

Gathering around him to administer an exam, one of the girls leans over him in such a way that her breast grazes him. It sets off another chain reaction, and his catheter pops off.

—Hey, get a load of this. He's doing that trick again!

—Rounds will be much more interesting for now on.

—I will never be able to look at him in the same way.

Since Culprit is unable to speak or express himself through other means, forward-thinking Nightingales get a kick out of making his sheet rise below his belly, like bread dough. It's a way they could make him show them that he wasn't dying, that he appreciated their care.

—I think he does that catheter trick on purpose because he likes when I put it back.

It pops off again.

—I can see why nurses love their job! Back home while I was growing up, I always heard about how filthy the human body is, but I disagree. I could do this sort of thing every day. We need more patients to practice on.

—Samantha, I really think you ought to wash your hand now.

—I think we should all wash our hands.

At a long row of basins, they are able to wash up at the same time.

•

A strange breeze washes over them. Imagination carries them away. The air blowing in from the open window doesn't feel like Haiti. It's warm and dry, a desert breeze, and sends them to the Desert of Arabia where there's nothing, save an oasis over here, a mirage over there, camels and magic carpets, men in turbans with beards and a gaze that can cut you in two, and they drink wine, just like the Nightingales. The nights are warm, and the wine never seems to run out. That's the mood the breeze carries.

—Arabia is so mysterious.

—It just makes me think of the time my moron brother slashed up his hands after boxing with a cactus. No gloves.

—Shh, don't ruin the mood.

—Our daddies are all sultans.

—Mine's a sheikh.

—Shh.

—We are the Daughters of Babylon, and I can turn myself into a belly dancer and turn all our good-looking dark strangers into sheep.

—Do any of you girls remember the Evening Aires? They're a musical group back home, and they sing this one song I like so much.

—I know the Evening Aires, but it's not one of their melodies I'm hearing.

—What is it?

—Snake charmer music. We've left Haiti. This place must be Morocco.

—It's just like being there, Polly Jean says, her eyes closed. —I can feel the sand between my toes and lips tasting like wine. I hear chimes blown by a breeze, a breeze you don't feel, all I feel is the warm evening air. The camel is tied to a post.

—You foolish girl!

—Tonight I'll dream of a sheikh with rings on every finger, wire rim sunglasses so dark you don't see his eyes. Look at his eyes and see yourself reflected back to you on his glasses. It doesn't mean he isn't looking at you and giving you the look, you know the look I'm talking about.

—You mean this? Nora says, making a funny face.

—His eyes are fixed on me, and the two of us won't need a camel to go for a ride.

—He has a secret he's keeping from you. No, it's not that he's not married. He's got a book stashed in the sleeve of his robe; he likes to read. He sneaks a page or two when no one's looking.

—What's he reading?

—*Dracula.*

—Are there countries in the world where the desert meets the ocean, on one side you have rolling dunes, and the other an empty beach?

—I think California is like that.

—Nah, in California, you have a million people and nearly as many oil rigs in between the desert and the beach. I'm wondering about a place more uninhabited.

—I don't know.

—Maybe more uninhibited is what you mean.

There is a sign over the entrance of the dormitory of the St. Marc school that reads, MEN FORBIDDEN. The sign doesn't stop the Wandering Egyptian who perhaps knows no English.

—A man?

—A phantom.

—There's no such thing!

—How do you know?

—Because if there were phantoms, we'd all have heard about them by now.

—Who has never heard of phantoms?

—How do you know the Wandering Egyptian is a phantom?

—Our phantom is an Egyptian?

—What would a live Egyptian be doing here?

—Why would he be here if he's a ghost?

—How do you know it's not all a dream?

—I just saw him in the flesh. Do I look like I'm dreaming?

—What makes you think the phantom is an Egyptian?

—The headdress, the braided beard. He's straight out of one of the funny drawings on the walls of the mummy's tomb.

—This couldn't be any more strange.

—It could be a joke. Not everyone has seen him.

—That's because he's not here. These walls, this embroidered tapestry, the bookcase, they are real objects, nobody's imagination. The phantom is just a figment.

—I'd like to agree with you, that this is a tasteless prank, but I've seen him, too.

—Stop trying to scare people.

—How do you know he's real just by seeing him? Did you touch him?

—Heck, no! He's not wearing much, and his skin is rubbed in oil.

—He smells of sandalwood.

—Strange!

—It's the wine, gone to your head.

—What does he want out of us?

—What do we want out of him?

—Look at how you're blushing! I know what's on your mind, missy!

When Jill leaves the others, she neither doubts the reports nor hopes to confirm them. She has all but forgotten the talk of him when she rounds a corner and finds herself face to face with the Wandering Egyptian. She sidesteps around him to her left, he steps around her to the right. They note everything they can about each other, and then she doubles back to where the girls are gathered.

—He was smaller than I thought and darker, Jill reports.

—The school is haunted. I can think of so many phantoms who might haunt this place, priests, slaves, witch doctors, American G.I.s. An Egyptian is not the phantom I would imagine.

—Who were you expecting?

—Napoleon Bonaparte.

—Where is he now?

—I just saw him outside the kitchen.

—For Pete's sake, he is imaginary! How many times do I have to tell you?

—He's in the dining room, having a bowl of Henry Greathead's chicken soup.

—The whole infernal island is haunted!

—What about the Dominican side?

—I've never been there. Maybe it's just Haiti that's haunted.

Nora walks back in the room. —He's gone, she says.

—What do you mean he's gone?

—He's nowhere to be found.

—How can he be gone when he never was here?

—I'll ask next time I see him.

Jill is the type who sneaks out of the house only when she knows she won't get caught. Yet another head nurse has been run off, so there is no one to catch her, and the other Nightingales are too tipsy from the wine to notice Jill's gone missing.

Nor do they notice Nora is missing (for she leaves with Jill) and that the flashlight and spare bulbs and batteries are not in their proper place.

—When you said bring bulbs, I thought you meant tulips, Nora whispers.

—Shh!

—I was kidding, golly!

They walk in the dark down the narrow road that leads toward Le Cap, their path littered with debris and rotten fruit. They don't need the flashlight as their eyes adjust. It isn't all dark and foul. At times, they meander along a lane illuminated by rows of kerosene lamps hanging from the trees and made pleasant by the aroma of coffee beans roasting.

After a while, they know they are getting close. The drums are nearer, and they can smell the smoke of the fire. Jill is the one who has been reading about voudoun, wanting to see it for herself, wanting to see if magic is involved. By day, she'd seen traces, clearings in the scrub where there's corn flour spilled on the ground, their strange hieroglyphics.

They hide behind a bank of shrubs peeking through the spaces between the leaves. The fire is on the other side along with the drummers and dancers.

—It is Africa, after all.

—What is?

—Haiti.

Nora has no idea what Jill is talking about.

—It's just like in *National Geographic*, but no magazine makes sounds like this, how strange everything smells, and the odd dances.

—They aren't exactly trained by Arthur Murray, Nora whispers.

—I don't even think it's beautiful, but the way it brings everyone to life is magnificent.

—I wonder, what's the point?

—It's a congregation, they're calling forth a spirit, a Loa, and the question is who will the spirit mount. It could be anyone, a man, woman, or child.

Then it happens. An old woman seated near the fire flies from her chair. It is if she has taken a wallop on the back, thrusting her chest cavity forward while the rest of her body catches up. An object shoots out of her mouth like cannon fire.

—Yuck, she spit out her gum.

—That wasn't gum. Those were her teeth.

The woman regains her composure, and it is as if she wasn't herself anymore. She is not in possession of her faculties. A spirit is in possession of her.

—Erzulie takes her, Jill says, narrating the scene.

—Erzulie who? Nora asks.

—Shhh, Jill replies, then breaks her own silence, —I read all about this.

The old woman dances about, leaving Nora to wonder if she was secretly a younger woman wearing stage make-up to age herself and fool everyone. Her old bones and decaying muscles, the skin hanging off the bone and her ankles, knees, and elbows all so swollen, her body worn out by years of hard work, it is unbelievable seeing her now, the life and energy left in the old dame, and for Jill, there is no other explanation than that they are witnessing magic. The old woman twirls her skirt, her arms and legs moving with abandon to the drummers' rhythm. She dances faster and faster, a twirl, a spin, a leap in the air.

—We're lucky this doesn't happen to us, Nora says.

—I wouldn't mind.

Nora rolls her eyes.

—This doesn't happen to Americans, Jill says.

—Thank God.

The drumming stops, and the woman collapses on the ground. The men prop her up against a younger woman's knees, and they hold her arms up over her head while her body convulses then becomes still. She is still alive, though her dancing has left her worse for wear.

—I swear I saw a cloud fly out of the top of her head, but it was so fast I can't be sure.

—I don't like all this hocus-pocus, Jill. Please let's go home.

Tonite's sensational entertainer in black top hat and Inverness cape sets the birdcage down on the table. As he drops a cloth over the top of it, the cloth falls flat across the tabletop. The cage vanishes, but what becomes of the bird? The entertainer opens his white glov'd hands and a dove flies out. Maybe, just maybe, he had been holding the dove in his hand all along and Culprit hadn't noticed because the bird and gloves blended together. There is more Culprit had not noticed. The entertainer is a giant. He hadn't seemed so tall when he was far away, but it is now too late because the entertainer towers over him and drops a cloth down upon him. It's uncomfortable, it's suffocating, and Culprit struggles to get out from under it. When he does, he finds himself behind bars.

He's looking out from inside a damn, human-sized birdcage, and all he can hear are the voices of the Nightingales.

—I hope you didn't use up the penicillin supply, too. This man is burning up.

—Let's give him a shot.

—Let's draw him a cool bath.

—Not with him in all that plaster. Cold rags will have to do.

When the fever breaks and the hallucinations subside, Culprit is left with a feeling of physical well-being, just like being in love.

In the doctors' absence, it is a quorum of Nightingales who decide it is time to remove Culprit's casts on the chance that his bones have already healed. They use sharp blades and small saws to cut away the plaster casts that cover his arms and shoulders. His muscles have withered away so much over the last several weeks, his skin hangs loosely over bone.

—At least your bones seem strong, even if you're not.

—Your wrists seem fine, and the neck brace, we only put that on for good measure, but your legs took the worst of it, and those casts must stay on!

—The good news is we can roll you around in a wheelchair.

—We can wheel you to the kitchen, and you can drink a cup of coffee with me.

—We've become accustomed to taking care of you.

—It'll be a shame when it's time for you to go.

Culprit lifts his arms in the air to stretch them out. He extends them out like wings. He splays the fingers on both hands, and an instant later he doesn't know what his right hand is doing. Nor does he want to know. His left hand reaches down to pull up one girl's skirt, and the right hand slaps the left hand before it goes too far. All's he knows is he is in love with one of them. He thinks he will know when he sees her.

There appears at the door a ghostlike apparition, a young woman like the others, but in a denim skirt and wash blouse.

One of the uniformed Nightingales attending to him grips her index finger and thumb on Culprit's chin and turns his head away from the girl at the door. She pokes a long hypodermic needle into his cheek.

—That's Novocaine. It will numb you before we remove the apparatus from your jaw.

Minutes later, the contraption is removed, and he tries to speak but his mouth is too numb to move. Like a ventriloquist he manages to get words out without moving his mouth.

—I can speak, he says and the Nightingales cheer.

His next vocalizations sound less like human language as he can't feel his tongue. The cheers are replaced by fear as one or two of the girls wonder if their Culprit had suffered a stroke unknown to them.

The feeling comes back and Culprit's voice is found, —My jaw was one of the bones that was never broken, he says. —I've been trying to tell you that.

—I would have thought your first words might have been thank you.

—There's still swelling. Maybe we should put the apparatus back on you.

—No, don't please.

—You may need it.

—The apparatus is what's causing the swelling, thank you very much.

—So this is what he's like, our darling Culprit Clutch, an ingrate, Samantha Sound whispers to the others.

—Culprit, I'm so glad we can have conversations with you now. You're lucky we didn't lose you. You could have died from that fall. You could have survived the fall, then died when we brought you here.

—We lost Nurse Pisgah.

—We didn't lose her while she was here.

—Nurse Pisgah was headstrong. She was the only head nurse we couldn't chase away. She not only took everything we dished her way, it all went to make her stronger. In the end, it was illness that drove her back to the U.S.

—It says everything that she didn't think we could nurse her back to health.

—Her cancer was so bad, she was beyond nursing. All's there was left for her to do was die. She wanted her family near. I am not going to begrudge her that.

—That funny smell, it was her breasts rotting, both of them. All the perfume she used to wear, the smell cut right through it, a horrifying smell.

—I liked that old dame.

—It wouldn't surprise me if she were dead already, no one's heard from her.

Culprit wants to change the subject. He turns to the Nightingale holding his hand and asks, —How did a nice girl like you wind up in a place like this?

—I was booted out of the WAC.

—How about you?

—I came up with my best friend from my hometown. It was our dream to do this together, meet our husbands together, and settle down in homes right next to each other. She's not here anymore.

—What happened to her?

—They shipped her out to Diego Garcia. It's more inhospitable than Haiti.

—No place is more inhospitable than Haiti.

—It's an atoll in the Indian Ocean.

—In the hot atomic zone.

—I've seen the Meneer Bros. filmstrip and know better than ever to want to go there.

—Do you know the Meneer Bros.? You'll meet them soon enough.

—How long have you been nurses?

—Culprit, dear, there are no nurses here, only students. We are all equals. No one's in charge.

—Am I the only patient?

—You are our first and only patient.

—Who was that earlier? I saw someone at the door.

—Did you? That was no one.

—That's Josie. She's a student like us, though it's been ages since she's put on the uniform. She has headaches, and oh, brother, are her headaches ever our headaches!

—I want to meet her.

—Oh, brother.

—She's sick. Doctors think she might have a brain tumor, although all she ever complains of are her headaches. If it is a brain tumor, it doesn't explain why she's fine some of the time. Brain tumors don't just dry up and come back, dry up and come back.

—We haven't read the chapter yet on brain tumors.

—Don't get any ideas about her, Culprit. She won't like you anyway. She prefers the company of Haitians.

—I'm not shocked that she would be the one you like. The doctors like her, too.

—There's something about that one.

—I'll never understand all you men chasing after a wretched little number like that.

—I don't know anything about her.

—Don't bother with her, Culprit. You know what they say about her.

—She has a needle habit, and by that, I don't mean sewing.

—Nor is it a habit like sisters wear.

—None of us likes shots, on either the giving or receiving end, but shots are a regular part of the nurse's day.

—Josie likes shots.

—We're not talking about the polio vaccine. We're talking about morphine.

—The school ran out of morphine a year ago.

—It's why she hangs out with Haitians.

—I don't believe it.

—She was talking about morphine all the time. I only thought she was fascinated by it.

—Josie likes giving shots to herself.

—The day we practiced giving shots, she was the only one who wouldn't look away.

—When we found out she was one of the ones skimming the school's morphine and taking it herself, she said it was medicine for her nightmares, whatever that means.

—Her headaches. I get headaches, too. I don't know what Josie has to complain about!

Yet there she is again, Josie so ghostly back in the room standing right behind them. They flinch when they see her. Josie acts like she hadn't heard anything they said, and the others act like they hadn't said anything.

The other Nightingales parting around her, Culprit takes his first long look at Josie.

She is what the government would call a student nurse of the standard issue. She's slim, and her chestnut hair, she wears up in a bun. Culprit sees more to her than that. She is a green-eyed Jenny fair, a whisper of a girl in her skirt and blouse. She casts an air of self-confidence missing in the other girls. The Nightingales have no idea what they are doing here, but Josie gives the impression that she knows and is content. From seeing her, he can hardly tell there is anything wrong with her.

—Pleased to meet you, Culprit said, extending his hand to Josie.

She gives him her hand. It falls into his and goes limp. Her hand is cold to the touch. On impulse, he wants to keep her hand, rub it to warm it up, resuscitate her, but instead he takes it, shakes it, and gives it right back.

Without a word, she turns and leaves the room.

—There is really something wrong with her, P.J. whispers in his ear.

Confident she is out of earshot, the Nightingales resume their conversation about her.

—I've lost count of the times I've seen her riding around in that topless red car with those outskirt characters. She wears a mauve scarf and dark sunglasses, a lighted cigarette in her hand, and the men she is with are all as dark as midnight.

—One of them works at the dispensary, which is how she gets her dope.

—She told me her headaches started a year or two before she came to

Haiti. They come on all the time and make it so bad that there are times when she cannot drag herself out of bed.

—While the rest of us students were in lecture or lab or studying, she would go lie down in a dark room in the infirmary wing and curse to high heaven anyone who would come to check on her.

—I'm afraid she's lost her mind.

—She's started talking about herself as if she were somebody else.

—That's what happens when a headache takes hold.

—Don't bother with her, Culprit. You'll find yourself a nice girl. You'll do better.

The endless days spent uselessly taking each other's blood pressure and pulse give way to a period of flopping down on the Great Room sofa, drinking wine before dark, and smocks left unbuttoned at the top, all a play for the wheelchair-bound Culprit's attention. Girls who don't even like him want Culprit to like them best.

He only has eyes for, of all people, Josie, and she's never there, and when she is, she walks around listless with red rings around her eyes.

Culprit sees her again on Saturday afternoon, this time down in the kitchen where the others had wheeled him so he could keep them company. He sees how Josie's hand shakes when she holds her cup of coffee. He offers to pour her a second cup. She hands it to him, her hand brushing against his, and it emits a soft shock.

They wheel him back to his bedroom that evening, put him to bed, draw his blinds, turn off the light, and carry on their tipsy conversation in the hall right outside his room.

—Has anyone noticed we spend less time out of uniform? I always look forward to nighttime, because when I wear my nightgown, I feel more like myself. All day long, I feel so pent up.

—The uniform doesn't stop some of us.

—I still can't believe the way you examined him that one time.

—I wish I had been there.

—It was nothing.

—So what was it like?

—Culprit lists to port.

—Oh, you are awful.

—What are you two laughing about?

—Shh!

Culprit wakes up restless in the middle of the night. He drops his pillows and blankets to the floor and leverages himself to drop from the bed. Lucky for him, none of the sleeping Nightingales hear the thud of his plaster legs dropping to the floor.

He crawls to his wheelchair in the corner of the room. He pulls himself up and into the chair, rolls to the counter, strikes a match and sets his kerosene lamp aglow. Rolling from counter to table to cabinet to drawer, he searches madly for a saw or pair of scissors, any tool he can find to free his legs from his casts.

He rolls his way out of his room and into the hall and outside the door of another room, which he opens. There's Josie, lying in her sickbed, a candle beside her, a rag across her forehead, her eyes focused on him. He lurches forward and backward in awkward circular motion until he arrives at her bedside.

—Do you know where I might find scissors?

—She's not listening to you.

—I'm only looking for scissors.

—Ask someone else. She's not here.

—Where is she?

—Away.

—Josie, right?

—She doesn't want to see you right now.

—Tell her I'm not around. I'm only looking for some scissors.

•

1955. The flight is bumpy, so much so that the pilot thinks it best to land the airplane before its final destination, Jamaica. It makes no matter how they try to shift around passengers and their luggage, asking them midflight to lean one way or the other, the wing'd crate won't fly straight. The plane lands in Haiti's north country, near Le Cap, along a seasonal riverbed that is, for the moment, dry.

The student nurses hanging their laundry on lines see it all and follow the forest trails downhill toward where the plane must have crash landed, although there is no crash sound. The pilot is outside the plane already, and it takes no time to discover the source of the plane's bumpy ride. There is a plane hopper along for the flight, hanging on to a tailfin. He is quite cold; frozen actually; stiff, they say; and stuck in the same death grip that kept him from slipping off the plane and into the Atlantic.

—He's alive and in need of nursing care.

—Good luck, there are no true nurses in this part of Haiti.

—We Nightingales will have to do.

They take his pulse, count his breaths, wrap the strap of the blood pressure instrument around his arm.

He speaks, —You'll get you a stick of gum, if you mend me socks, he says, smacking the gum he's already chewing.

—You're British, by golly, how I do so admire your accent! I am such an Anglophile!

LYDIA

It was true enough, his socks were in dire need of mending. The wind hitting the plane not only knocked the plimsolls right off his little English feet but also unraveled his stockings, pulling out threads for what may be a mile. He did manage to keep a packet of chewing gum tucked neatly in the vest pocket

of his windcheater. It's the type of gum you can't get in the
States, let alone the West Indies. I can mend those socks. I'll
take him up on his offer of a chewing gum stick.

—I'll do your mending and darn them while I'm at it.

—They are so darling, his purple socks.

—He's not listening to you. I don't think he can hear.

He approaches shrubs to see what's behind them.

—Must be all that air flowing into his ears. He'll hear again soon.

—Beware of the plane hopper, Dinah says in an ominous tone.

—Is he a criminal?

—A spy!

—See that holster beneath his jacket. He's trying to hide it, but I saw it
nonetheless.

—You read too many spy novels.

—Shh, he's coming back.

As if he had overheard their concerns, he takes the jacket off. The black
straps across his chest are holding a camera, which he pulls out, and begins
taking photographs of the passengers and bystanders.

—Hey, mister! You're missing your plimsolls, and I got your socks for
you right here! What do you say? Rule Britannia!

—Will you look at that? He dropped a book.

—A spy book, no doubt.

—Give me that. *Why Not Try God?* by Mary Pickford. What business
does a regular sort of fellow like that have reading a book like this?

—Hey, will you take a look inside. It's filled with radio diagrams.

—That ain't Mary Pickford's writing.

—See, I told you he's in the spider biz.

—I'm glad, because otherwise I would have some questions for that man.
Reading a book like that, I swear!

•

It's the secret that Culprit is keeping from the Nightingales, that his legs are now free. The legs feel fine but his knees hurt like hell. They're stiff from all that time encased in plaster. His other secret is that he's escaping, sayonara sisters, *c'est tout*! One good night's sleep, and he's gone, vamoosed. The door's locked, the Nightingales locked him in, so when he goes, it'll be through the window.

Sleep won't come easy. Maybe it's the Haitian jazz playing on a radio somewhere within earshot of his window. Maybe it's Josie on the other side of the sickroom wall. She isn't well, he knows that. Their previous interchange was odd. It doesn't put a damper on his desire. He cannot leave without seeing her again.

With his door locked, the wall is the closest he can get to her, the wall with an ecclesiastical face, a depiction of Mary with a most Italian countenance. He takes the painting down, it's in the way. He rubs his hand against the wall. The texture of the wall doesn't feel like wallpaper as he runs his fingers over it. Expecting to feel nothing other than the wall, instead he feels her, though dimly; the signal's weak.

She feels him, too, and rolls from her bed onto the floor. She crawls toward the wall adorned by acoustic tiles with their pinhole pricks. She presses her hand against it, just opposite his. The electricity that flows between them doesn't come as a shock. It flows to their hips, and broadcasts itself low and center.

They press their bodies against the wall and their hips will not hold still. It's all they can do to keep their souls from wriggling loose from their bodies, their thumping against the wall makes the windowpanes rattle in a slow jazz rhythm, syncopating with the song that's playing on the radio.

The wall buckles, and a lightning-shaped crack creeps across the ceiling. Powdered plaster drops from above. Culprit is surging with strength. His door is locked, he's not the type to bust through doors, he cannot see her face to face. His knees don't hurt. He hurls himself out his open window and into the limbs of the tree outside. All he can do is flee.

1955. —Do you think they've forgotten about us?

—Who?

—Washington.

—Why do you think that?

—They never sent a new head nurse.

—That's not all they forgot.

—What else?

—They forgot to send me home.

—What makes you so special?

—My final semester was supposed to have ended months ago. There's no head nurse to end it. The doctors never came to administer our exams. I've had enough. I want to go home.

—I think there's more to it than they've just forgotten us.

—Then why are we still here?

—They're planning a sneak attack on the Russians, and they know the Russians will strike back with all their might and main. They are keeping us offshore so they can load us onto planes and fly us back to the mainland the moment after an American city has been hit.

—I believe it.

—I say we all desert. When they come looking, we'll be long gone.

—The door's open.

—What do you mean?

—I mean, you can go. We all can.

—If I leave now, I might not ever get to see Culprit Clutch.

—Today, it's Culprit Clutch. Tomorrow, you'll think up another reason to stay.

—Sweetie, it's like I've been saying all along, he's not that wonderful.

—I say let's stay and work through it ourselves. We can govern ourselves.

—Who will teach us about nursing?

—They tell us we need to know how to follow doctors' orders, but really there's nothing more to it than making beds. All that fiddling doctors do doesn't help.

—That's right, in time the body heals itself, and a well-made bed helps it heal. Clean linens and fresh air work wonders.

—I don't mind staying as long as they want us to stay. I only want to know how long.

—Go ask Doctor Bast. He's in the kitchen.

—What's he doing there?

—Eating.

—He brought us a new head nurse?

—No.

—Why is he really here?

—He looks like a maniac, and you'd never believe what he was eating.

—What?

—I'm not going to say what it was, but you or I would never dream of eating what he's eating without removing the feathers first.

—He ate the casaba bread, too. Every last crumb.

—We had enough bread to feed forty girls.

—He came in and pretended that he wasn't hungry, that all he was looking for was a snack, but after he started to eat, he ate everything in sight. The cupboards are empty.

—See, this is exactly what I am talking about. They treat us like second-class citizens. 'Hungry? Let's go to the St. Marc school and eat all the students' food. Those Nightingales, they weren't going to eat it anyway.'

—'Those girls don't need to eat.'

—He didn't touch the spinach.

—I can't eat that.

—Why not?

—Too salty.

—Then more for us! Spinach is the best bone builder.

—We all need a little salt in our blood.

—Death has a salty taste, same as tears.

—We come from the sea.

—Do I ever have a surprise for you!

—You know I can't stand surprises.

—Carla and Dorie were down in the cellar looking for more wine.

—Are we running out?

—No, but what they found were rifles, crate after crate of guns. Bullets, too, just the right size.

—Has anyone told Annette?

—Upstart Annette?

—She was the first person they told. She said that all the guns were American made, probably surplus from the First World War, though I don't know if that matters. They fire just the same.

—Annette says it's all right to talk about the guns among ourselves but to keep it quiet to the outside world. She says that if the outside world finds out we have them, they will come and take them away by force, and that we should take up arms and protect ourselves.

—Oh, dear!

—Have you never fired a gun before?

—Never. Have you?

—My brothers used to take me to the firing range. Every so often I would fire off a round.

—What does it feel like?

—You feel such force flowing through your body, it feels like the gun becomes part of you. It's loud, it shows you mean business. It makes you feel nine feet tall with muscles this big. It makes it so you can see better, nothing will escape your attention. All your senses are keen with a gun in your hand.

—I can't wait!

—Let's just wait for Doctor Bast to leave, and then we'll find a spot in the middle of nowhere where no one can hear us.

—It shouldn't be hard. All of Haiti is the middle of nowhere.

JILL

The discovery of the guns elevates Upstart Annette to the role of ringleader. Marcy is her Number 2. When Marcy is around Annette, she starts acting like Annette. It's like having two Annettes when one Annette is all we need, and both are armed to the teeth.

—To stage a coup, you have to start somewhere, says Upstart Annette, cradling a rifle in her arms. —We may as well start with these.

—What about Doctor Bast?

—Gone.

—Shot dead?

—He went back to the hotel. He's bored around here.

—The government won't answer our questions. They won't let us know when our business here will be through. They won't send us a boat to take us home. My message to them is, fine, we'll stay, but on our own conditions. If they want us, they can come get us.

Annette puts on a tin bucket helmet found in another crate alongside the cache of weapons. She's ready to wander the jungles of Haiti, rocky and sparse as they are, looking for evidence of the U.S. Government and its outposts and not knowing where to look. She looks in the sky. She pokes the surface of the water with her bayonet. In the stream, all you see is your own face in the ripples. Who am I trying to fool? she asks herself.

NORA

Outside, the drumming never pauses, and now you hear cracking in the distance. It's less rhythmic than chaotic, at least to me it is. It's the girls at a makeshift firing range, taking

target practice. Wonder of wonders, let's just hope no one
gets hurt.

—Keep yourself on this side of the line, Chihuahua. We have some poor marksmen in our ranks. Cross that line and risk getting yourself shot, and no one here's been trained yet on treating gunshot wounds.

They practice marching in formation, like they've seen in parades. They storm the hillside, fox crawl in the lowlands with black grease paint dabbed underneath their eyes. Their white training uniforms, once so delicately laundered, become filthy and ragged, not that they care. The further from white their garment, the harder it will be for their enemies to spot them in the brush. They train each day, because soon their day will come.

In the room with the low ceiling, they smack their gum and blow bubbles to hide their dirty faces. They will stage a revolt, just as soon as the enemy commanding officer shows the whites of his eyes.

—His eyes? We've decided already that the enemy is a he?

—Yes, ma'am.

—Why is everyone so angry?

—I am sick and tired of Josie getting all the perks. I get headaches, too, and I still make it to class every day.

—She should be made to sleep here in the dormitory, just like the rest of us.

—All the doctors are sweet on her.

—When they come visit, it's only to see her.

—She gets away with murder.

There's a commotion on the other side of the room by the door. Nightingales left and right are stepping aside, leaving Josie standing exposed where everyone can see her.

—What's she doing here?

Josie's body bends at the knees and shoulders. She's speechless. She holds her hand over her mouth to hide her shock.

—This is fitting. Now you know what we all think about you, Annette says, then spits in the direction of Josie's feet.

—Let her be! Jill screams.

Calmly, Annette raises her rifle, directing the muzzle toward Jill's face.

Nora raises her rifle, aiming the barrel in the direction of Annette's ear.

The battle line is drawn, and the Nightingales in the room scramble to choose sides and position themselves behind either Annette or Jill.

A shot is fired, a sound so loud it could have ripped the room apart.

The girls are in shock, momentarily deaf, turning this way and that to see who has been shot, to see who fired her weapon.

There stands beside Josie an older woman, with two long, braided ponytails resting on her shoulders. Her white uniform is similar to the others, but the stranger has two holsters hanging from a belt over her hips. She holds a pistol aimed at the ceiling, smoke seeping from its barrel.

—I am running this outfit now, and I will not run it as a circus.

Jaws drop in silence.

Nora lowers her rifle, though Annette turns hers on the older woman. Annette squints, not so much as a prelude to firing a shot as to say she means business.

—Put the gun down, sweetie, the older woman says. —You don't scare me.

Annette stands down.

—Besides, I am on your side, the woman says.

—Who are you? Jill asks.

—The name is Luckie, and I'm the new head nurse in town.

—Luckie?

—Good thing you got here, Luckie. We were about to do something stupid.

—I can see that.

—Tell me what this is all about, all this artillery, Luckie says.

—We are staging a revolt.

—I beg your pardon. Against whom?

—Against anyone around.

—It looked like you were staging a revolt against each other.

—If you say so, Annette says. —We were just playing around.

—You are grown women, I shouldn't be telling you not to play with guns. Now will someone please tell me what this revolt is all about, what's bothering you?

—Luckie, it's just awful, says Samantha Sound.

—What is?

—Don't trust her, Annette advises Samantha. —She was sent here by the State Department, and she will report right back to them.

—It can't hurt just to talk, Samantha says.

—What is it, sweetie? Tell me what's troubling you all.

—We've figured everything out, the reason why they sent us here.

—I'm curious to hear this myself.

—There's going to an atomic war, and they're going to ship us in to care for the wounded.

—That's interesting.

—I've seen photos of people burned so badly they look like a dirty ashtray.

—That's true.

—I heard the blast isn't as deadly as the radiation in the air afterward.

—That's also true.

—I am happy to give my life to nursing but I don't want to get sick and die because someone pushed a stupid button. If I'm dead, I can't give my life to nursing.

—That's what's bothering you? That's why you think you're here? I'm glad you are all gathered to hear what I have to say. Atomic war is not the reason why you're here.

—My final semester was supposed to end sixteen months ago. I should be home. Why am I still here?

—You're still here because you've been forgotten.

—You're pulling my leg!

—At the State Department, there are only a few bureaucrats who know St. Marc's exists, not because it's secret, but because no one gives a damn. The bureaucrats in charge of your care are preoccupied, their minds drift, they are forgetful men.

—Luckie, you have to get us out of here.

—We will all leave, and we will all leave together, when it's time.

—Why wait another moment?

—Because you're not nurses yet. When I send you home, I will send you home as a nurse. You'll have a mind and a career. Girls, I am not here to hold you back, but rather to equip you. We're all in this together, joined at the hip, guns a-blazing, if that becomes necessary.

—We're with you all the way, Nurse Luckie.

On the plaza outside the United Nations building in New York, there is a sandwich sign hanging from thin chains over the shoulders of a hatless stranger in a toga. The sign's message is ominous, I AM IN TOUCH WITH THE DEAD. Sirens are in the air.

Culprit Clutch and the stranger in the sandwich sign are on opposite ends of the fountain, and although there are tourists and New Yorkers wandering through their sightlines, the two of them see each other. Culprit had never seen the man before. He tightens his grip around three pieces of paper in his hand.

The sirens grow louder then diminish, and people are running in all directions. The air smells like smoke; there must be a building fire nearby. The plaza empties. The wind picks up and blows the long row of world flags, waving them out and filling the gray sky with color.

A gust yanks the papers out of Culprit's hand. He gives chase as they cartwheel through the air in the direction of the sandwich sign man and paste themselves to the face of his sign.

The man peels off the first sheet and begins reading it aloud before handing it back.—A Guggenheim Fellowship award notification letter, how impressive.

Culprit takes the letter, folds it, and places it in his lapel pocket.

—An itinerary for a sea-liner voyage from New York to Cap Haitien. Your boat leaves today.

Culprit takes back the itinerary.

—A shipping claim for a 16 mm motion picture camera and other paraphernalia.

The thought strikes Culprit, —Have we met?

—Haiti is about as old as the New World gets.

—I've seen you somewhere.

—The Americans want to control the Haitian people like marionettes. The Loa have a jump on them.

—What do you know about the Loa?

—People, like planes, have pilots. Planes, unlike cars, don't have brakes.

—My plane didn't have brakes. What do you know about that?

—Nothing.

—Greathead?

—No.

—I know you, you're Henry Greathead.

—I am not.

—You're the butler from the nursing school south of Le Cap.

—You got the wrong bum, mister.

A wind stream high above them begins rattling the ropes against the aluminum flagpoles, creating a succession of zings and pings.

—It sounds like starship ray-guns firing in a science fiction matinee, Culprit says as an aside to the stranger.

—If you say so.

Tonal and rhythmic, it is the sound of the new atomic age, the sound of the future, more electronic than acoustic, more like radio static than a trick of the wind. The sound mixes in with the fading sirens and the squawking of seagulls flying above; it distracts Culprit from hearing eight million New Yorkers sigh all at once.

—Listen, it's music, Culprit says.

—It's not music, no one is playing it.

—It sounds like music. You can dance to it.

—You want music? Try Leonard Bernstein. Now that's music.

—A woman, a wigmaker, and a wild horse are not to be trusted, Culprit says.

It's a non-sequitur that causes the man in the sandwich sign reading I AM IN TOUCH WITH THE DEAD to to look at Culprit Clutch as if he were out of his mind.

—What is that? A kind of spy talk? Are you a spy?

—It doesn't mean anything. It just shows me that you're not Henry Greathead. You look like him. You could be brothers.

Culprit turns to walk away when the stranger calls out to him, —I have something for you to take to Haiti.

It catches Culprit off guard until he sees the object the stranger is handing him. He catches the drift that maybe this is not a chance encounter after all. The object is a 16 mm film canister.

—Well, well, what have we here? Culprit asks.

—A film about Haiti for American schoolchildren.

On the canister, there are block letters written on masking tape, ILLUMINATE THE REEL. Culprit opens the canister to find a companion piece of masking tape with a variation of the message on the inside, ILLUMINATE THE REAL. He unwinds the head of the film, letting it spill onto the concrete floor of the United Nations plaza and thumbs through a few frames. It shows scrub shrubs on a rocky landscape and black people in hats with their bodies in strange contortions, apparently dancing. It is a Haiti film, indeed. He winds the film back onto the reel, and the stranger is gone.

Culprit Clutch is going back to Haiti, this time as a VIP, as a Guggenheim Fellow, with an assignment to create a movie.

At the New York harbor, it is a world-class send off, a gala departure as passengers gather on the dock before boarding the luxury liner that will take them across the ocean. A brass band is playing, colorful paper ribbons fly in every direction, rice and confetti; there is champagne, laughter. It is an air of jubilant pandemonium.

That ship, however, is bound for London.

Culprit meanders through the celebration as he makes his way to a tiny French freighter bound for the West Indies. He will be the only passenger not on the ship's crew and he braces himself for six days' adventure at sea, salt water splashing against the port windows and the hydrochloric acid splashing against the walls of his stomach.

The year is 1955, and despite the best efforts of the Haitian Bureau du Tourisme with the assistance of the U.S. Department of State and UNESCO, Haiti is not yet a glamorous vacation destination. The world has not yet learned of Haiti and its plum-colored brocaded satin draperies, the mahogany hotel furniture with rattan seats suitable for tropical temperatures, the flimsy huts serving rum cocktails constructed so close together that you can touch one from the other; and how can you talk of Haiti and not mention the the cocks crowing, the pariah dogs howling, the sound of drumming in the distance and the ever present scent of woodsmoke.

For Culprit, his return to northern Haiti means one thing: seeing Josie again.

It is not the ship's diesel engine that provides the locomotion that transports Culprit back to Haiti. Rather it is an invisible rope, one end tied around his waist, the other tied around Josie fifteen hundred miles away across the Atlantic Ocean. Culprit pulls himself along the line, one arm's length at a time.

He cannot see her soon enough.

Better Get Hit in Yo' Soul

The Top Hat Man appears mostly in visions and always in haze. He travels no other way. When you walk past the cemetery, he's outside locking the gate with a key he returns to his vest pocket. You'd swear you've seen that sinister, monocle'd Mr. Peanut of a man a hundred times doing just that. It's as if that's all he ever does, leave the cemetery and lock up after himself, return the key to his pocket without saying anything.

JILL

I remember him the way I remember my dreams, which is to say I remember just enough to remember I remember. The lesson here is that I need to stop taking walks away from the school at night. I need to find a way to sleep. I need to stop taking walks away from the school at night.

Far from the cemetery, on the grounds of the St. Marc school, under hazy sun, the freckled Nightingales hang their clean linen on lines that stretch across the courtyard and shoot the breeze, talking yet again about the Nightingale they always talk about, Josie, and the stories Josie tells about an old blind sheepdog who lives in M. Budé's tool shed, though no one else has ever seen the pooch. No sooner do they mention the old dog than up he comes running.

Once all their laundry is hanging, the sole item that stands out is a striped pillowcase someone must have brought from home. All the others are white.

It's early. The humidity and heat are not yet chasing them indoors. The mosquitoes are not yet biting. The drums are not so loud that they are all you can think about. There is a breeze, and the sun tints their hair, giving it a golden sheen that won't show up until later.

NORA

My first day in Haiti was the strangest of my life. There was a balling swarm of bees, changing its mind about which of us to chase just as often as it changed shape, droning all the while. 'Close your eyes and don't move,' I remember Gilda saying. 'They won't bite you if you don't move.' It was madness, trying to hold still, but I held my breath and got used to it. 'Close your eyes and try to enjoy the sound.' She was right. The buzzing was beautiful in its deafening way, though I still had the heebie-jeebies.

—Jill, tell them about the corpse in the laundry cart and the roly-poly man in the nurse's uniform.

—I love that story. I want to hear it again.

—One of the oddest things I've seen in Haiti, Jill begins, —was as American as apple pie. Afterward, we figured out that the nurse's uniform was stolen from the school. It must have belonged to one of the head nurses because none of us wears that size.

Nora picks up the story, —It all started as we were taking an afternoon stroll along the river, and in the distance we see him, the roly-poly nurse person and his cart.

—You've got to be pulling my leg.

—You haven't heard them tell this before?

—They've only been telling it since yesterday.

—It only happened yesterday.

— . . . His back was turned, so he couldn't see us, and we wanted to keep it that way. We crept along the trail, from tree to tree, hiding, to get a closer look.

—Spying!

—Of course we were spying, silly! It's not every day you encounter something so ridiculous and strange! Finally, we were right behind the roly-poly man, still hiding. He seemed nervous, fidgety, pushing his cart along, which was piled high with towels and linens, just like he was making rounds in a busy ward.

—Keep in mind, it's still the dry season. He's not going to find anyplace to do laundry down by the river, if that's what he's thinking.

—I'm not that sure what he was thinking, his linen looked fresh to me, nicely folded. So he's sunburned and sweaty, checking over his shoulder as if someone might be following him. He pushes his cart harder and faster, then bingo! He hits a rock, the cart flips, and a body tumbles out.

—Dead!

—Pretending maybe, but not dead. The body belonged to, from appearances, a young Haitian, a boy really, and once he rolled onto the ground, he pretended very hard that he was dead. He lay on his back with his tongue hanging out the side of his mouth. Then he'd seize up in a conniption and follow that with a fit of giggles. His giggling was how we knew he was still alive, thank God.

—We haven't read the chapter yet on how to revive dead boys.

—Cynthia is an expert on that chapter, just ask her.

—We were still well hidden, and neither one of us made a peep, but somehow the roly-poly man heard us. He fixed his gaze right at our hiding place and bellowed, 'I see you there peeking out at me. There's no use in hiding, show yourself!' Did I get that right?

—Right as rain.

—We stepped out of hiding, our arms in the air just like they do in movies. He took one look at us, and it was as if he were seeing a ghost.

—I remember perfectly that look on his face. It was shocking. It was like one eye was swollen shut, and his mouth trembled as if he had something to say but couldn't get it out.

—Then what?

—He fell over.

—Dead!

—Not dead. Dead drunk, maybe.

—What was it all about?

—We didn't stay to find out.

It's another quiet Saturday afternoon at the St. Marc American School for Nurses. In the conservatory, there's Vanessa sitting in the corner sun window, reading a Pearl Buck paperback. There's Lydia in a mahogany chair, soaking her feet in a tub of Epsom salt solution, trying to soothe her aching bunions. There's Samantha Sound, the sweet little country gal, saying something like, 'You're still the same jealous lunatic you always were.' (She's reenacting a conversation she once had with a boyfriend back home and drawing shrieks of laughter from the girls she's with.)

Then the noise begins, banging piano from the parlor, and the Nightingales converge.

—That sound can only mean one thing: Men are here.

—Not men. Buffoons.

—Women don't play piano like that.

The Nightingales enter the parlor and find two of them pounding away at the keys of an out-of-tune piano, hitting as many as they can at once in a caveman rhythm barreling up and down the keyboard. Their elbows are a blur of motion. They've been intruded upon, but that won't stop them from playing.

—That's the by-Goddest sound I ever heard.

—It's strange, but I think I hear a trace of melody in there somewhere.

—You can't call that racket music!

—I bet if you ask, they call it rock 'n' roll.

—I've heard rock 'n' roll. This is worse.

—Why is it whenever men show up, they bring pandemonium?

—Where are the others? Men, like wolves, travel in packs.

—Luckie's not here. Where is Henry Greathead?

—Shh, their antic melody is winding toward a big finish!

ABBOT JAFFE

What thoughts must be cracking in their brains? The parlor
door swings open to reveal our gruesome crew standing there,
Yanks in sheep's clothing, which is to say wool-knit shirts of
the Arrow brand and chinos.

LYDIA

They were such an odd sight, the six of them. Their leader,
looking untidy with sweat stains under both armpits, stood
in the doorjamb striking a pose, while his fellows hid behind
him peeking out from around his shoulders, hips, and knees.

If the unspoken question lingering in the air is, 'Who are you? ' a smirking
Abbot Jaffe adopts an air and blurts out the answer, —It's Humphrey Bogart's
double, here's looking at you, sweetheart.

The only response is the hollow ticking of a cuckoo clock.

Jaffe sheds Bogart and changes to an opposite tack, addressing Jill
directly, for she's the one brave enough to stand within an arm's length of him.
—Doesn't that drive you mad? he asks her.

—How do you mean?

—The ticking.

—I'm used to it. I live here.

Jaffe changes tack again, —Where are you hiding Culprit Clutch?

—Good luck, we ain't seen him, says Samantha Sound slipping into her
southern drawl.

—That don't mean he ain't here, Jaffe replies, her drawl rubbing off
on him.

—You don't think you're fooling us, saying you're here looking for Culprit Clutch.

—He's carrying something that belongs to us.

—You all are just using that as an excuse. You all just wanted to come out this way and meet the pretty girls. You are men, after all, and I know what men are like, says Belinda Ballard.

Abbot Jaffe turns and winks at Dinah, which startles her. He shifts gears and pretends he has a speck in his eye. She responds with a concerned look, falling for it.

—We have not come to mix business and pleasure.

—Like I said, mister, Culprit ain't here.

—If you see him, can you deliver a message?

—As you wish.

—Tell him we can't make the, ahem, movie without him.

—Movie?

—You're in show biz? You don't look like Hollywood types.

—Svevo, show her the light meter so she knows we aren't pulling her leg.

The obligatory Swede emerges from behind Abbot Jaffe and waves the instrument near Nora's face as if to make it dance. Annoyed, she swats the air at it.

—We're not from California. New York City is the hub for educational filmmakers.

—Is Culprit Clutch supposed to be your movie star?

—Our type of movies don't need movie stars.

—Educational movies come off better with regular type persons.

—So what's Culprit Clutch got to do with it?

—He is a Guggenheim Fellow, says Lafferty, one of the piano players.

—That's not why we need him, says McKenna, the other piano player.

—Yes, he was also named by UNESCO as our cinematic director, says Lafferty.

—God knows, that's not why we need him, says McKenna.

—We need him because he has our camera, says Abbot Jaffe. —They were supposed to send us here with a camera, but all they gave us is a projector, and if you know anything about film, you know you can't shoot film with a projector.

—You can, but it requires extensive modifications, says Keith Clone.

—With a projector, you can show movies, Nora says. —That sounds like fun!

—They didn't send us prints, just stock.

—We have no way to shoot film and nothing to show.

—You're trying to tell me you don't make Busby Berkeley-type pictures?

—No.

—Give me an example of the kind of movies you do make.

The last crew made one about the American doctors who give free medicine to Haiti's poorest citizens.

—Oh, brother!

—It was quite informative.

—You don't know the American doctors like we do.

—The doctors we know are worse than useless.

—That film crew should have made a movie about voudoun. It's much more appealing.

—Why don't you make a movie about voudoun?

—UNESCO hasn't given us the subject of the film they want us to make yet.

—Are they paying you well?

—Peanuts.

—Do you stay in the Little America?

—There's a Little America in Haiti?

—Just the hotel where the doctors and diplomats stay.

—Nope, they put us up at a small base camp just out of town. There ain't room service, but the supply truck is well stocked. There's clean linen.

—All's we need to get by is booze, though a 16 mm Bolex would be nice

69

and maybe ice. I keep asking them for ice and mosquito netting. Show her your mosquito bites, hey Neil.

As the roly-poly man who Nora and Jill had seen the day before dressed as a nurse begins pulling up his shirt, Jill interrupts, —How long are you fellas staying in Haiti?

—I don't know. How long will you girls be here?

—According to Washington, how long we stay is none of our business.

—That's the State Department for you, mister.

—UNESCO ain't no different.

—Bayard Pumphrey Huffy, says Jill.

—Who's that?

—He's the boss.

—You know what I would do if I wanted to make a movie and didn't have a camera? Jill asks. —I would put on a play.

—Have you ever heard of M. Lyle Mislove? asks Lafferty.

—I can't say I have.

—He's a New York City playwright, Lafferty says. —These days, he's working off-Broadway.

—The East Village? McKenna plays along.

—Farther.

—Tribeca?

—Farther.

—Jersey City?

—Not even close.

—I give up.

—Haiti.

—Shut up! yelps the unassuming man in the corner.

—Ladies, I wish to introduce you to the Ineffable and Inestimable M. Lyle Mislove, McKenna says, sweeping his arm in the direction of their irritated colleague.

—Him?

—I have never met a playwright in person before.

—Mister, can I have your autograph?

—Why does he have that look on face?

—That caged animal look? He's trying to work out the kinks in his latest.

—He never shuts off his writing mind.

—It's because you annoy me, comes the voice of the playwright in the corner.

—Maybe if he tries talking about his play, we girls can help him write.

—I loved *Music Man*.

—All right, here is our man's quandary. He's working out the details of a murder mystery.

—Oh, do let us help!

—All's he got so far is the first act. The set is an English drawing room, and two servants bring in a heavy trunk and set it down on the stage floor. The trunk is heavy to lift in such a way that the audience can easily surmise its contents. The servants exit, and two constables from Scotland Yard enter, amid a discussion of how a crime has been committed only the victim's body is missing, making it impossible to prove there was a crime. All the while, they banter on and on and don't put two and two together. The two actors exit leaving the trunk alone on the stage. The trunk opens and a living man climbs out. He sits down in front of a mirror and removes his false whiskers and makeup, puts on a Henschel Deerstalker cap, lights a pipe, and reveals himself to be the legendary Sherlock Holmes. First act curtain.

—Bravo, Mislove.

—I wrote no such thing, pipes the playwright in the corner.

—Don't you think it's strange to go on about him while he's standing right there?

—What do you find strange?

—You're expressing his thoughts and opinions without letting him speak for himself.

—Isn't that what he does when he writes his plays?

—Come again?

—Isn't that what he does when he writes his plays? He puts words in our mouths.

—That's different, Mislove snipes from the corner.

—He puts you fellas into the plays he writes? asked Jill.

—Yes, into his off-off-Broadway plays.

—His off-off-off-off-off-Broadway plays. You're in them, too.

—We are? We only just met.

—That doesn't mean he isn't writing our conversation as a play in his mind.

—Oh, brother!

—The thing about Lyle Mislove's plays is that I'm better at writing them than he is.

—Stick it in your ear!

—Then why don't you write plays of your own?

—Because a genuine Lyle Mislove play is better than anything I could ever dream up. Let me give you an example of dialogue. 'The ice is breaking up, hurry and jump!' That's a bonafide line from a Lyle Mislove play.

—That's not one of mine, Mislove proclaims. —I didn't write that.

—You didn't write it, but you sure did say it. You were talking in your sleep last night.

—Then it is one of mine, and you can't use it.

—Why not? You said yourself you didn't write it.

—It's my line. I need time to know its meaning. I don't recall dreaming about ice.

—The best dreams are the ones you can't remember.

—If you can't remember, how do you know they were the best ones?

—I will now use 'The ice is breaking up, hurry and jump!' as an example of how to write a Lyle Mislove play.

—If you do, you'll be hearing from my lawyer.

—We can put something together based on that one brilliant line.

—If you want to keep your friend happy, Jill interrupts, —I have another line to try out, something I overheard.

—Let's hear it.

—'You're still the same jealous lunatic you always were.'

Samantha Sound gasps. —That sounds like something I might have said.

—Sweetie, it was.

—Don't worry, after we finish our experiment you'll get your words back unharmed.

—Let them use it, this might be fun.

McKenna begins, —Two young lovers quarrel on a dusty airplane runway. She's trying to leave him, and he's not getting the message. Lafferty, you play the part of the man. She says to him. . . , that's your cue, my love.

—You're still the same jealous lunatic you always were, says Samantha Sound. She then slaps Lafferty with a smart blow across the cheek.

McKenna turns to Lafferty, —As the jealous lunatic, your reply to her is?

—Since I am an indelicate brute, I don't say a word. I grab her arms to keep her off the plane.

—Get your hands off of me, you gorilla.

—Bravo, my love. See how this works? The scene is unfolding before us. What's next?

—I break free and board that plane and fly as far away as I can from that sorry excuse for a man.

—The jealous lunatic takes it lying down?

—Not quite. I climb back on my horse and watch the plane as it begins to taxi across the runway.

Jill turns to Samantha and says, —Your George was a cowboy?

—Shh, I want to hear this.

—I have a change of heart, Lafferty says. —I ain't letting her go. I give the horse a squeeze, and we chase that plane.

—A horse chasing an airplane? Now I've heard everything!

—What happens next, does your horse grow wings?

—I draw my lasso and hoop that plane around the nose. I hang on tight, and away I go. Next stop: the wild blue yonder.

—Ladies and gentlemen, says McKenna, —that is how you write a Lyle Mislove play.

—My dear, I don't think it's possible to lasso a plane from a horse.

—We had a plane hopper just the other day. He flew all the way from New York riding on the airplane's wing.

—Never in a million years would I write that, Mislove complains. It's worse than contrived.

Outside the window, two men spy on the scene inside. They keep themselves out of sight, although anyone who looks their way would see their two sets of eyes and thinning heads of hair. One of the men is reading lips, and the other holds his ear against the glass in hopes of following the conversation. Neither is in luck.

The sky is purple, the moon yellow. It's a night brighter than the darkest of days, a night bright enough to read the paper though neither has seen a paper printed in English for months.

They turn to walk away from the building.

—I don't understand, sir, whether you are coming or going, says the man in chartreuse slacks, Patrick Fitzpatrick.

—It's all stagecraft, a trick of the light, replies Bayard Pumphrey Huffy, the gray-eyed senior American diplomat stationed in Haiti's Nord Department. —Stagecraft and statecraft are far more closely aligned than our colleagues in the State Department would have the world believe, eh, Fitzpatrick?

—I beg your pardon.

—The night is our only light.

—Yes, sir. I just don't get it.

—A day as warm as the sun at night, the kind of night you only get in places like Haiti.

—I don't follow.

—You know what your trouble is, Fitzpatrick? No poetic imagination.

—You're right, because I have no idea what you mean.

—Now here's the plan: The student nurses and New York film crew will believe that I've returned to the mainland on official business, while in truth, I shall remain in Haiti.

—Why the charade, sir?

—It's the Heisenberg principle, Fitzpatrick, as it applies to Foreign Service. The presence of diplomats in a host country changes how a host country acts in the diplomats' presence. I want to see how the Nord Department behaves when I am not here.

—It's putting yourself through a lot of trouble.

—These are new times, and as emissaries of the most powerful nation in the history of civilization, we have only one purpose.

—I've forgotten it, sir.

—The prevention of nuclear war.

—I thought you were going to say the defeat of Communism.

—No.

—Haiti is not under threat of Communist takeover?

—No.

—Then we have nothing to worry about. Is the rumor true that Vice President Nixon will be visiting Haiti?

—I wouldn't know.

—I don't see what's wrong with Dick Nixon, Fitzpatrick says. —He's the horse I'm backing in 1960.

The two of them stop when Huffy startles at the sight of a person hunched under a tree in shadow of the moon.

—Hallo, man, you gave me a fright, Huffy says.

—The Nixon team is so on the ball, they will be putting together their campaign staff next year, non-paid positions that can lead to high-ranking appointments five years down the road.

—He's not answering. Maybe he's asleep. Or drunk.

—If Ike dies in office, there's nothing I can do, since I'm stuck offshore in Haiti. The point is Nixon needs to know I'm with him. He's never met me. He's never heard my name. My father was a grocer, just like his. I'm working just as hard to pull myself up through the ranks.

—Fitzpatrick, what are you going on about? Give me a hand assisting this man.

—The man is dead, sir.

—Dead drunk?

—Dead.

—How can you know for sure?

—He's not breathing. His body is cold. It's not an act.

—Good God, what a way to go.

—The question is did he die here or did someone leave his corpse?

—Give me a hand lifting the man.

—I'd rather not.

—Let's carry him back to St. Marc's until his family can be notified.

—That's not the Haitian way.

—How so?

—In the Third World, citizens don't feel death the way Americans do.

—That's not what I've seen.

—In the Third World, death is more commonplace.

—The man deserves our respect.

—I say we get ourselves two shovels and lay him to rest right here.

—His family would want to know of his passing.

—The Haitians put their dead in the ground as fast as possible. If they don't, wizards will come and turn the corpses of their beloved into zombis. If we bury this man, it's doing the family a favor.

—There are no zombis. You've seen too many Italian movies.

—Take a look at Haiti in the mirror. It's a living hell. The people are stupid, because they don't know how bad they have it. These Haitians were dragged here in chains, so long ago that they've forgotten it.

—It's not true. They know the reason they're here.

—They are so proud that Haiti is the first democracy in the New World, and the first black democracy on earth, and that their revolution was a slave revolt and that they repelled the French. They act as if there were nowhere else they would rather be, but that's only because they've never been anywhere else. If they had been anywhere else, they would hate it here as much as I do.

—Where is Henry Greathead?

—Asleep, most likely.

—He was supposed to meet us here, under this tree.

—Isn't it just like a black man not to show his face when expected? You know darn well that if we didn't want him around right now, not only would he be here, we wouldn't be able to get him to leave.

—Henry Greathead, at your service, sir.

—Greathead, have you been here this whole time?

—I have, sir, Henry Greathead replies, then under his breath, —Isn't it just like them to think I don't hear their insults?

—What on earth has happened to you?

—I cannot rightly say, sir. Last night, I went to sleep at a quarter to eleven, and I awoke this morning like this.

—Fitzpatrick, are you seeing this?

—It's happened twice since I've been here. Something in the air. Nothing a few days of sun won't clear up.

—By God, Greathead, Haiti turns your skin white.

—If you say so.

—Greathead, you need your dark skin back. I'm going blind just looking at you. Think of it, Fitzgerald, if we could take whatever this is, make it permanent, bottle it, take it with us back to the mainland, and mass produce it, we could end racial prejudice once and for all.

—Because all we'd have are white people?

—American Negros would like that, wouldn't you say, Henry?

—If you say so.

—You would like that, wouldn't you, Henry?

—No, sir.

—It's that pride of yours that holds you back, Henry.

Patrick Fitzpatrick chimes in, —The problem, sir, is even if we turn their skin white, they will still be black on the inside. Their mumbo jumbo is more than skin deep. The problem is we wouldn't be able to tell people apart. We wouldn't be able to keep people separate.

Henry Greathead, again under his breath, —How I would love to give this Fitzpatrick a piece of my mind.

—What's that?

—When my proper skin tone returns, it will ease my mind, Greathead says.

—To each his own, Fitzpatrick says.

—I am not sure I can carry on with our rendezvous with a dead man in our presence, Huffy says.

—I doubt he's listening.

—Let's move to another tree. I am sure his friends will be along shortly to dispose of him.

—What was it we were meeting about?

—Hawaii, Greathead reminds the older man.

—Yes, now the plans for the Nord Department include a luxury hotel, amusement park, public baths, swimming pools. The best of all is when you get to the beach, and there's surfing. What young person of today won't be taken in by the sport's charms? You straddle the stick and the water carries you forth.

—I'd like to see you try it.

—I've had far too many ham and egg breakfasts for the sport, Fitzpatrick. Surfing is for the younger generation. It's our gift to the children. As you know, Greathead, the State Department's objectives in Haiti are extremely, oh, what's the right word?

—Hazy?

—Delicate is the word I had in mind. As you know, you are better off knowing only what you need to know and leaving the rest to the foreign policy team back home. What you need to know is that the surfing film is of the utmost importance. The idea is to remake Haiti in another image, that of Hawaii. We wish to recreate Haiti as a haven for American tourists along the Eastern Seaboard of the United States, and surfing is a crucial element in encouraging American tourists to bring their children along.

—So all's I need do is keep the surfing film on track? Greathead asks.

—Yes, and please, if you wouldn't mind, do take care of this corpse.

—You want me to take care of it?

—Fitzpatrick here tells me it's Haitian custom to put the body in the ground so wizards don't turn it into a zombi.

—I'm not Haitian.

—You're of African descent, same as this man.

—I'm French-Canadian.

—Yes, and I'm Santy Claus, Fitzpatrick says, mocking.

No sooner are Bayard Pumphrey Huffy and Patrick Fitzpatrick walking away than Henry Greathead hears a noise above him in the tree. A man standing upon a low branch drops himself to the ground beside him while cradling a bottle of wine and two glasses under his arm.

—Only the worm is clothed, Culprit Clutch says.

—The worm is our little brother, Henry replies.

—Thought those fellows might break out with 'Melancholy Baby.' Care for a glass?

—Well, if it isn't you.

—Not exactly back from the dead.

—If you say so. Your limbs seem to have healed.

—Henry, your skin has turned as white as mine.

—It'll clear up in a day or two. The sun will clear it up. I'm the same in my soul.

79

—Haiti performs strange magical feats on the body. My hair hasn't grown since I first set foot on the island. I haven't been to the barber in two years.

—So you came back.

—They sent me back. You're still here?

—Not going nowhere. 'Come with us to Haiti, Henry Greathead,' they say. 'Henry Greathead is perfect for our interests in Haiti. Henry Greathead can pass himself off as a Haitian without the possession of a Haitian spirit.' 'You want someone who looks the part but is just playing the part.' 'You want someone who keeps a distance and his heart out of it, and Henry Greathead is nothing if not aloof, really quite cool.' One day, they say, 'Sever your ties with the Continent of Africa, and come with us, Henry Greathead.' The next day, they say, 'That Henry Greathead, all he does is complain about the heat and humidity. You'd think with his African ancestry, he'd be used to it.' Yet can you truly feel your ancestor's world? I close my eyes and feel nothing.

—Good to see you again, Henry, says Culprit, pouring wine into a glass.

—The Nightingales have been expecting you. The Bums hope you brought them a movie camera.

They raise their glasses and clink.

—Good to see our two friends, the crusty old crocodile and the man in chartreuse slacks, are up to old tricks.

—Those two are so, I can't think of the word.

—Indescribable.

—Baffling is the word I had in mind. So why did you come back? Don't tell me again it's because you were sent.

—I came back for the honey.

—It is love then. Love, love, love, what would Doctor Freud say about that?

Culprit adopts an erudite air, —Our top-flight analysts have diagnosed Mr. Culprit Clutch as an obsessive compulsive.

—Meaning?

—In lay terms, he never knows what he is going to do next, nor does he let that stop him, no sir. His abilities as a social catalyst are his only dependable qualities.

—Social catalyst? You? Give me a break.

—I took a Dale Carnegie course on how to win friends and influence people.

—Good for you.

—Some of my new friends turned out to be Commies.

—Oh.

—That's not the reason the HUAC began to pester me.

—It's not?

—The summons to speak before Congress was because the ghost of a dead Red uses my body as his vessel. He takes over at the most inopportune moments, when I'm on a crowded street corner. He blurts out things I would never say, things I can get thrown in jail for saying.

—Like what?

—'Long live the Great October Socialist Revolution!'

—That one can get you in trouble.

—'Long live the indissoluble union of the working class, the peasantry, and the intelligentsia!'

—I wouldn't go around saying that if I was you.

—'Proletarians of all nations, unite!'

—There you go again.

—The joke's on them. Despite my poor standing with Senator McCarthy, I maneuvered the American diplomatic corps to hire me and send me here. They even gave me a Guggenheim Fellowship and a movie camera. I owe it all to Dale Carnegie.

—If you can't beat 'em, join 'em.

—Henry, what do you make of the objective to turn Haiti into the new Hawaii?

—Project Magic Island is what they're calling it.

—Shit.

Now it's Henry's turn to adopt an air as if he were someone else, as if he were Bayard Pumphrey Huffy or another like-minded soul, —It's not the Communists we fear in Haiti, oh, no! Communism is a people's movement, and it's fluid. Over time, people will have a change in heart and move in another direction. My suspicions about Haiti are spiritual in nature, African in origin. No one in the Americas has ever seen anything quite like it.

Culprit Clutch gets in on the act, —Let's have the RAND folks get to the bottom of it.

—Those trigger-happy sons of bitches do not have the capacity of understanding Haiti.

—I believe you're right!

—Their impulse is to destroy what they cannot understand.

—I don't understand Haiti, either, sir.

—That's because you are thinking from the perspective of the Bomb, and the Bomb does not have an effect on a spiritual enemy, that is if *enemy* is even the right word. The most powerful tool at our disposal is Capitalism. There is no force in the known universe that runs more roughshod over the soul than the mighty dollar.

—Hear, hear.

—Let me lay down your mission for you. You will recraft Haiti in Hawaii's image. You will build airports and high-rise hotels and swimming pools, and turn Haiti into a tourist wonderland a short air voyage from the Eastern Seaboard of the United States.

—Hurrah!

—In Hawaii, they flooded the market with tourist souvenirs and plastic Tiki dolls, and in so doing, the spiritual power of the Tiki idol has not only been diminished but extinguished. It's a profit deal, the Hawaiians are on the take and richer for it. Tourists are thrilled to take home a genuine trinket of the Hawaiian culture.

—Everyone's happy, and the war is over.

—Unless the Japanese decide to attack again as retribution for what we did to their cities.

—Then again, if they do, they face massive retaliation with Tokyo as our next target.

—The Japanese are firmly in our camp. In the end, American businesses profit while Hawaii's spiritual forces are kept at bay, and the nation can focus on problems back home, like this rock 'n' roll music that's making kids dance like Negroes.

—I hear the Communists have brainwashed an American boy in Memphis into singing like he's black.

—The United States will counter by introducing the masses to folk music.

—That will surely stop the dancers in their tracks.

—As agents of the United States Department of State, we must counter the recommendations of the RAND Corporation who wish the Haitian theatre placed under the auspices of the War Department.

—Sir, the name has been changed to the Department of Defense.

—It's still War to me.

—Defense makes the department sound less aggressive.

—Then why not change its name to the Department of Peace?

—That's supposed to be State's area.

—Then why not change State's name to the Department of Peace?

—Because the Department of Defense would then declare war on its sister agency.

—It sounds so complicated.

—Think of it this way. War's answer to the Haiti problem would be to drop the Bomb on Port-au-Prince. State's solution is to commission Rodgers and Hart to write a Haiti musical.

—The government moves in mysterious ways, but as long as they keep paying me, I go home happy. Speaking of going home happy, I heard there's an endless source of fine wine at St. Marc's. Care to join me for a nightcap?

—First let's take care of this poor dead soul.

—Did Bayard Huffy and his underling carry him off?

—They left me to figure it out.

—Did he come back to life and walk off?

—No.

—Where did he go?

—I don't know.

—Let's go drink wine.

A quarter mile away under another tree, Bayard Pumphrey Huffy without Fitzpatrick arrives for another rendezvous, his last of the evening, a meeting with Luckie the new head nurse at St. Marc's. He's brought a bottle of wine and two glasses, but to his surprise discovers a man's body lying beneath the tree.

—If I were of a weaker mind, I would believe this corpse was following me. This is the second time I have run across him tonight. Last time was under the tree where I was meeting Henry Greathead.

—Maybe someone was carrying him and set him down to rest, Luckie says.

—Who?

—*Le Garde d'Haiti.*

—In that case, they will come back for him. Haiti takes care of itself, and I admire that. Can I pour you a glass?

She speaks to fill in the silence while he's pouring, —It's a beautiful evening.

—I'll say. I don't remember seeing such a purple sky and yellow moon back home.

—The drumming stopped.

—Stopped? I hadn't noticed.

—The drumming never stops.

—No, listen carefully. It's faint, but you can hear it.

—I hear it now. I didn't a moment ago.

—When I hear drumming, you know what I hear? A clock ticking. Ticking down to zero.

—If I only had a dime for every one of your dreadful obsessions.

—This is the one.

—You let it get under your skin

—The planet has never known the likes of the atomic bomb before. Our times could lead to the end of time.

—You called me out here to tell me this?

—Dulles' New Look policy ensures massive retaliation for minor squabbles. Want to know why?

—Why?

—To save money. As opposed to building a conventional army large enough to take on the Soviets or Red Chinese.

—You can't let it worry you. *Que sera, sera.*

—Cutting costs. I say the day we engage in massive retaliation is the last day money will have any value.

—This man over here, he looks like he's sleeping.

—He's dead. Fitzpatrick couldn't find his pulse.

—Fitzpatrick couldn't find his own pulse. You're going into hiding?

—Yes, and I am leaving your nursing students under the direction of Doctor Boldieu Bast.

—They say he's not quite himself these days.

—Aren't we all?

—The man is not with it. That's what I've heard them say.

—He's out of his mind is what they say, and I'm a damned fool for leaving him in charge.

—He's been letting his hair grow out. It's long on top, and he slicks it down and winds it together and lets it be.

—It's like a plate of jet-black spaghetti noodles on his head.

—Why make him the boss?

—I want to see for myself. I want to see what he's like when he's the authority.

—Patrick Fitzpatrick is the one you should watch.

—Shh, do you hear that?

—The drumming.

—I thought I heard a Tarzan call.

—That's McKenna and Lafferty, two on the film crew with a childish sense of humor.

—How do you know?

—Because I heard one of them saying, 'If you hear drums, it's voudoun. If you hear Tarzan, it's McKenna.' They have a grand idea of introducing more strangeness into the theatre of Haiti.

—They're funny.

—They're not funny.

—*Yo ap-di-m yo kôn wè zôbi.* [Trans. They were telling me they used to see zombis.]

—Oh, my, he's living!

—He speaks the language of the dead.

—*Bâ-m moso mâjé.* [Trans. Give me a piece of food.]

—It's creyol. He's Haitian through and through.

—What's he saying?

—*M-ap-fè zôbi prâ ou.* [Trans. I'll make the zombis get you.]

—I believe that's the Haitian way of saying, 'The missus and I had a fight.'

—Very funny.

The girls prone to wandering alone in the pine scrub forests discover a camp neither too near nor too far away, and however long it takes to get there, the walk is just right. The camp is where the film crew is staying, the film crew with Culprit Clutch as director, although for whatever reason, Culprit also has a room in a pension in Le Cap.

JILL

His pension room is small, or so we've heard, a single bed, a hanger, and chest of drawers, not that we'll ever see his room. Such quarters are as off-limits to us as our dormitory is to everyone else.

NORA

It looks like hell, their camp, like a pack of dogs lives here, not what you'd expect from a set of Hollywood types even if they are from New York and only make educational pictures. They are all booze hounds, that much is clear, and all their garbage winds up on the ground, bottles everywhere and cigarette butts. They sleep in tents and cook their meals by fire, and their world turns around their supply truck, which is where they store the microphones, stage lights, and film, not to mention their booze, and they always seem to be running out of it, and they invade Le Cap looking for more. How can people live like this and wake up in the morning and make pictures? I always thought that to make pictures, you had to be neat in your habits. If dirt gets in your camera, your film is ruined, and with these bums, dirt is everywhere.

ABBOT JAFFE

The linen in the back of the supply truck was sent by the United Nations. It appears UNESCO wanted to make sure we had a fresh supply of linen. Yet linen hardly stays fresh when you are sleeping in a tent on a floor of solid dirt. After a while, the linen disappeared, and who's to say it wasn't stolen. Or someone around here just gave it away. I don't care. There's not much use for linen here.

SAMANTHA SOUND

Silly Billy! You went to the Useless Bum camp all by your lonesome to find Culprit Clutch, and believe you me, you're not that different from the rest of us. Now we're here, and we still haven't seen hide nor hair.

Jaffe says, —If you girls see him, will you let him know we're looking for him. He has an icebox at his fancy pension, and we need a cool place to store the Ektachrome. I won't let the heat get to me, but I'll be damned if I let it ruin our movie before we even begin to shoot.

NORA & JILL

I feel worst of all for Sheila. The rest of them are Useless Bums through and through, and she doesn't belong with that lunatic crew. She answered the movie crew want ad just like the rest of them, but she got a raw deal, and not just because the ad forgot to mention that it was government work and they were sending her to Haiti. They brought her on as the film's editor, because that was her experience in working on her father's films. She says they hired her to do it because to them it seems like sewing.

—Which is funny because she doesn't know the first thing about sewing.

—Then UNESCO decided that the film would be edited back in New York City, that the Useless Bums would send all their exposed stock back to the mainland. This gives Sheila nothing to do, yet she's still here.

—Of course, none of them have anything to do, until they get their hands on a camera.

—They keep screwing Sheila over, you see, and it's the

same way they're screwing us, telling us we can leave when we finish our studies but not letting us know what we need to do to finish them, and there's still talk of a revolt.

—I used to be angry, but now I just don't give a damn.

—I am not sure if that look on Sheila's face is a scowl because of the situation she's in or if that's the look she was born with. If she didn't look so angry, she might even be pretty.

—It doesn't help that the other Useless Bums are men. Since there won't be film to edit, they told her she can be their Continuity Girl. She will make suggestions on the set to give Mr. Director the fewest headaches, but I know how men are, and I know right now that as long as men are in charge, they will never listen to a word she says. They are a pack of turds, men.

—Swine!

—Calling Sheila a girl is selling her short. It's not that she's older, because she's only a year or two older than the rest of us, but she has the self-confidence of an adult. There's no kidding around with her, and kidding around is the only way some of us keep from going mad.

—Have you ever given it thought how Haiti sounds like Hades?

—Not really, but it's just as hot.

—Do you realize how much Haiti sounds like hate? Haiti sounds like hate with an i at the end, because then it would be hait, pure and simple. I hate, I hate, I hate, I hate Haiti.

—Oh, brother!

—The irony around Sheila is that she knows more about motion picture photography than the lot of them. I can tell just by talking to her. They make fun of her and dismiss her for it.

•

—It's only natural, says Stuart Scales-McCabe. —A woman knows things like shutter speed and how to gauge exposure, while a man just wants to get closer to the subject and see more. A women knows her stops and sets them correctly.

They chuckle at the innuendo.

Sheila has a reply, —A man typically lights a scene too much, because it makes no matter what you show, a man always wants to see more. A woman understands darkness and shadows.

—It's all about that shadowy place, says McCabe, —that shadowy place right between her legs.

—You're a swine, talking that way in mixed company, talking that way in any company.

—No matter how hard I try, he goes on, —I've never been able to see it closely enough to see it all. As much light as you throw on it, and you shine on it brightly when shooting stag films, I'm always left wanting more.

—I would say that under more light, the less appealing it is, adds Neil the Feel.

All this seedy talk has Sheila wishing she could throw herself off the nearest sea cliff, or perhaps do something less dangerous and more ameliorative, perhaps paint. She mentions the desire, and they have a mouthful to say about that, too.

—Paint? The brush is just another substitute for the phallus.

—You can sexualize painting all you want. You know Freud would.

—Wasn't it Nietzsche who used to say Freud is dead?

—The camera is always a woman. A camera traps light inside of it, if you catch my drift. The brush just pushes paint around, producing nothing on its own.

—Women who paint have a bad case of penis envy is what I'm saying.

—Shut up! Sheila cries out and runs off. She can't get away from them fast enough.

They carry on with the same conversation they were having, ignoring her presence when she is with them and ignoring her absence when she's gone.

—Aren't all photographers talentless hacks who wish they could paint but don't have the patience to learn? I am saying that from my own experience as a photographer.

—I think the two art forms are so different, each one beautiful in its own particular and peculiar way. I would never knock photography, and I would never knock motion pictures.

Sheila hauls an easel, canvas, and her wood box of paint and brushes up the trail to the Citadelle Laferrière. After she's set up, you'd never know the struggle it was for her to get here. It will take longer creeping back down than climbing, especially with a freshly painted canvas to protect. Other painters who climb this high may delight in the tableau the Citadelle presents at such a close vantage. Not Sheila. High on the rock, she's in a linen bonnet and painting the landscape below, the cliffs, the mountains with their scarce patches of green. She paints the view of the valley with the Citadelle at her back.

Here comes Belinda Ballard, climbing the bumpy road to the Citadelle on her bicycle, riding all the way to near the top and walking the rest of the way, just to prove to herself she could make it.

While Sheila and Belinda have seen each other before, they have never spoken. There are always so many people milling about, there is never any privacy. Not to mention, Sheila's family back in New York has been sending her money so that rather than sleep at that pigsty campsite, she has her own pension room.

Belinda is curious to see how the painting is turning out. Sheila has just started and there's not yet much to show.

From their point of view, the sea doesn't seem real. The horizon is a razor edge with dark, billowing clouds rising from it.

—I'm amazed you were able to paint a line so straight. It looks . . . real.

Sheila doesn't say anything but paints.

Belinda watches fishing boats with colorful patches holding together their tattered gray sails cross paths with an American war ship on patrol from Guantanamo.

—It's a comical sight, really, Belinda says. —I'm not sure why.

She can't stand still. She takes a look all around her. On one side, there are stunning peaks; on another, the green northern plain; and always the sea in the distance. She wanders into the Citadelle fortress, running her fingers over the rusting hinges on gargantuan doors, and she discovers a crate so heavy it would take a crane to lift as it's piled high with rusting cannon balls. After exploring all she can without wandering too far away, she returns to Sheila.

—See, I knew if I gave you enough time, you'd really have something. The painting is marvelous!

Sheila remains silent, then addresses Belinda as if Belinda were not there, —I am not such a religious type that I would say yes, but this is God's art, and it does lead you to wonder, and indeed, if this is true, you can call God a metaphysical realist. Please excuse me, I have this habit of talking to myself even when other people are around, and for all I know I'm full of beans.

—You make good sense to me.

It's a painting simply of the sea with a horizon as straight as a carpenter's square.

—Do you ever paint people? Belinda asks. She's seen art created by the Haitians: colorful townscapes and market scenes with boundless people moving about, the women with wicker baskets of fruit balanced on their heads, the scene stretched across the face of the canvas.

—When there are people to paint, I paint them.

Haiti is brimming over with people, so Belinda doesn't know exactly what Sheila means.

—Sometimes, you have to climb this high to paint a scene without people in it.

Belinda takes that as a cue that Sheila may wish to be alone. —I can leave, Belinda says.

—No, stay. That's not what I was saying. What I mean is that the people here never hold still long enough for me to paint them, and I am unskilled when it comes to painting people blurring about with such frantic, kinetic energy. New York is the same way. Landscapes are more my cup of tea.

—I know what you mean.

—Have you ever posed for painters?

Belinda, of all the student nurses, is the one who prides herself most on her worldliness, her far-reaching collected experiences, her exposure to the arts and sciences, her two semesters at Washington University in St. Louis, and if she wanted to say yes, she had posed for painters in the past, she would be able to recall past experiences and relate it in such a way to make it sound like she knows what she's talking about. There was the time in grammar school when the boy showed her a finger painting and said that it was supposed to be her, something like that. This time around, Belinda doesn't feel like playing that game.

—Not really, I mean no, Belinda says. —I mean, I didn't bring any nice clothes with me to the island, and all I have is my student uniform, she stammers, answering a question other than what was asked.

—You don't have to wear your uniform.

—I thought only homely girls pose for painters, and it's the artist's skill that makes them beautiful.

The two of them find themselves standing with that their faces near each other until Belinda steps back. There will come the inevitable downtime when it's just the two of them talking, the two of them relating to each other. Where will this lead? If Belinda holds still long enough to pose, the two of them will become friends. Over the course of time, their stay here will end, and they will return to the U.S.A., Sheila back to New York, and with all the talk of her family back in Missouri, Belinda has nowhere to go. Maybe now she'll go to New York, too. That way, she could continue posing and maybe even get good at it, and they could stay friends and not just pen-pals. Maybe Sheila could teach Belinda how to paint, and then Sheila will become the one who poses. Maybe Sheila will become a famous painter, and her paintings of Belinda will become her showcase works. They will have conversations like this:

—That first time, up near the Citadelle . . .

—Yes, I remember.

—You were wearing a bonnet.

—I don't own a bonnet.

—I don't know why I remember that, but the memory is so clear, it could have been five minutes ago.

At first, Belinda is too shy to take off her clothes, so she leaves her uniform on, and Sheila paints the way she imagines Belinda may look with her uniform off. Belinda had seen herself often enough dripping wet in the mirror after stepping out of the shower to see that the paintings do not quite capture the truth about her body, and not for any kind of lack of artistic skill on Sheila's part. As soon as the uniform falls to the floor and she steps out of it, Belinda no longer feels the fear of people seeing her body. The problem now is mosquitoes, but Sheila's paintings are so beautiful that the bites are worth it.

Before long, the Useless Bums catch wind of what's going on and beat on the door of Sheila's room at the pension, demanding the film stock they were storing in her icebox, which is their ruse. Their real reason for knocking madly at Sheila's door is the prospect of taking a peep at those nude paintings of the tall Nightingale with even higher hopes that she may be here now, posing at the moment when they bust inside.

Of course, no one's home, and the only paintings they find are the landscapes that Sheila used to paint and an experiment or two in abstract expressionism.

(Before leaving that day, Sheila took care to hide the nudes behind the curtain in the bathtub.)

It isn't their intention to meet in secret. Josie is never where she's supposed to be, and no one has seen Culprit. The only evidence of Culprit's return was the mysterious appearance of a 16 mm motion picture camera in the back of the supply truck at the camp.

To Culprit, it's as if just a day or two had passed since he was last here, and nothing has changed. Yet he has been gone long enough, it is like seeing everything for the first time, the traffic policeman under the wooden umbrella with a whistle in his mouth, the procession of dark nuns and a donkey train behind them, the long curtain in his pension room that poofs inward with every clap of thunder.

To Josie, Culprit himself is strangely familiar. She never really knew him last time.

The water churns below the sea cliff where they stand. She takes her belt off to play with it, then puts it back on, while he studies a conch shell he found earlier when the two of them were walking closer to the water.

The wind causes rocks to roll down the cliffs behind them; they stay out of the way. You'd think the danger here is water below reaching up to grab you, but really the danger comes from above.

—There is no beach down there.

—So?

—It's amazing what the wind does to these islands.

—It's the surf that does it.

—Do you hear that flapping sound?

—It's the wind on something.

—The wind on what?

—They stopped a suspicious boat a few miles from here.

—Communists?

—Pirates.

—So how long are we going to keep up this charade?

—What charade?

—This.

The Cosmic & The Comic

—May I? he asks in crisp English. —I wish to show you this little pearl of a map. The three tones, they are the Haitian colors. Crimson is for the bougainvillea of Haiti, and blue is the sea. Lavender-lilac, that's the sky at sunset. In the corner, it is the Haitian national seal. I would give this map to you for 25 cents American.

—Does it show where to find the town the zombis built?

The boy grins, raises his eyebrows, shrugs.

—It's supposed to be a secret, put it that way, the Yankee says to his mates gathered beside him. —You're not supposed to ask about the town built by zombis.

The boy no longer looks confused. —It's not a secret, he says. —All the world knows about the town the zombis built. If you buy this map, I will show you where to find it.

The Yankee drops two bits into the boy's open palm.

The boy lowers his eyes and when they come up again, it's like looking into someone else's. His eyes become devious and mocking. What they are witnessing is a voudoun possession in the works. Then the boy lets a giggle slip, and the Yankees realize he's faking, though the boy sure had them fooled.

—You're just doing that, trying to scare people.

Next time, they won't fool so easily.

—Back home, voudoun is so sensationalized. If you believe everything you read, they are cannibals performing rites of human sacrifice, witch doctors placing hexes on people, making dolls in their image and inflicting pain on them. If you believe what you read, Haiti is abounding in Black Magic, but there's no Black Magic in Haiti. Even the voudoun possession of the soul might be nothing more than playacting.

—I sure would like to find that town built by zombis.

—You've seen too many Italian movies.

Three Nightingales are hanging their laundry on lines while a balloon passes overhead. Nora had the smarts to bring the opera glasses from the drawer of the secretary in the great room, just in case they should see the mysterious balloon again. There have been several sightings. It isn't the balloon itself that piques their curiosity as much as its cargo. The balloon drifts across the sky, tugging along a large hook-shaped object.

—It's a house, Nora proclaims while seeing the object more closely through the glasses.

—How can you tell?

—I see windows.

—That sure is a funny shape for a house.

—I see people.

—In the balloon?

—In the house. I see a person in an open window with binoculars.

—What nerve! Some people are as nosy as we are.

—Is he looking down at us?

—No, he's staring out to sea.

—Let's get his attention: Hey, mister! Samantha yells.—Hey, mister, down here!

Nora feels a tap at her elbow and thinks it's either Jill or Cynthia wanting her to pass along the opera glasses. As she hands them off, she sees it's a strange man who must have walked up while their gazes were fixed to the sky. He takes the glasses and holds them up to his eyes, lowers them, shakes his head.

As Nora is gesturing to ask the man who the heck he is, a moment of high drama ensues. The cord attaching the candy-cane shaped house to the balloon slips. Was that supposed to happen? The structure begins its free fall, and it takes their breath away. The people inside are falling to their doom! A parachute sprouts from the top, then cushions its descent. Safe! The structure drifts slowly into a grove of mahogany in the direction of the Useless Bums' camp.

—That's the best news I've had all day.

—You can say that again.

—Are those your people in there? Nora asks the stranger standing elbow to elbow with her.

—Formerly.

From his looks, he's a scientist, the glasses, the serious manner, all the stereotypical trappings.

—You're American like us?

—Yes.

—Your name's Claypool? (The name was on a small plastic plate pinned onto his shirt.)

—Yes.

—What do you know about that flying contraption, Mr. Claypool?

—It's one of our fleet of aerodynamic domicile capsules, lightweight living spaces designed for balloon transport.

—No kidding, what a kick! Nora says. —Flying houses.

—Why not build houses that stay put? It sure works back in home in America.

—Because.

—Because why?

—Because unless you live in Texas with access to an oil well and can refine the crude in your kitchen, a gas-powered engine won't do you any good.

—Why do you need an oil well to build a house that stays put?

—It's based on a principle, the Dynaflow philosophy. Wealth is measured as the time you can survive on earth by your wits alone.

—How fascinating!

—The trick is to harness the earth's resources without destroying or depleting them.

—That paints a rosy picture!

—Hanging laundry is an excellent example. No byproducts and nothing is used up.

—I knew we had the right idea this morning.

—Yet with smarts we don't need to live like primitive people. We can have our creature comforts.

—I would love it if we could have a vacuum cleaner at St. Marc's.

—It's in the design. Determine the problem and design the solution. Inventiveness.

—You're an inventor? I don't think I ever met a real live inventor before.

Nora adopts a serious air,—My question is, why are you down here while the rest of you are up there?

—Because the old man has been like an old man to me.

—What old man?

—Headminster Gully.

—I've heard of him.

—Is he famous?

—He's the inventor of the geodesic domes, Jill says.

—That's someone else, Claypool says. —Gully is the inventor of the Quonset hut and founder of the Dynaflow Institute, my former employer.

—What's a Quonset hut?

—Arched T-frame, semi-cylindrical, corrugated sheet metal naval housing. They're sturdy and go up quick.

—That still doesn't explain why you're down here, and they're up there.

—I'm a conscientious objector.

—What does that have to do with it?

—Do you have any idea how many people have died because of Quonset huts?

—It's a building, not a weapon.

—It's war machinery. I'm not in the business of building tools for military purposes.

—Like those flying houses? Nora asks.

—They seem pretty harmless to me.

—You can drop them on top of people, Jill says.

—Like the Wicked Witch of the West, Samantha says.

—Droll, Claypool says.

There's a sudden disturbance in the distance, two pariah dogs in pursuit of a rabbit. The dogs fly under the linens hanging on the line, creating a wind that poofs the sheets outward, and are gone as soon as they arrive.

—Why are you no longer with the Dynaflow Institute? Jill asks.

—I've had it up to my ears.

—I know what that feels like. I've wanted to run away for years.

—Disappearing is easy, Claypool says. —The hard part is finding a way they don't come looking for you.

—They might send me to the tee-hee farm for saying this, Jill says. —There are times when I've wanted to disappear so badly that I've dreamed of pretending I'm dead.

Along the same path the dogs had flown, they hear the voices of laughing men, Useless Bums.

—It sounds like the fellows will be joining us, Jill says.

In that moment, she sees Claypool out of the corner of her eye, and in that same moment he's gone.

—Now where did he go? Samantha asks.

—He must have walked off when our backs were turned. Such a strange man.

—No, Jill says with a mix of urgency and confusion in her voice. —He was here.

—Of course he was here, you dingbat! We were talking to him.

—He disappeared, just like that.

—Dingbat, that's impossible.

—He disappeared before my eyes.

—You gals see a funny-looking capsule on a parachute fall somewhere around here?

—It's a gift for us from the Dynaflow Institute.

—A man's capsule is his castle.

—We won't have to sleep in a tent anymore.

—They said they would drop by with one. They truly meant 'drop by.'

—What do you bums know about the Dynaflow Institute?

—They're a bunch of eggheads who build flying houses and dome cars.

—What else do you know about them?

—They build gizmos for people who want to live like savages and not give up their creature comforts.

—They're here to work in peace. Certain members of Congress call them Communists.

—Have you seen their car? It runs without gas.

—That's a Communist idea for you, right there!

—They believe the world's coal and oil supply will run out in thirty years.

—They say that mankind will soon return to its hunter and gatherer roots.

—The State Department is funding them.

—Now it makes sense.

—It does.

—The secret reason we're here is the same secret reason they're here.

—It's bad manners to keep secrets.

—Do tell!

—It's not my secret. I don't mind telling.

—I think I know what you're going to say.

—The government has set its sights on an atomic war.

—That's no secret.

—They won't send us home because they want us to call upon if we lose an eastern city. They're stashing the Dynaflow Institute here, because after the destruction, people will live like nomads in houses carried by balloons and drive cars that run without gas. Why else would they make us watch these slideshows filled with photographs of burnt-out bodies from Japan?

—At least we're safe because we're in Haiti.

—Not if they send us to an atomic blast site. Radiation poisoning is worse than burns.

—What a horrible thought!

—I knew it all along but didn't want to think it's true.

—I can't speak for the rest of you fellows, says Stuart Scales-McCabe, —but if World War III leaves us the last living Americans, I know damn well that it's my responsibility to get the ball rolling on repopulating our great nation. Which one of you girls would like to stand first in line?

First silence, then Jill slaps his face so hard that it appears on its way to flying off his neck before snapping back in place.

—My parents live in Poughkeepsie and my sisters in Jersey. I do not wish them dead just so you can get it on!

She yanks her linens off the lines, crumples them into her basket, and stomps back toward St. Marc's. Stuart slinks into the grove until his face stops smarting and his pride returns.

—You'll have to excuse Jill. She gets touchy.

—Stuart provoked her. I don't understand all his bluster about his way with women when all he does is upset them and try to get a laugh out of the fellows. His big secret is it's the men he's out to impress.

—Jill has other reasons to be sensitive.

—She's not sleeping.

—She's shaken up because she thought she saw an invisible man.

—That's impossible.

—I know, that's what I told her. There is no such thing.

—That's not what I meant. It's possible, I believe, for a man to turn invisible, but not possible to see him.

—I saw him. He wasn't invisible. Mr. Claypool slipped away when no one was looking.

—I wouldn't put it past the Dynaflow Institute to develop a top secret cloak of invisibility for American G.I.s. The flying houses are just to throw the Russians off their trail.

—That would give the Americans an unfair advantage, wouldn't you think?

—If anyone has an unfair advantage, I just hope it's us.

They hear a loud whistle. It's Keith Clone down the hill, waving to get their attention.

—He must have found our capsule.

Its parachute had caught in a tree and it's swinging a few feet off the ground. When they find it and look inside, it's empty. The person in the window must have walked away, just like how Claypool had walked away. Lowering the capsule proves to be a simple task, and the men raise the lightweight capsule upon their shoulders like a casket and march away with it in the direction of their camp. Nora and Samantha balancing their laundry baskets on their hips follow. No one notices when she rejoins the party, but suddenly Jill is with them, too.

—Tonight we're going to christen our new pad with booze and jazz records.

—How much do you know about Headminster Gully? Jill asks Abbot Jaffe.

—He's the Dynaflow Institute's resident genius. It's his brainchild.

—I always confuse him with Buckminster Fuller.

—The difference is Buckminster Fuller looks old. Gully is old.

—No one's seen him since they moved to Port-au-Prince. The rumor is he's gone off to the Great Hereafter.

—What I heard, Lafferty chimes in, is that they are keeping his brain alive in an aqueous solution with two live wires plugged into an electric socket.

—The brain communicates with his minions through mental telepathy, says McKenna.

—Now I know you're putting me on.

Back at the camp, they open the capsule's flaps, press a button, and spring-loaded gizmos snap the object into an open and comfortable living space. The Useless Bums file in with Nora, Jill, and Samantha behind them. Egg-shaped seats descend from the ceiling.

—What a nifty place to live! Samantha says.

Keith Clone, —I'd love to get my hands on one of their dome cars that don't run on gas.

—What's the trick?

—Instead of a motor, it's got a flywheel. You have to pedal to get the flywheel going, but once you do, it keeps going on its own. Going downhill gets the flywheel revving pretty fast, creating the power to sustain you over the next hill and then some. It's the miracle of the conservation of energy.

—What will they think up next?

—They're more like magicians than scientists.

—We live in a magical age.

M. Lyle Mislove, who has been silent, gestures that it is his turn to speak, —As a man whose father was a professional stage magician, I can tell you the Dynaflow Institute is bad for the art. Magical entertainers can't keep pace with scientific progress. Every time a scientist invents something wonderful and new, the magician must go back to the drawing board to dream up something even more spectacular. The world is full of scientists, while the brothers of the American Society of Magicians are the loneliest artists you'll ever meet. How on earth are they supposed to keep up? That's why I took up playwriting. A man's gotta eat.

—I didn't know you aspired to be a magician.

—That was many years ago.

—I wonder if the Dynaflow Institute has the know-how to build a time machine.

—Or invent a magic ring that turns people invisible.

—There's a rumor that they are working on the problem of invisibility.

—You've seen too many matinees.

—There may even be an invisible man among us.

—Not me.

—Of course, not you. We can see you. The invisible man is the one we cannot see, McKenna says.

—I saw someone with binoculars in the capsule while it was still attached to the balloon.

—Where did he go?

—I don't know.

—Maybe he's gone invisible.

—When he's around, you can't see him. When he's not invisible, he likes to hide.

—He might even be standing right in front of us.

—You're just saying that, trying to scare people.

—There is one way to prove we are alone in this room. Bolt the door and pull a sheet out of your laundry basket. We'll use it as a net to try and catch ourselves an invisible man.

—Oh, please!

—You do realize that if there were such a man in the room right now, he's invisible and not deaf. If he doesn't want to get caught, he would have slipped out already.

—Close the door, bolt it shut, and let's give it a go. Toss me that sheet!

Before the door closes, in fly the two pariah dogs pursuing a rabbit. The dogs fly in circles around the capsule, their windy cyclone causing the sheet to hover flat near the ceiling. They speed faster around the room, up along the walls, and the only way to get them out is to unlatch the door and hope they go. With the door open, their hind legs digging over their shoulders, they barrel away and into the Haitian twilight. The sheet falls to the floor as the nerve-wracked inhabitants of the capsule shake themselves off.

—Oh, damn, I spilled my drink.

It becomes a regular occurrence, mixed-company get-togethers, now that they have a Dynaflow pad where they can drink, smoke, and speak freely about those not in the room. They are a Godless Bohemian Congregation.

—Neil the Feel is lucky to be alive.

—Aren't we all?

—The humiliation would have been enough to kill me.

—Strangely, Miss Penny is the only one who doesn't know about the entire escapade. She slept right through it.

—Neil the Feel has this odd notion that if he never talks about his boozy exploits, no one else will talk about them, either. We all know he's the biggest lush on the island. He'll drink anything he can get his hands on, but don't let on that you know.

—He's the type you ask if he's a drinker, and he'll say no just as long as he doesn't have a drink in hand right then.

—That's because he never knows where his next drink is coming from.

—He's always broke. He spends all his dough on booze.

—Everything worked out. He brought Miss Penny back in one piece and got away with his shenanigan.

—He even got his jacket back, which shows the Nightingales have their heart in the right place.

—So let me get this straight. He rang the dormitory bell in the middle of the night, and then ran away as fast as his short, stubby legs would take him.

—He ran because he thought he could get away with it. What he didn't realize is that we all sleep on the building's second floor, and those who woke up startled by the door chimes were less inclined to race downstairs than to look out the window. That's how we saw him running away.

—I would know him a mile away. He's the Yank whose belly bounces between his knees when he runs.

—Fleeing the scene of the crime wasn't bad enough. He left behind his jacket. A true gentleman, he had coaxed Miss Penny's sleeping body on top of it when he loaded her onto the wheelbarrow.

—I can't believe it didn't wake her up.

—Not only did he leave his coat behind, an unopened bottle of rum was in the lapel.

—Later, when Miss Penny was back sleeping soundly in her bed, and Neil the Feel was long gone, we passed the bottle around and shared a good laugh.

Neil the Feel, —Father, I have three sins to confess. I haven't gone to Mass since coming to Haiti. I drink more than what's good for me. Saturday night, I found myself plastered on the grounds of the nursing school.

—How did that happen?

—I don't remember. Geezus, how do you think?

—Hoping to make friends.

—All's I know is that when I got there, there was a student nurse lolling around the grounds in nothing but her nightgown with this bed-sheet wrapped around her. When I saw her, I almost pissed myself, pardon the expression. I helped her get home safe and sound.

—Had she been drinking?

—Sleepwalking.

—How did you manage to get her home?

—M. Budé left a wheelbarrow out. I lay down my coat and placed her inside.

—She never woke?

—No. Before loading her on board, I had to run clear across the lawn to get the wheelbarrow and then run back with it to where she was out cold against a tree. I don't know if you've ever tried running with a wheelbarrow, let me tell you.

—I haven't.

—It makes this sound like rolling thunder.

—You don't say.

—I am surprised half the world didn't wake up, let alone the girl.

—How exactly did her body feel, when you lifted her?

—What are you driving at?

—You're sure she never awoke.

—She never made a peep.

—How did you lift her?

—Beneath the shoulders.

—Did your hand by chance overreach and graze her bosom ever so lightly?

—Hey, why are you reading me the riot act? I should be in line to get a medal for this.

—To grant you forgiveness, I need to know the sin.

—I may have copped a feel. Then again it might have just been the material in her nightgown. All's I was trying to do was get her home in one piece.

—What are this young lady's bosoms like?

—It was dark. I couldn't see much.

—Bosoms the size of sand dollars, to the eyes and to the touch.

—Bosoms the size of jokes, if you ask me.

—Now we're getting somewhere!

—I didn't touch them.

—Did you feel any freckles?

—How would I do that?

—Freckles can be raised from the skin ever so slightly. Shows how much you know about women, kid.

—I hold my own, Father.

—Do you have more you wish to confess?

—Nothing comes to mind.

—Did you like the feel of her skin?

—Easy does it, Father. Like I said, I never touched her anywhere. Just this nightgown material, all bunched up.

—Other than the rolling thunder sound a wheelbarrow makes, what lesson have you learned?

—That even if you don't cop a feel but think you may have copped a feel, you may as well have copped a feel, because apparently, it's all the same in God's eyes, and I really need to give up the drink and start going to Mass.

—Add fifteen Hail Marys, and all is healed in God's eyes.

NORA

Molasses isn't as slow as a procession of nuns in the Nord Department. In sun helmets that cover their hair, they inch across the market square in a single-file line. They make a dividing line that's impossible to cross. We're thirsty, and on the other side of them, women are selling juice in cups made from green coconut halves. We'll be stuck here all day waiting for them to pass.

JILL

To our left is a tall pile of thick rope that lost its way from a seagoing vessel; to our right, a waist-high pile of dry beans, and children are playing king of the mountain on top, causing the mound to spread. I don't mind waiting for the nuns to pass.

KEITH CLONE

I don't mind waiting for the nuns to pass. It gives me a moment to stop and survey the landscape. I'm seeing many wood poles driven into the ground along the sides of roads, up and down the mountains. It's a British project. They are establishing a pan-Haitian telephone system. The next step involves stringing lines of wire across the tops of the poles and hoping that hurricane winds don't knock them over.

M. LYLE MISLOVE

This procession of nuns reminds me of the last time I acted, a bit part in a production of Saint Joan at Columbia. I studied with Lee Strasberg. Nothing came of it. I'm a wooden stage presence, but I can't imagine spending my life away from the theatre. After Saint Joan, I took up the playwright's cause, thinking I could still inhabit the theatre without going onstage. The more I wrote, the more I found myself writing parts for myself, which wasn't my intention. I think it's my subconscious telling me my love is to be on stage.

—So who are the stars coming to Haiti to make this picture?

—You're looking at 'em.

—The stars in the sky?

—No, you silly dame, all of you. All's you need is to carry yourself like a star to make out as one.

—I do that already.

—See, there you go. You're halfway there. Someone just needs to put you in pictures.

—Why don't you do just that?

—Someone with a camera needs to put you in pictures.

—I forgot to mention, there's a camera in the truck. He must have dropped it off.

—Thank you, Culprit Clutch, wherever you are.

—Hey, I've been seeing signs for *Cat on a Hot Tin Roof* at the cinema. We could go Friday night.

—I have something better.

—Better than Paul Newman?

From under a pile of folded linen, Lafferty produces a 16 mm film can.

—Where did you get that?

—A little bird gave it to me.

—A stag film?

—A film about Haiti.

—How dull. I already know more about Haiti than I ever wanted.

—It's a film by those who came before us. It's in English, shot near Cap Haitien.

—It will be refreshing to see what we're up against from a production standpoint.

—At least we have a print to show.

—Once it's dark, let's roll film.

MOVIE NARRATOR

You were expecting maybe Florida and its orange groves, or Cuba and its cigar factories and nightclubs. But what you'll find isn't of the New World. What you find in Haiti is deep, dark, truthful Africa. After Africa, the major influence is an Indian tribe, the Arawaks, whose customs strangely mirror those of their more recent African compatriots.

—I love the narrator's voice. It's a full octave below mine.

—All's I know of Africa is what I seen in *National Geographic* magazines lying on my brother's bedroom floor.

—I won't ask why you know so much about your brother's magazines.

—Haiti does seem older than other places I've been.

—The thought of Josie riding around in cars with Haitian men. Is it really so bad?

—I bet they want our film to be more up-tempo.

—Shhh!

MOVIE NARRATOR

The citizens of Haiti call themselves Catholic, though

in spots they accompany their ceremonies with native drumming rather than ecclesiatical music. The cathedral in Cap Haitien is majestic, tall with stucco outer walls and magnificent spires. Yet once you are out in the sticks, the language spoken is creyol, and the religion is voudoun. The peasants hold community fires in clearings far from any town, and their ceremonies take place after dark. The Haitian peasant worships a pantheon of voudoun gods in a tradition similar to the mythology of the Ancient Greeks. The difference is that voudoun has withstood the test of time while the cult of Zeus has vanished from the face of the earth.

—That's not true. They still worship Zeus on Easter Island.

—The voudoun spirits are more like eccentric aunts and uncles than gods.

—You really know your stuff.

—The so-called voudoun gods sneak up and slap you on the back, laughing and stinking of Scotch.

—I thought it was rum.

—I don't think the Haitians can be called Catholic, at least not in the strict sense like when I was in school back in Dearborn. The sisters from St. Ignatius Legion Street would beat those Haitian drummers silly if given a chance.

—Oh, Nora.

—Catholics don't beat drums. They beat children.

MOVIE NARRATOR

As the Haitians are fond of saying, the god mounts you, the way a rider mounts a horse. You can always tell when a mounting has occurred. The bodies of the possessed are unchanged in their physical appearance, but the manner in which the person walks is now different, and when you look into the person's face, you find yourself peering into a different set of eyes.

—Do you believe in voudoun?

—Do you believe in method acting?

—I asked you first.

—I asked you the better question.

—Voudoun has nothing to do with the stage.

—Nah, they're clearly connected.

—There's a connection between voudoun possession and method acting?

—You New York types have to slow down when you talk. What is method acting?

—It's the style of acting that means you live the part.

—It's about giving a performance so real it's unbelievable.

—Now you really lost me.

—It's about coaxing the audience into believing what they're seeing is happening before their eyes.

—It's the opposite of slapstick, melodramatic acting.

—One of my problems with the Method is that there is no way you can make spectators forget they are in a theatre, witnessing a company of players.

—That's where the actor's art comes in. Go as far as you can but never all the way.

—How does all this fit in with voudoun?

—Possession is like method acting. You lose yourself in your role so completely that you become the character you are playing, physically and spiritually. It's like self-hypnosis, and after the performance, when you do it right, you can't remember anything. When a Loa possesses the body, it's very similar.

—But acting is fakery, and voudoun is a religion. Religions are supposed to be real.

—Oh, brother.

—With all the hocus-pocus, voudoun is all just play-pretend. Take a look around, and there's your proof.

—To me, it makes no matter if voudoun is a religion or make-believe. It's a powerful force in these people's lives, just as acting is the guiding light of an actor's life. The problem in America is that no one takes acting seriously. Even in New York where there are more actors than anywhere, acting is some kind of joke. Acting is thought of as playing, but the secret actors keep is that their calling is a heightened spiritual experience. What if praying on your knees all day gets you nowhere near God, but acting does? Those moments when you live the part so deeply that you can't feel any trace of yourself and you become the role, those are spirits flowing through you, just like in voudoun.

—That's a beautiful sentiment, bravo. The problem is that parts in plays are based on fictional characters, products of a playwright's imagination. Last time I checked, fictional characters don't have spirits floating around in the ether.

—Maybe they do.

—Are you trying to tell me these Haitians know something we don't? They are collectively the dumbest people in the world. The taxi drivers kill their engines at stop lights because they think it saves petrol. They live in huts they can't even line up on a grid. They lay down tracks of railroad here and there that don't connect. Worst of all, they think the rest of the world is just like Haiti, which is a good thing, because if they ever caught on, New York would be overrun with Haitians, and that's the last thing we need.

—Spiritually, they have one up on us, just like method actors.

—The actors I know are a soulless bunch.

—Not every actor in New York is a method actor, and even among method actors, there are failures. Hello, you're looking at one.

—I get this strange feeling that we are on the set of a play. When you stare out at the sea, the horizon walls are painted backdrops illuminated by rows of footlights. If it is a play, that makes us all actors.

—No more wine for you, Sweetie.

—Shh, I want to hear what she says.

A breeze rattles the leaves high in the trees, a pause, then: —I get this strange feeling that we are performing a play for the Haitians. They laugh like hell at our antics and gimmicks, all the while we pretend we can't see them.

—They exist beyond the stage's fourth wall.

—I'm the same way. I've noticed over and over how we all project our voices, enunciate so clearly, strike these grand poses as if we were playing our parts to the nearsighted fellow in the back row.

—We're straight from the Lee Strasberg school for comics and clowns. We are so engrossed in our roles, we forget we're playing them. We never stop to see the world for what it is, and that's our hubris.

—Our pubis.

—I didn't understand a word a one of you just said. You talk like you're in college.

Neil the Feel, who hasn't had a drop to drink, mentions offhandedly that he's not drinking because he's begun going to Mass and doesn't want to show up in the morning stinking and hung over. He changes subjects away from himself and begins saying that the Catholic cathedral in Cap Haitien is a one-of-a-kind building, best you'll find in the West Indies, right up there with Italy and France.

Because it's the Godless Bohemian Congregation, he braces himself for jeers. Instead the girls ask if it would be all right for them to tag along. The Bums want to go, too. The girls want to be near God, and the Bums want to be near girls.

It's a blue-sky Sunday morning, and the scent of smoke hangs in the air, although its source is now more smolder than flame, and you can still hear drums in the distance, but now even the drumming sounds tired.

—The poor drummer must be about ready to fall over!

They find themselves on the cathedral steps, smoking cigarettes and shooting the breeze, waiting fifteen minutes for the last Mass to end and seating for the next one to begin. On the cathedral steps, Josie recognizes a young man, —Pascale! she exclaims.

—Josie! he answers.

LYDIA

We trip over ourselves to say hello to Pascale, because it's the right thing to do. Someone calls him Pascale the Rascal, which takes him aback. Aside from Josie, he's never met our crew. It shows we have nothing against Haitians. They are people, just like us, even though they are black, and not just black but dark black.

—The change, Pascale demands, his hand held out; he's trying out the English he's learning from Josie.

—He wants money.

—I just have a fiver, and I need to hang onto it.

—*Non, non, non*, the change!

Now he's off across the way at a telephone booth, trying to shake a coin out of the slot.

—He's got me. I'm baffled.

—Hey, here's a coin. Go buy yourself a cup of coffee.

—Yes!

Pascale catches the coin flung through the air and holds it in his hand, showing it to all of us. He waves his hands in the air, and it's gone. He shows us his hands, front and back, fingers splayed then closed, the coin has vanished. He waves his hands in the air again, rolling them in front of his head, then up high, now down low, and the coin reappears in his hand again, and not just one coin, but two or five, and then so many that he can't hold all of them in his hands. They pour onto the stone steps of the Catholic cathedral.

—That's a neat trick.

—You can keep the change, Pascale announces, the punch line, but he's lost his audience as the Yankee men and women climb the steps to enter the cathedral.

JILL

We'll see Pascale many times in the days ahead. We'll see him serving ice cream to kiddies in the cleanest uniform you'll ever see. We'll see him as a schoolteacher with a pencil propped above his ear and chalk coating his hands. We'll see him as a witch doctor putting on an African mask several times the size of his head, and performing a dance that leaves 'em in a trance. We don't know him well enough to know for certain it's him. On the dock with the crab cage, Pascale shows Josie how to catch them. Pascale is everywhere. It's true what they say about him. He is the face of the place, smart, funny, charming. I don't think they noticed me within earshot in the central city café veranda, while they were sipping their coffee. I wasn't hiding from them, although I was wearing a scarf and sunglasses. Josie acts like she's the only one who strays from the school, though I do, too, and no one knows.

—Pascale, Josie says, —I understand you were born here, but you don't belong here. You should go to New York. Haiti was never your ancestors' chosen destination. They came here because they didn't have a choice. You can start history over by going to New York. You can take your magic act with you.

—But the manner your country affronts its black people.

—It's awful, I'm not defending it, but you can do better for yourself than here. Americans have so much they can learn from you. What exactly are you afraid of?

—The effigy.

—It's New York City. They don't burn effigies in New York.

—In America, the black people don't get a vote. The law prevents their voting. That is not a democracy.

—That happens in the South. You'll be in New York.

—I don't know, Josie.

—The New Yorkers will love your exotic magic act!

The U.S. State Department's outpost in Honolulu sends a large manila envelope addressed to MOVIE CREW care of the St. Marc American School. It's stuffed with photographs and a memorandum introducing a new sport called surfing. It involves wearing a bathing suit and standing aboard a long, flat stick balanced on the crest of ocean waves. Their mission is to make a short film featuring the sport on the beaches of northern Haiti.

—It's not like I always lived in a cave. I know what surfing is; it's Polynesian.

—They call it a surfing board; it's not a stick or ski.

—What's the difference?

—If Hawaiians heard you saying stick, they would hit you over the head with one.

—It wouldn't hurt. They're made from balsa. My head would probably shatter it.

—All's you have to do is stand on the board and keep balance halfway up a curling wave.

—Does the board stay in the same place?

—No, the wave moves you. According to what this says, you ride it.

—How do you hold still?

—You balance yourself.

—Are there oars?

—No.

—Do surf boards have Evinrude motors?

—They get their locomotion from the waves, as mad as that sounds.

McCabe thumbs through the photos, stopping on one and showing it to the others, —It looks like that wave is chasing that poor bastard, and he's riding it as fast as he can before it swallows him.

—Does that happen, do the waves catch up to you?

—If he had any brains, he'd get off that thing.

—It says here that if you crash in the water, it's called a wipeout.

—Surfing doesn't look so hard, really. Not much of a sport, McCabe says.

—It might be harder than it looks.

—Now baseball is a sport, it's just not a sport for Haiti. I brought my mitt thinking I'd find a sandlot and kids who play, but haven't seen a field since I've been here.

—These photos are lovely. The water and sky in Hawaii are so blue. I wonder if Washington knows it's not like that here. I haven't seen a beach here that looks anything like that.

—A beach is a beach. At least Haiti's not Bikini Atoll.

—I can't wait to try it out, McCabe says.

—Too bad, we don't have the sticks.

—We do. They're in those crates over there.

—Boy howdy! That was fast.

—There won't be much time to learn.

—It looks easy enough. You just stand there and balance. Either you have balance or you don't, McCabe says.

—Fine, we'll shoot surfing footage tomorrow late afternoon in the twilight sunlight.

—I hope the water's warm.

—The water is always warm below the Tropic of Cancer. Haven't you tested it?

—We need ourselves a surfing player.

—I nominate Culprit Clutch.

—Culprit's too accident prone. He'd drown.

—What's in that tiny box?

—Those are the bathing suits for the girls to wear in the movie. They're called bikinis.

—Ooo la-la!

—They don't leave much to the imagination, that's for certain.

—I wish I had known they want us to wear something so skimpy. I could've started my diet.

—I have the same measurements as Marilyn Monroe, but you'll never catch me in one of those.

—Did you see this last crate? It doesn't have surfing boards in it, just soil.

—It's not addressed to us. The man must have dropped it off by accident.

—Shipped from Romania, uh-oh.

—I don't like the looks of this.

—That's Count Dracula's crest.

—How do you know?

—Because I'm pulling your leg.

—It's just soil. It's not like there's a body buried inside it.

—How can you know that? Let's see you dig your hand deep inside there.

—No thank you, the last thing I need is a handful of maggots.

—What might happen when the crate's owner comes looking for it?

—In the dead of the night.

—If makes you feel any better, I'll steal some garlic from M. Budé's garden and plant it in this crate, just in case you're thinking what I'm thinking.

—Werewolves?

—Vampires.

—There used to be a werewolf infestation in Haiti.

—What changed?

—American G.I.s came in and brought DDT.

—I'd feel better if they had left some for us.

•

—Stuart Scales-McCabe, by unanimous decision you've been selected to be the star of our movie.

—Why me?

—Because of your self-inflating stories of yourself as an athlete. Congratulations.

—Why me? I never said I knew how to do this.

—You did!

—You said it looks easy.

—I said baseball's my sport. I don't know how to swim.

—Swimming's easy. You roll your arms like windmills and flutter your feet like hummingbird wings.

—There are sharks in the water.

—I'd worry more about German submarines.

—McCabe, here's what it's like, you paddle out with your belly on the surfing board. Then you find yourself face to face with a wave as high as a mountain. It lifts you right up. You'll feel tightness in your calves as you take the position. You hold on tight and ride with the wave back home.

—Now what? You're a playwright, Mislove. Write me some dialogue.

—Who made you boss?

—Culprit's not here. I'm taking the reins.

—George Bernard Shaw is what I know, Arthur Miller. When it comes to writing for a surfing film, I don't know where to start. A surfing film, I don't even know what that is.

—Get husky with it!

Mislove draws a pensive look, then proclaims, —Where grows the winter cherry, in what land?

—Will you listen to my friend here? Every word he speaks is poetry, Lafferty says.

—Winter cherry, my eye! People don't talk like that, says Abbot Jaffe.

—People do talk like that, because M. Lyle Mislove makes them talk like that, McKenna says.

—Ain't you ever seen a Lyle Mislove play? asks Lafferty.

—Just write me some dialogue, and I will be done with you.

ABBOT JAFFE

McCabe runs out to the water, the surfboard under his arm and three Nightingales in their new bikinis tailing him. He drops the board in the water, places himself across the top and paddles out toward the open sea. He waits for the waves. This may take a while. There don't seem to be any waves. Cut. Let's not film the waiting. We'll run out of film.

SAMANTHA SOUND

Not only are we wearing these skimpy, humiliating bathing suits, the tide is filled with shards of broken glass bottles, and the water is so filthy that I have black oil rings around my ankles. Other girls were lying on towels to get a suntan, and fleas jumped on them. This sure as heck ain't Myrtle Beach!

Miss Penny wears a long-waisted bathing suit with a voluminous skirt and long, striped stockings and a bathing helmet and bathing shoes so that her toes will not be pinched by crabs. The thin waves of a tidal pool are nipping at her feet.

—How 'bout these waves?

—They are the perfect size for surfing fleas.

—How long can McCabe stay out there?

—We'll never get this movie shot until there are waves.

—The worst part is the saltwater and sand in the gash on my foot.

—Worse than the fleas?

—The more skin you show, the more places they bite.

—Darn these skimpy things.

—Just kidding. I love the way you look in your bathing suit.

—McCabe is still out there, bobbing on the board.

—He's hanging on for dear life, afraid of getting wet. Some movie star!

—That McCabe fellow is a J-bird. I wonder why they let him out. I wonder why he's here.

—He's a photographer.

—He's a criminal.

With their light stands, cables, and sound recording gear on the beach, they didn't see the crowd of Haitians gathering behind them. The Haitians have come because the commotion sounded like there might be an emergency. They stay because the sight is so strange, the young women in bathing suits that show off their stomachs and the lone Yankee belly down on a floating board just off the shore.

With their heads hanging low, the Useless Bums carry their equipment to the supply truck, brushing shoulders with the Haitian men and women as they pass.

—They're wondering what the hell we're doing.

—I'm wondering what the hell we're doing.

—They look at us as if these are the strangest rites on earth. It makes no sense to them.

—It wouldn't make sense to anyone. There are no waves.

—They could have told us that.

—In their otherworldly pidgin no one understands.

—I am deflated, defeated in a battle against stupid waves, and not because the waves put up a fight.

—They must think we've lost our minds.

—There's nothing left to do other than admit failure.

—Where is Culprit Clutch?

—Absent as always.

—This is his movie. How I'd love to give him a piece of my mind.

—Hey, the boys are building a bonfire. There are sandwiches and wine. Want to stick around?

—Someone yell to McCabe it's time to get out of the water.

It's a dirty fire. The driftwood burns with an oily smoke that coats their sunburned faces. They neither notice nor care. It has been the kind of day that leaves them wondering what they're doing here, leaves them thinking about the other places in the world they wish they could be.

—UNESCO wants its Haitian surfing movie.

—If it were left up to me, we'd make a movie on the Devil's Triangle.

—It's not up to you.—Have you heard of the Bimini Road, just north of the Bahamas. There are rectangular stone formations there that prove the existence of Atlantis.

—Atlantis Shmatlantis. Poppycock.

—If it were left up to me, we'd make a movie about Atlantis.

—It's not up to you.

—Atlantis is coming back. It's supposed to resurface in 1968.

—I can prove it won't.

—Not unless you can see inside the future.

Abbot Jaffe turns to the tall, silent lad standing beside him.

—C.B., in 1968, will Atlantis return?

The boy whispers a long message in Abbot Jaffe's ear, then walks off.

—What does he say?

—He says it won't, but from how it sounds, 1968 will be a pretty strange year.

—How so?

—C.B. says that in 1968 there will be soldier apes riding horses and treating human beings like animals, but not to worry because there are a few chimpanzees who are kind and smart and help the humans, but the gorillas are mean, and the whole show is run by these blond apes with bangs.

—It's on the kid's authority that Atlantis won't return?

—I believe everything he says.

—Is he with you?

—Don't tell me you thought he was Haitian?

—He's Curly Batson.

—He's so young.

—He's seventeen.

—He's tall.

—He's also so dark, she whispers.

—We've noticed that about him.

—Is he Haitian originally?

—We brought him with us. He's a ward of the United Nations.

—Technically, he's of mixed lineage. His mother is Jewish, and his father, an Argentine. He was raised in New York, and though he looks black, he isn't.

—The name Curly Batson sounds neither Jewish nor Spanish.

—It's a made-up name the U.N. gave him. We call him C.B.

—His real name is classified, top secret.

—We don't even know it.

—We are the last to know anything.

—There are people who would hurt him if they knew what he can do.

—What's his secret?

—The remarkable ability to see across the sands of time.

—What are you saying?

—He's saying the kid's a time traveler.

—No, I ain't.

—You're right, he doesn't travel through time. He's a seer. He stays put.

—Poor kid, the bigots back home must hate him for the wrong reason, although if they knew he was an Argentine Jew, they would hate him just the same.

—Why, he's just a boy! What a shame, racism is. He's so adorable.

—You don't have to worry about good ol' C.B. He's going to go far in this world.

—Tell me more about his psychic power.

—The way the rest of us have memories of what has already happened, C.B. has memories of what's ahead.

—We can all see into the future to a degree. The trick is how far.

—C.B. can see pretty far, right up until 1973.

—I can't see past five minutes from now, and that's only if nothing happens in the meantime.

—Hey, C.B., get yourself back over here. These nice ladies want to hear some of your priceless stories. Tell them who the president is in 1973.

—President Nixon.

—He's well spoken.

—Hey, C.B., are you pulling my leg? How can a red-baiter like Richard Nixon get to be president?

—I don't know, sir.

—He's trying to tell us Nixon will be president twenty years from now. By then, Nixon will be old enough to be dead.

—Adlai Stevenson will be old enough to be dead. Nixon's young. He just seems old.

—So what else does the future have in store for us in 1973?

—Your guess is as good as mine.

—I wasn't asking you.

—At least Richard Nixon will be president.

—Yes.

—He's a hawk on Communism. Those apes won't stand a chance.

Nora whispers to Lafferty, —I worry about the boy.

—Why? He's a great kid.

—He can't see past 1973.

—I can't see past five minutes from now.

—What do you think that says about the future, that he can't see past 1973? Do you think it's the End of Days?

—I think it's the year the kid dies.

—He'll die young.

—He'll be thirty-three. That's my age now.

Abbot Jaffe jumps upon a log and addresses the crowd, —I remember something I seen that can help explain this.

—Explain what?

—Our lack of waves. It was this painting of the sea. I don't remember where I saw it.

—Sheila's painting. You don't need to say another word.

—Why's that?

—I know why you men are such fans of Sheila's paintings.

—I don't know what you mean.

—Do I have to wink to spell it out to you?

—Ahem, what I saw in this painting was a neat strip of white water halfway off the shore.

—What's that got to do with anything?

—There are waves; they're just breaking way out at sea.

—So what?

—So what, it's a barrier reef. It slows the waves down before they reach shore.

—What's that mean to us? We take a boat way out to shoot our surfing movie? McCabe ain't gonna like that.

—Maybe we try Port-au-Prince.

—This is getting more complicated all the time.

—What it means is we can't make this movie, period.

—I see you writing everything down in that notebook of yours, says McKenna.

—Do we amuse you so much you must write down every word we say?

asks Lafferty.

—That's typical of the *genus M. Lyle Mislove*. Head always buried in notebook.

—Would you care to tell us about the play you're writing, hey Lyle?

—I'd rather not, Mislove replies.

—How would it hurt? It might give you some fresh ideas, putting your ideas into words.

—All right, it's set in San Francisco. The villain is a fake swami from Brooklyn, and all the heroine's lines are drowned out by the foghorn on the Golden Gate Bridge. It takes place at the Presidio.

—That must save you time, not having to write her dialogue.

—I still have to know her psyche, her inner life. She's more difficult to write than a regular Charlotte Chatterbox.

—What's the play called?

—*The Depths of My Caress.*

—Is a caress ever measurable in terms of depth?

—It depends on the caress.

—I'm writing a play about the crates that contained the surfing boards, says McKenna.

—Do tell.

—The crates in my play contain Frankenstein's monster and are padded with shorn yak hair.

—I enjoy the exquisite details, says Lafferty.

—How will your theatre audience know it's shorn yak hair specifically? asks Jill.

—That's a challenge for the actors. They will have to express it through their tone of voice and body language.

—I think you should give up playwriting and try your hand at the novel, says Mislove.

—What's the title of your play? Jill asks McKenna.

—*The Ferris Wheel of Love.*

—How does the Frankenstein monster in a crate figure in?

—I'm taking that part out. It's the story of a tennis player, Gillemand, and the debutante apple of his eye, Daisy.

—It's so exciting to meet these writers and learn about the creative process!

—I don't think you're writing a play. I think you merely say you are writing a play to get under my skin, says Mislove.

—I didn't catch your name.

—I didn't tell you my name.

—What is your name?

—Stuart Scales-McCabe.

—McCabe, I knew I knew you from somewhere. I know all about you.

—Nah, you have me mixed up with someone else, same name, different bum.

—You don't have to hide anything. Your secret is safe with me.

STUART SCALES-MCCABE

When I boarded the freighter back in New York Harbor, I thought I was leaving this behind. On an island more remote than Mars, I still can't get past it. To my way of thinking, there are two types of people in the world, those who know my name and those who don't. Those who know my name don't know me. The other, more famous, infamous Stuart Scales-McCabe is up the river at Sing Sing.

—It's nothing to be ashamed of, Stu, Justine says, treating him familiarly although they'd just met. —My uncle did ten years, and you'll never meet a nicer guy in an alley late at night.

—Shut up, listen, I'm no jailbird, just a shutterbug, nothing different.

Justine, freckled and bespectacled, taking him by the arm, says, —It's all right if you want to keep on the straight and narrow. I won't let the cat out of the bag around the other girls. But you just don't come crying to me if they know already. You're famous, Mr. McCabe, but why am I telling you that?

—You are all mixed up.

—So how long have you been out, really?

—Unbelievable.

—Stu, I love giving you a hard time.

Not ten feet away, Svevo the Obligatory Swede is falling fast in love with the Nightingale named Libby, whose habit it is to slap the tops of your hands while she's joking around with you. It's like a game she doesn't know she's playing. She's of the jovial sort, her eyes curling into half moons when she laughs, which is all she ever does other than slap the tops of your hands. Svevo, ever the smart one, quickly learns a trick: If you keep your hands down and behind you, she'll lean in far enough to slap them that she's almost close enough to kiss. It sends a thrill straight down Svevo's spine.

Neil the Feel pulls the Swede aside, —Stop it, Svevo! Keep your damn hands to yourself. The last thing we need in Haiti is any of your Swedish hanky-panky, and I swear it didn't even take you five minutes!

—Shh, they're going to sing a song for us.

—Who is?

Lafferty and McKenna step into view from the other side of the fire. Both are wearing necklaces made from flowers, Hawaiian-style shirts, and holding ukuleles. They begin strumming in unison, getting as much sound as they can out of the tiny instruments and drawing everyone's attention. On the beat, the two of them break out in song:

At words hysteric, I'm apoplectic
I'd rather not let them all burst
That's why I keep my lips pursed

Play 'em off as unrehearsed
I hate charading and masquerading
Play pretend I know the whole plot
But my two cents 'bout both of us, dear is
I'm the dearest friend you ever got

You're the hat
A pillbox topper
You're the cat
Now that Fido's got ya
Oh dear me, you're a symphony for timpani
A well sung trill, my thrill
You're a daffodil
I'm the bumblebee.

You're a pie
Florentino pizza
I'm a fly on the Mona Lisa
I stutter, flutter in the gutter, I pop
Baby driver, I'm your putter, chop-ty chop!

I'm a pill
Shakespeare's ass named Bottom
I'm the shill for Gomor & Sodom
You're Lotte Lenya
Keeping ol' Macheath at bay
I'm H.L. Mencken
You're Mary Lincoln
Notta lotta like Doris Day

Marmalade
Duncan Hines' choc'late cake
Marinade
For a Heinz sauce beefsteak
With friends so fickle you're in a pickle
Better think up something quick
My heart beats frantic at your cartoon antic
and bounces around on a pogo stick

Legionnaire
I'm Mortie Adler
Evening air
I'm Li'l Abner
Live crabs, they hurt
Where did you lose your nerve?
You're a seafood mama
A Chekhov drama
A Chevrolet with verve

You're my Valentine
A thrill divine runs down my spine
Arabian knights dance sheik to sheik
My old bones may start to creak
The chair I broke was granny's antique

Lose your shirt
Lose your mind
Drop me a line
'Cause if baby I'm the roof then you're the house!
'Cause if baby I'm on the loose you broke me out!
'Cause if baby I'm the hoof then you're the mouth!

'Cause if baby I'm the woof then you're the howl!
'Cause if baby I'm a goof, you're Mickey Mouse!
'Cause if baby I'm the wolf then you've flown south!

The song ends not so much because it reaches its end as because they have given up on thinking up new lines. As happens in the tropics, the sun sets quickly, leaving them on the beach in the dark, the fire their only light.

—That was a nice tune. You guys make that up?
　　—Yeah.
　　—On the spot, just like that, all those words?
　　—Yeah.
　　—The music?
　　—Yeah.
　　—That song was all right. You two guys are all right.

—Pardon me, but do any of you nurses know anything about the piano at St. Marc's? asks sunburned Keith Clone in the formal tone he always uses with the Nightingales. —It's an old player piano with the automation taken out, and I was wondering if you've seen the missing apparatus lying around? Boy, I'd like to get my hands on that!
　　—Boys and men, men and boys, Nora says. —You're all the same, when you're not obsessed with taking things apart, you're obsessed with putting them together.
　　—Have you heard the big secret the Vatican has been keeping? Abbot Jaffe asks. —Jesus' voice was recorded in the grooves of an old vase. An artisan was spinning the vase on a potter's wheel while Jesus was speaking and the vase has been holding the voice of Jesus in it ever since.
　　—That's impossible.
　　—I read about it in *Look* magazine.

—Who has time to go through all the vases from ancient times and play them like records?

—Benedictine monks have the time. You can only pray so much.

—I'm not buying it.

—What I would give to be able to hear something like that.

—I have the hots for one of the girls, says McCabe.

—The chicken little who was following you around?

—The one with the pin-up boobs, as in they look pinned up, their eyes aim toward the sky.

—That bathing suit leaves less to the imagination than it covers.

—You won't get a complaint out of me.

—Talking like that in mixed company. You are shameless.

—I don't feel well, Miss Penny says. —I think I need to get to sleep.

—It's the Haitian food. Have you thought about fasting?

—No.

—After three days' fast you find yourself drifting into a curiously inexplicable peaceful mind.

—What's that up there? Jill asks pointing to a searchlight shining from the top of a cliff.

—That's P.F.C. B.J. Roper-Melo, the last of the U.S. Marines in Haiti.

—No kidding.

—He's that stocky man with the transistor radio that plays nothing but static.

—He tunes in just in case there's a broadcast.

—I climbed up there. The searchlight is U.S. war surplus. The mystery isn't why he shines it down into the inland valley where the voudoun practitioners dwell, the mystery is why he shines it at all.

—He has nothing else to do. If he ever looks up, he has a nice view of the stars.

—Talk about the sparrow looking like a toy.

—What's that?

—Just the words from a song I like back home.

JILL

Culprit Clutch had a way of coming back to Haiti without coming back to us. He is here, but he's missing. He's a hummingbird, come back for the nectar of Sweet Li'l Josie, to be exact. We all knew he liked her last time he was here, and while he didn't like her enough to stick around, he liked her enough to come back, this time as a Guggenheim Fellow, a movie director.

NORA

Josie is a puzzle to us, starting with how well she fits in among the Haitians. She can change out of her nurse's uniform and slip into a calico dress and bandanna head scarf and fit right in. She doesn't change clothes as much as the clothes change her, and she always seems just like one of them, as if everything that is American about her goes poof the instant the nurse's uniform falls to the ground. She can dance like them, which is no easy feat, all those herky-jerky movements, it's not exactly Arthur Murray. While Jill has taken it on to learn about Haiti and its customs, Josie seems more interested in becoming Haitian. All the while, her skin stays white, so no it makes no matter how she tries to have us fooled, she is still white, and she is still one of us.

Back at St. Marc's in the evening, the Nightingales uncork another bottle of wine.

—The rest of us like to try on a new dress before buying it, Nora says.

—Josie is trying on a Haitian soul.

—Josie is a classic voudoun possession case, Jill says, drawing gasps from the other girls.

—I didn't think voudoun worked on Americans, says Dinah. —Possessing one of us means dispossessing the American spirit, and the Uncle Sam in us won't back down without a fight.

—There's just one thing I don't understand about voudoun.

—What's that?

—How do you know who you're talking to?

—What do you mean?

—If a spirit comes along and throws a sucker punch at, let's say, Dinah here, clean shot knocks her soul out cold, props her up in a chair, takes possession of her body's temple, forces a smile across her face, and then say I come along to engage Dinah in pleasantries, who is it I'm speaking to?

—The possessing spirit.

—Poor Dinah!

—When I talk to Josie, it's like I'm talking to Josie. I don't think she's possessed, just strange.

JILL

So maybe it was never a spell Josie was under, but certainly Culprit is under her spell. No one thought it unexpected when she returned from the beach damp from the waist down. She and Culprit tried swimming in the ocean and changed their minds only hip deep.

—I saw them together out on the beach, Jill says. —Josie didn't recognize me in my floppy sun hat. I tried to get as good a look at Culprit as I could without him noticing. They were far away.

—I've seen those two before and didn't know it was them.

—I saw them up close.

—So what's Culprit like?

—Culprit has beautiful feet. Who would ever have thought someone with a name like Culprit Clutch could have such beautiful feet? The rest of him leaves much to be desired.

—What were they like?

—The skin on his feet is thin and perfect, the hair on his toes is bleached from walking barefoot in the sun, and his arches, I have never seen such arches.

—Was there fungus on his nails?

—Not at all, and they are the most well trimmed nails I've seen on a man.

—He likes the ocean, likes walking out there with Josie. It's such an ugly beach for the rest of us, but when that pair is out there, it dresses itself up, puts on its Sunday best, makes itself beautiful.

—It's just like a beach back home.

—Except the waves.

—Except there are no waves.

Belinda Ballard sees them on the beach and takes off running. It takes long enough while she runs to catch up with Culprit and Josie for her to think about it. Does she really want to play the fool? She's been waiting to see him, and now here he is. He's the closest thing they will ever have to a movie star. She's come this far already. Out of breath, she makes herself run faster.

Face to face with Culprit and Josie, she cups her face into her hands. She won't raise her head to meet his eyes and not because she's shy. It's because everything the girls were saying is true. It's because she can't get past his damn feet, Culprit's beautiful feet. If only the rest of him could be so nice!

CULPRIT CLUTCH

I didn't know where Josie was taking me, what any of this was about. All's she said was that we were in store for a thrilling adventure and bring a sweater. In the end, it lasted a day, a night, and then another day, and while there was never enough chill in the air for me to need a sweater, I could have used a change of clothes and toothbrush and wouldn't have worn my best chinos and brown oxfords. Everything was ruined on this thrilling adventure.

It is late Saturday afternoon, and she takes me by the hand and says our destination is the Source.

—The Source? I ask what that is, guessing it's the origin of the ghostly drumming always in the distance, the origin of the wood-smoke that blankets the rocky paths through sablier and mapou forests. I had wondered about the Source. There were places in Haiti out in the sticks, clearings with crude chairs set in a round, hieroglyphics drawn on the compacted ground, and a smoldering fire. Whatever happens here at night, you never catch it in the act. Unless Josie brings you, that is.

I pretend to know what I am talking about, —The first problem is the only way to discover the Source is by not looking for it. The second problem is that when you find it, you won't know what you found.

—We're not looking for it. We are moving toward it, she replies.

—Maybe we'll look back one day, and be able to put a finger on it, and say, 'That was the Source.'

—We'll know sooner than that.

—Do they call this place the Source? I ask her.

—It's the *hounfor*.

—Is that their bumpkin French for the Source?

—No.

—I've never heard that word before.

—Try thinking of it as a church.

—Church? It's built by hut architects. If you ask me, it's not exactly a cathedral.

—You can think that way, if you like.

—Is that all it is?

—No.

—What are these? I ask, pointing out the hieroglyphics on the ground formed from corn flour carefully poured.

—*Les vevers.*

—I have to write these words down, I say, patting down my pockets for a pen.

—Please don't.

—Why?

—Writing it down will distract you from the experience. You'll remember what matters.

THE FIRST NIGHT'S CEREMONY

Every seat in the round is filled, and the drums are deafening. They beat those skins so hard, you can feel your soul come apart from your body, which may be the intention. One musician plays a trumpet made from a conch shell. Others shake rattles also made from shells. The hiss from the rattles is so powerful, they may as well pour sand in your ear.

The drummers in a circle are accompanied by a musician playing a red accordion and a boy in short pants beating a tambourine. The boy's belt flops around his waist as he dances, and his feet move so quickly, they blur before your eyes. Another boy lies in wait, crouched, ready to spring and trip the boy with the tambourine when his dance carries him in that direction.

Any ordinary object you can hold becomes a musical instrument, all you need is a small stick to beat it with to unlock the rhythm trapped inside.

I lean toward Josie and whisper, —They really do make use of what they have, don't they?

—Shhh.

The ceremony is led by an older woman, Mambo Peto. With a rattle in her hand, she begins to dance, her arms and legs flailing to the drummer's beat.

—She's not exactly Ginger Rogers.

—Shhhh.

In their dance, they fall and they catch themselves, all within a single beat of the drum. You can jump in any time, but you have to dance your way in. It means you have to find the rhythm of the others. The drummers beat it into you.

I stand and ready myself to join them, —My feet feel so heavy!

—Shhhhh.

A coconut thrust through the air smacks me on the side of the head, causing me to lose my footing. It's the boy with the tambourine and his friend, children with a homemade catapult and bad aim, laughing at me just the same. Their laughter is a sign that I am welcome, while it's also a sign that I'm the odd duck in this picture. I retake my seat, content to watch the others dance.

Then the clamor begins, bells from every direction outside the circle. Twelve young men, walking their bikes, wheel them to the center of the circle, ringing their bells all the while. The audience laughs, applauds, and the ceremony draws to a close.

That is all. It is over. Quite the experience.

RESTLESS SLEEP

Later in the night, the dancers and drummers are gone, but Josie tells me that we aren't supposed to go. I doze off in the hounfor, first upright in my chair and then lying on the ground beside Josie underneath kerosene lamps and citronella candles hanging from a wire. The sweater I brought becomes a makeshift pillow we do our best to share. The pillow is small, and our heads are hard and keep bumping into each other. It's hardly enough for us, but it's what we have, and in Haiti, you make use of what you have.

I stir to see that in the empty center of the round, they have brought in a bed, a perfectly good bed, covered in silk linen and pillow covers, embroidered with fanciful designs. Beside the bed, Mambo Peto rocks in her chair, smoking her corncob pipe. Seeing her is like seeing a painting, an old Dutch master of a night scene in Haiti, circa 1955.

My limbs heavy with sleep, I drag myself across the ground in the direction of the bed. Seeing what I am up to, Mambo Peto raises her bony arm and points me back in the direction of where Josie is sleeping. It's a perfectly good bed over there. I don't know why no one is sleeping in it.

Dawn's first light brings heat. A truck rolls up, its engine rumbling, rattling rods and burning oil, and too many voices speaking all at once in their bumpkin French disrupting my last few moments of shut-eye. The way they talk, it's a miracle they can understand each other.

Mambo Peto is nowhere to be seen, and the group hoists the bed into the cargo area of the truck. They then hoist themselves into the truck, standing on the tailgate and holding on tight. Josie reaches down from the truck and pulls me up with the rest of them.

—Where are we going?

—Out to sea where the boat is waiting.

THE SECOND DAY'S JOURNEY

Later that morning, under a daylight moon with phantom church bells in the distance, the truck is off, slowly trudging along the road made from jagged stones with wild grasses growing out of every crevice. Barefoot Haitians hear us coming and join the caravan. They had been sleeping on the stony roadside, awaiting our arrival. So many riders climb on board, and we are packed together so tight, it can squeeze the existence right out of you. Those who join the caravan late run alongside the truck, holding onto it wherever they can or just touching the side. There are children with them, boys in khaki and girls in white blouses and pleated skirts. Elders are picking up the rear. They wrap themselves in coats and scarves, others in tattered sheets that make them look like Arabs. It may be early, but the sun is hot.

—The more, the merrier, I say.

It's reassuring that with no chance of finding a filling station out here in the wilderness, we can all pitch in and push the truck if the need arises.

The Haitian countryside never stays the same for long. We pass cocoa plants and plantain trees with limbs bowing from the ripe, heavy fruit. There are plenty, free for the taking. Along the side of the road, women are picking the leaves off of shrubs I've never seen before and a border collie is rolling on his back on the dusty, yellow soil.

In the distance, clouds tumble in the blue above a distant mountain and to our immediate right, bamboo trees are bunched tightly together to form a natural fence-line. The bamboo clumps keeps us from seeing what's on the other side: a primeval forest. Mambo Peto is telling Josie the names of the trees in English, —Mahogany, mapou, sablier, ebony.

—Giant trees like these have almost vanished from Haiti, Josie explains. —That's why they planted the bamboo clumps along the road. The forest is off limits unless you want to hack away with a machete at the clumps, and that could take all day.

—Does anyone have a machete? I ask around in English.

—Hold your horses, Culprit. You don't have to see it for yourself, Josie says.

Her explanation appeals to the worst part of my nature, my obsessive compulsions, my social cataclysmic tendencies, the spirit of the dead Red taken residence inside my psyche. I will jump off the truck and either find an opening or wrestle my way in. My imagination is not good enough. I want to see it for myself.

—What's that for, that crazy look in your eye? Josie asks. —Culprit, sometimes I don't know about you.

She deflates me.

Josie says we should walk a while so that others can take our place on the truck.

When the road is soft it feels like quicksand. When there are vines along the roadside, I can almost feel them wrapping around my ankles, the ankles that never healed right after my skywriting fiasco. Does she know she's the reason I came back? If it's love, it's certainly not always pleasant. Most of the time, it feels like hell.

After a few minutes, the road is hard, and our shoes are covered in lime dust. Walking is much more pleasant than riding in the back of the truck jammed together like sardines. Walking lets us see more of the island's spectacular beauty.

Hanging back far enough back to avoid the stench of diesel, we follow the truck up a narrow twisting mountain track with gorgeous views of the sea. Then we climb higher along the steeps high above a town. It looks like the same town we saw earlier.

The farther we travel, the more it seems to me that we've seen it all before, the same landmarks, that we are going in circles, but Josie's not buying it.

—The caravan has a specific destination in mind, she says.

—You'll know it when we get there.

The Source.

The farther we travel, the more it seems we're lost. So many people have joined the caravan, we can't all be lost. If worse comes to worst, we can follow the ones home who seem to know where they are going.

Below us is a beach formed in a graceful, curving inlet.

—That's Chou Chou Bay. That's where they're building a hotel once the roads are improved, she says, as if to assure me the caravan is not lost, that she knows where we are, that the world where places have names still holds its sway.

The twisting hairpin curves of the road lead us back down the other side of the mountain. The view of the great plain is breathtaking with its chessboard squares of sugarcane fields under a now cloudless sky so blue that it's purple. The road down is even more overgrown. Our path is blocked by huge boulders, potato-shaped and the size of Volkswagens. They were spewed out by volcanic eruptions long ago. The truck empties so that the driver can focus his attention on maneuvering around the boulders without losing traction and sliding down the cliff.

—Why on earth would you build a road with a boulder in the middle?

—Beats me.

—It could be a meteorite, just fallen.

—Dingbat, I'm sure it rolled down the mountain.

—I've always wondered about boulders at the tops of mountains. How did they get there?

—Maybe someone shot them up there with a catapult, Josie says.

The driver manages to squeeze the truck around the side of the boulders, and the peril is worth it. Not long after, we pass majestic waterfalls. High stone walls with sheets of water raining down the sides. The truck parks for a break, and many of the riders and walkers still in their clothes run through the showers, splashing each other.

Back on the road, we wind farther down, our shoes slipping on the limestone gravel.

At last, we are near sea level, near our final destination, but the rest of the way is impassable by truck, even by burro, if we had a burro. It's only a mile, and it's not hard to walk a mile, but much of the mile we need to cross is over mangroves. The roots above water are like wooden arms and legs braided together. The limbs are slick and climbing on them is an invitation to fall right off. Not to mention slipping hurts like hell, like the collision of bone on bone. Yet we manage, the young and old, the men and women designated to carry the bed, Mambo Peto, Josie, and me.

THE BOAT LAUNCHING

The sea wants this, a lover's bed on a boat set adrift. The boat they brought is for the bed. Maybe one day they will get the boat back. They might even want the boat back, but not the bed. The bed is a gift to the sea.

They adorn the bed with a bouquet of palm leaves, a bouquet of roses. They sing, play music, and walk the boat into the water without letting go. They walk with it until they too are in the water up to the waist. They finish the song and set the boat with its brightly colored sails adrift.

It bobs along, it makes its way. I've never seen water so calm.

Paddlers take it out to the sea, then swim back. They stand along the shore and watch as the tide slowly pulls it away. At the mercy now of the wind and ocean current, it becomes smaller and smaller until you can't see it anymore and the sun begins to set.

How I want it to be us out there, on the bed, on the sea. Part of it is I'm tired and could use a snooze. Part of me desires to lie down with you, Josie.

—Erzulie and Ogoun are legendary lovers, Josie says. — The gift is theirs.

I want them to be you and me. The sun's fiery heat gives way to a cooling breeze. The invisible spirits flow around us. You can almost hear them hissing in the wind.

A Brief Spell Between Chapters

—Haiti is vertical, that's the most important thing to remember.

—It's a rare day you'll find a long, flat plain.

—It's like the New York skyline, with mountains instead of buildings.

—It's why baseball never caught on like it did on the Dominican side. Your outfield will have rocks and dips.

—Outfielders chase fly balls and fall off of high cliffs.

—In Haiti, it's better to lose the ball than catch it. You may lose the game but you'll live to play another.

—Where we are, there are dry riverbeds abounding, dry as a bone.

—During the dry season, Haiti's rivers flow not with water but with rocks.

—Haiti has no navigable waterways.

—You'd never know it during the rainy seasons when the rivers are full, the current fast.

ABBOT JAFFE

Among the road systems south of Le Cap, there are two dry riverbeds where the U.S. Army Corps of Engineers have planted survey stakes. One is where a manmade river will one day flow, a public works project. A series of dams will regulate the river's flow and create a reservoir, and for once, this will make it safe for watercraft. The other riverbed will see its flow diverted and will provide the runway for the soon-to-be-constructed airport. Haiti north has not seen projects of such ambition since the construction of the Citadelle Laferrière in the early 1800s.

—It's not easy to tell which bed is the river and which is the runway.

—The river has a newly built bridge spanning it.

—The bridge looks ridiculous those months when the bed is dry.

—The other day, in the late afternoon, along comes P.F.C. B.J. Roper-Melo, always the one with a bag of tricks up his sleeve.

—He's an imbecile.

—Though docile, a docile imbecile.

—Whose domicile is a shaky shanty shack built from driftwood right on the beach, what little beach there is, and outside the shack, he flies Old Glory, or at least a flag that used to be Old Glory. The elements have weathered it, bleached it white. If you haven't been here for ages like we have and don't remember back when the flag still held onto its stars and stripes, then you might think Roper-Melo's flag signifies surrender.

—Surrender? Who would want this place? Who would want Roper-Melo's beach?

—Even Communists have to start somewhere.

—He has something in mind, apparent designs to line torches ten meters apart on both sides of the riverbed.

—Anyone could have asked him what he was doing; no one bothered.

—We just watched in our nonchalance; the curiosity was killing me.

—The rows of torches seemed in a word *poetic* in their ornamental elegance. Art's beauty need not have any purpose or rely on anything other than its own aesthetic sense. In Haiti, the summer sun fades fast, and as darkness spreads, the P.F.C. uses his Zippo to set flame to each of the torches.

—Dinah, bless her heart, put forth her theory, chalking it up to conjuring, suggesting that the P.F.C.'s intent was to call upon sojourners of the afterlife. Others scoffed, for how would Roper-Melo, such a simpleton, know how to do that?

—This is the type of ceremonial pomp you'd associate with Africa.

—It was a warm Friday evening, we brought wine, and there was nothing better to do than sit on the bluff overlooking the P.F.C.'s Torch Spirit Conjure Show.

—If you'd listened to me, we would have gone to *Cat on a Hot Tin Roof.*

—It was dark enough that we could only see the P.F.C. because he was holding a pair of ignited automobile flares, the type that resembles dynamite sticks but rather than blow up, glows red on the ends. He shakes and spins the flares in the air, like they were a drum major's marching batons. It's a show of sorts. He never stands facing us and never acknowledges we were observing him, even when it was light enough that he could still see us.

—What impressed me most is the trick the light plays on the eye, the afterimage of the flares' glowing red tips swirling in strings of light floating in the air, following the movement of the P.F.C.'s hands.

—Oddly enough, the P.F.C.'s herky-jerky movements seem familiar.

—Then it strikes me what he's doing. He's playacting the role of an airport runway worker, guiding an imaginary airplane out of flight and back onto land.

—Turns out the airplane wasn't so imaginary. Behind us, a rumble broke up the peace of the night. The airplane soared over our heads, just on top of us, and bounced in for a rough landing on the P.F.C.'s makeshift runway.

—Turns out I'm not the only one who gets confused trying to tell the difference between the two dry riverbeds. The P.F.C. coaxed the plane down on the wrong one, the one with the new bridge. We didn't see it, but we heard it as the bridge's supports clipped the plane's wings as it passed through below. The wingless plane rolled a few more feet as we ran to aid the crash's survivors.

—Meanwhile, the P.F.C. himself seeing his error trickled off into the night.

—We helped the plane's passengers pour out of the two large gashes in the fuselage where the wings used to be. They are disappointed to find they are in Haiti and not their final destination, the Bahamas, but all they need from us are directions to the nearest pension and our last bottles of wine. They need it more than us.

—No one was hurt. The plane was destroyed.

—It was ridiculous.

365 Is My Number
–The Message

It's a showcase attraction on a muggy June evening. The makeshift stage is enclosed by an embroidered curtain with designs of stars and planets and is enough to draw a crowd of local characters not accustomed to such entertainment. It also draws a scattershot crew of Nightingales and Useless Bums intrigued to witness the spectacle. A fading hand-painted sign announces:

FABIO LE FANTASTIQUE

VENTRIOLOQUE EXTRAORDINAIRE

SABIAN ET ELF

MUSICAL PROFESSORS

Yet it's a magic act on the stage. A bearded magician stands beside an armoire painted with suns and moons. He opens the door to reveal it empty, drawing a gasp from the crowd.

Nora standing next to Jill gasps not at the trick but at seeing a young woman poking her head from behind the stage curtain to see who's in the audience.

—It's Josie!

—Where has she been?

—She missed the surfboarding movie. I still have a bathing suit to give her.

Josie steps out from behind the curtain in an outfit that exposes her legs, drawing the applause of the crowd.

—It doesn't look like she misses it.

The magician introduces a trick. He guides Josie to lie down across a wood door set atop three sawhorses. One by one, he pulls out the sawhorses from beneath her, first the one on stage left, then on stage right. She balances perfectly on the makeshift seesaw, until he pulls out the center sawhorse, creating the illusion that she's floating on air. He waves giant hoops through the air over the door where she lies to show the audience that nothing is holding her up.

—This trick is called the Princess of Karnak, says M. Lyle Mislove, the failed magician.

—How do they do it?

—With wires, Mislove says.

—Isn't there a magician's oath not to reveal how the trick is done?

—It doesn't apply if you figure it out with your own smarts, Mislove replies. —If you want to see the magic behind the magic, keep your eyes peeled to the opposite direction of where the magician directs his hands. He leads you away from what he doesn't want you to see. It takes discipline not to let yourself be distracted.

Jill looks up, above the magician and the makeshift stage. They are in the open air, there is no roof overhead, just a few shoddy bamboo posts that hold up the curtains. High above are clouds mixed with stars.

—If he's using wires to suspend Josie in the air, what the wires are attached to? she asks.

—Don't look up there, keep your eye on the stage!

Jill looks closely at the magician and he seems familiar. His beard droops, the spirit gum attaching the beard to the kid's chin loses its tackiness in the humidity. It's Pascale the Rascal, the face of the place, Josie's Haitian confidant.

JILL

It was puzzling but made sense, the two of them are thick
as thieves. What didn't make sense was how the trick was
done with wires under an open sky. I looked all around the

stage for any explanation then did exactly what the playwright told me not to do. Pascale winked at the audience, but it was like he winked just to me. I fell under the spell of his hands. He waved them slowly in circles in the direction of the stars embroidered in patterns on the stage curtain, as if to suggest that the wires supporting Josie were latched to the stars in the sky.

In July, on the road along the mountains in the north of Haiti connecting Milot and Dondon, there appears a cart drawn by a short train of donkeys, itself not an uncommon sight. On its stage is a cage with a man canaried inside, which is strange, even for the Nord Department. It passes slowly along its way as if its business were nothing more than transporting a load of bananas to port. A crowd of spectators gathers on the side of the road.

—That man is carried to prison, says Svevo the Obligatory Swede.

—Who?

—What's he done?

—No, the question is *whom* has he done. The answer, a woman, says M. Lyle Mislove.

—Oh, brother.

—A Haitian woman?

—Another American.

—He's American, she's American. So where is the offense? asks Samantha Sound.

—Groping for trouts in a peculiar river, says Svevo.

—I don't understand.

—His goose is cooked.

—Does anyone know him?

—Know him? Not in the sense that brought about all this trouble, says M. Lyle Mislove.

—Miss, that is your dear Culprit Clutch, says Svevo.

—Jiminy Christmas!

—What's going on?

—Culprit impregnated one of your sweet, wholesome nursing types, and that rubbed the Powers that Be the wrong way, says Mislove. —Doctor Boldieu Bast, who they say is not acting like himself these days, sees himself as the new gun-slinging moral authority in these parts and wants Culprit Clutch to hang.

—What is this, the Spanish Inquisition?

—C'mon, gals. Let's go tell Luckie.

A small Nightingale party troops back toward St. Marc's, leaving the playwright and his sarcastic proteges.

—'A gun-slinging moral authority'?

—I have always had a fondness for the Wild West. I can't help talking that way, explains Mislove.

—I should listen closely to your speech pattern, McKenna says, — because I happen to be working on a play at this moment set in a Lone Star seminary some sixty years ago, and it's called *The Nun Slinger*.

—You're not writing a play, says Mislove.

—By coincidence, Lafferty says, —if you look around my sleeping bag, you'll find a manuscript called *The Nun Swinger*, and it happens to be set among the Manhattan upper crust. It's quite shocking, actually.

—I doubt either of you wiseacres is writing a play, and certainly not plays about nuns.

—Now you listen, mister.

—Another of mine is called *The Sister in the Cistern*, and another is *Habit to Break*. No one is telling me I'm not writing a play about nuns!

—Oh, my God, Jill says. —It just occurred to me it's Josie. She's the one having the baby.

—How did you figure it out? Nora asks.

—She's the only one Culprit pays any attention to.

—She's not having a baby. We just saw her in the Princess of Karnak, Samantha says.

—I'm afraid she is.

—We should keep this quiet.

—Why? By the time she's pushing a baby carriage, won't everyone know?

—That's true.

—I wonder if she'll give birth at the school, or if they'll send her home.

—How far along is she?

—She's starting to show. Didn't you see the bump underneath her costume?

—I was trying not to look.

—If you saw a bump, why didn't you say anything?

—I thought it was my imagination.

—Josie, it's one thing to bat your eyelashes at a man, but to let it come to this.

—Why are you talking to her? You know she cannot hear you.

—I've always had my suspicions about Doctor Bast. He pays more interest to Josie than the rest of us.

—That's because she's always sick.

—That makes him a pervert all the more, in my book.

—That pervert is our new provost.

—What happened to that other man?

—Huffy? Washington called him home, and he left Bast in charge.

—What a mess.

JILL

Josie always seems like the new-girl-come-lately but she's been here as long as any of us. When she first stepped off the boat, she was wearing a coat to her ankles and a great floppy hat that made her look like Ingrid Bergman. I never saw this myself, but I swear I remember seeing her stepping out from under a gaslight on a foggy night when no one else was around.

SAMANTHA SOUND

She is a head case and no, not just because of the headaches. She rides around in cars with Haitians and smokes cigarettes out in the open, as if she thought herself a Hollywood starlet. The rest of us, the only chance we have to smoke is down by the Ghost Quarry and it's been so long since I've worn anything but my uniform, I've forgotten what a pretty dress feels like.

Back at St. Marc's, word spreads.

—How time flies! It seems like it was just yesterday we were speculating on Culprit Clutch's arrival.

—Culprit Clutch is back all right.

—And now they say Josie is having a baby. What have these times come to when babies are having babies. All you daughters of Babylon, go to your ruin, run, see if I care.

—Josie isn't a baby. She just looks like one because her eyes are so big.

—Have you ever seen the moon through a telescope? Ruthie asks. —All those craters, the shiny glass ocean. The strange shadows. Scientists all say the moon is dead, which is just terrific. There can be no death unless there was life before it. Sometimes, I feel like Haiti is a dead island, or at the very least, dying.

—What's come over you? All this philosophic mumbo jumbo.

—Josie's having a baby.

—I dreamed last night of a face, an all-white face, Lydia says. —Not like yours or mine but one made of porcelain, and its eyes had no pigment. They were just as white as the rest of the face. The strange part was that the hair was made up of other faces, but these faces were alive, though at the same time, they were straight out of *Grand Hotel*.

—You really ought to lay off the bottle, girlie.

—Oh, I haven't had a drink in days.

—We can visit Culprit in jail. At least, those of us who weren't here last time will finally see his face.

—It may be awkward, seeing him for the first time in jail, knowing that he's been sentenced to death.

—It seems odd to me that it's called a sentence. It reminds me of high school grammar.

—A sentence doesn't mean anything until it's executed.

—We'll find an excuse to visit. He won't know it's just to take a good look at him.

—Why do you have opera glasses? Haiti doesn't have a national opera.

—That's not true, there are two Italian opera singers touring the countryside. I've seen posters and cards.

—Opera singers alone don't make for opera. You need an opera house, which is where you need opera glasses.

—All right, you caught me. I have them for spying.

—Spying!

—They do me no good. I still don't know what he looks like.

—He's got a gap in his teeth and a slack jaw.

—He doesn't exactly have the kind of face for musical comedy.

—That doesn't help me. I wouldn't know him from a jackrabbit.

—Hey, does the name Culprit Clutch rhyme with anything? I'm writing a poem.

—Double Dutch.

—Nice try, but Culprit doesn't rhyme with double.

—Can you do better?

—To me, he looks much better suited to a western, and I am not exactly sure I picture him in a white hat. But that's just me, and I am someone who's always been thrilled by anything to do with the Wild West.

—They say he was a real Don Juan the last time he was here. I think those girls need glasses.

—He's not my Prince Charming.

—Can you imagine kissing that mouth? I would rather kiss a dog's behind.

Les Gardes d'Haiti, the constabulary set, had loaded Culprit up into a cage, which they dragged onto a cart, which was pulled by donkey train. Off they went, down the mountain, passing by gawking onlookers, a mix of Useless Bums and student nurses. The train was en route to Le Cap centrale and the municipal jail when it passed a bearded man standing in the open with a briefcase.

Bayard Pumphrey Huffy has grown a beard for the first time since college when he grew it out to a sharp point for a theatrical production of *Uncle Vanya*. Back then, they used white shoe polish on the beard to make him look older. This time around, in his disguise, he's using black shoe polish on a scruffy beard, but rather than make him appear younger, he still seems old. His new beard transforms him into a Papa Hemingway of a man, a crusty old crocodile, less the lifelong diplomat and bureaucrat and one of Uncle Sam's boys than who he really is: an enlightened man with a taste for the theatre, garlic, and Italian wine.

He doffs a fishing cap as the donkey train passes and pulls a mirror from his vest coat pocket. Does the cap make him look Cuban? Like someone who doesn't speak English? His Spanish is passable, but is it believable? No, he's American through and through. He can disguise who he is but not what he is. He will play the part of an American, just not himself. He stuffs the cap into his briefcase.

As they had agreed, his protégé, Patrick Fitzpatrick, the man in chartreuse slacks, has no need to disappear. Fitzpatrick keeps himself a safe distance away, yawns, checks his watch, hides behind a tree, peeks around the corner while keeping an air of nonchalance.

Huffy weaves through a crowded veranda to the jail where he finds no one but Culprit's Haitian jailers whose English is worse than Huffy's creyol. When he sees a band of Useless Bums standing outside the jail, he puts his disguise through its most arduous test.

—Who's in charge here? Huffy demands.

—Doctor Bast, but he's not here.

Huffy attempts to pull back into character, while Jaffe whispers to McKenna as an aside, —I recognize him from somewhere.

—I bet he's an American spy, which doesn't explain why he's spying on us, says McKenna, under his breath but not so soft to go unheard.

With this cue, Bayard Huffy steps forward and introduces himself not as anyone affiliated with the U.S. Government, but rather as Herculano Cubana, swimming pool salesman from Poughkeepsie, New York.

—You're way off, Neil the Feel tells the man.

While the name seems odd for someone clearly without a drop of Spanish blood, the rest is almost true. In Bayard Pumphrey Huffy's vision of the Haiti in the future, there are swimming pools everywhere. Tourists will arrive in fancy airplanes at the state-of-the-art airport, and as they land, they will see bright blue orbs pocking the landscape everywhere the eye can see. It's a prosperity to be enjoyed by the American and Haitian peoples alike.

—How the heck are you carrying swimming pools in a case so small? asks cheeky McCabe.

Eyes dart to the slimline attaché case at Huffy's side, the type of object you'd casually associate with an emissary of the U.S. Department of State. He sets it flat on the ground and kneels before it, as if he is going to conjure flash-powder spirits from within. He opens the case and pulls out a stack of 8 x 10 color photographs of American swimming pools in a variety of designs. He had anticipated this question and came prepared.

—I have news for you, sir, Neil the Feel chimes in. —There is no one here who will buy a pool from you. We are all short-timers, and we're broke.

Abbot Jaffe,—Stranger, the only other Americans you'll find in the

Nord Department are nursing students who are just as broke. There are the American doctors who might be interested but they already have a pool at their swanky hotel. There are eggheads running around from the Dynaflow Institute, but they're hard to find because they're invisible.

—What business brings you to Haiti? the swimming pool salesman asks.

—I wouldn't exactly call it business.

—We're on the most cockamamie mission ever thought up by the United Nations.

—It's a secret mission.

—If your mission were really so secret, why are you telling a perfect stranger?

—What I mean, sir, is that our mission is kept secret from us, and that's no secret.

—We can't spill secrets, because we don't know a thing.

—We were sent to make a movie about surfing, but there are no waves.

—They won't send us home. The suspicion is they have something else in mind.

—Don't look now, says Jaffe, —but there's a person behind that building spying on us.

Stuart Scales-McCabe races after the spy, who takes off running in the opposite direction. McCabe tackles him in the center of the cobblestone avenue bustling with Haitian women on their way home from the market with baskets of fruit on their heads. The women gracefully dance around the two men struggling on the ground.

—That's no stranger, Lafferty says, pointing to the man with a fat lip in McCabe's grip. —He's the diplomat's protégé.

—I'd know the green slacks anywhere, says McKenna.

—What's this fellow's name again? All I can think of is F. Scott Fitzgerald.

—Patrick Fitzpatrick.

—That means he's royalty, a blue blood, says Lafferty. —All the Fitz names are royal, Fitzwater, Fitzsimmons, Fitzhugh, Fitzgerald, Fitzpatrick. That's why dogs bark at him.

—Ask if he knows where to find his superior who flew the coop and left Bast in charge.

—Mr. Fitzpatrick was keeping his eye on me, I'm afraid, the swimming pool salesman says.

—Why? You don't look Russian.

—Call off your attack dog. He's harming that man.

The swimming pool salesman transforms before Abbot Jaffe's eyes, not so different from the startling change that takes place in an old werewolf picture. In the salesman's place, Jaffe now sees Bayard Pumphrey Huffy.

The chain of events was set in motion a week earlier with Doctor Boldieu Bast unlocking Josie's second-flight infirmary room late at night and slipping inside.

He keeps the light off as he knows what he is doing and doesn't need to see. After warming his stethoscope with his breath to help prevent its chill from waking her, he presses it not to her chest where her heart is but to her lower belly where he listens for a heartbeat that isn't hers.

He finds it, damn it, and now it makes sense, why she's been twice as sick as usual. She's been throwing up for two. The question in his mind drifts from what might have happened to who might have done this.

The answer presents itself immediately at her open window. Bast turns his head to catch a glimpse of a face, a face on the outside looking in at him. It's that inept skywriter, certifiable turkey, that Culprit Clutch, here to rendezvous with Josie, the Nightingale he knocked up, damn it.

From the ladder, Culprit Clutch cannot see inside. The window is foggy and the room dark. All he can see is movement, and just enough movement to realize that Josie is not in there alone. He can't tell it's Doctor Bast, the Jesuit-with-a-screw-loose Doctor Bast, the bastard Doctor Bast, but he knows it's trouble.

He leans back, pulling the top rungs of the ladder with him, swaying away from the building so that the ladder stands perpendicular to the ground while he straddles it, an old circus trick. Swiveling his center of gravity, he spins the ladder around and hobbles away, the ladder performing as a fixed pair of stilts, and as this is no easy feat, momentum pushes him forward too hard and fast, and he teeters slowly one way, then the other.

At the open window, the doctor shapes a coat hanger into the form of a hook, its purpose to snare the clown on the ladder.

But for Culprit, he loses balance, and it's the same thing all over, the broken bones, the weeks in traction, all barreling his way yet again, no good, the fall coming fast, no way to slow or stop his crashing body.

As luck should have it, earlier that day, a Dynaflow balloon had run aground a few feet from the building. The balloon lies on the ground, its crew having abandoned it, half its air left, and when Culprit falls into its dead center, it cushions his descent. He rolls across the top, slides down its side, and he's on the ground, off and running, as good as new.

On the veranda sipping coffee, Bayard Pumphrey Huffy, out of his disguise, is apprising his protégé, Patrick Fitzpatrick, of his thoughts when the maître d' brings the phone to the older man.

—I won't take it. Tell the gentleman, or gentlewoman, that I am not here, that I am on my way back to the mainland.

—The gentleman says to tell you it's the Lip.

—I don't know any lip. Tell this lip that I'm not taking any lip.

—Sir, he wishes me to tell you it's the Stiff Upper Lip calling from the White House, and he wishes to speak with you now.

—Jesus Franklin Christ.

Bayard Pumphrey Huffy gestures for her to give him the phone. Up until now, the calls Huffy has taken were from the secretary pool. This call he has to take, as it's a Higher Up on the line, and in the natural order, the Highers Up have the ear of John Foster Dulles, and Dulles meets daily with the President.

BAYARD PUMPHREY HUFFY

I know, sir, yes, that Haiti policy is delicate, and all it would take is for the president to sneeze for it all to come down like a house of cards, but of course, what we have here is a mess, and yes, I did mean to inquire about the president's health. Did he receive the muffler the missus and I sent him for Christmas? No, I didn't actually send him a muffler. I don't know why I said that. It's a line from a play I'm reading. Of course, how would you know that. To the point, Lip, we have a mess here. One of the young nursing students is pregnant, see, and the director of our movie is in custody, sentenced to death by hanging. By whose authority? A doctor, sir. Yes, one of ours. Yes, I was the one who granted him the authority under the cover that I was leaving, while the secret plan was that I remain here under disguise. No, sir, this is not some kind of joke. I wanted to see how our agents here behave without the presence of an official provost. Yes, I do take Haiti policy quite seriously, sir, and I will not allow this to happen again, but that doesn't solve the mess at hand. It would seem that way, sir, that by removing my disguise, I could with a wave of my magic wand set everything right, but I have done just that to no avail. Yes, sir, the doctor will not relinquish authority, and he has won the backing of the Magloire government. The doctor has promised his free medical services in exchange for hanging Culprit Clutch. Perhaps this could all be resolved if you should step in, or Mr. Dulles. I know, sir, that you are a busy, busy man, and this mess is not your responsibility, but there are times when a simple act of Christian charity can save a man's life. Is Culprit Clutch innocent? Did he do what? I would never put it in such frank terms, sir. I have no way to know for certain what he did. I know this possibility of commingling between the student nurses and movie crew was accounted for and eliminated, and you can't pin that on me, because I had nothing to do with the psychological screening. Are there others on the film crew with the same appetites as Culprit Clutch? I apologize, sir, I know how annoying it is during a phone conversation when the other party repeats everything you say, but the connection isn't good. To answer your question, I have no idea, and again, this is doing nothing to address the mess we're in. I see, so you are saying the best course of action is no course of action. I know, I repeated your words back to you again, but I am not sorry. I am not sorry because a man is sentenced to die. I must end this call now, sir, and for that I do apologize.

—So what did the Stiff Upper Lip have to say?

　—An earful. They won't order Culprit Clutch's release.

　—What's their reason?

　—I can't say.

　—Classified?

　—No, there just isn't any reason.

—They say you'll hang unless Dulles or Magloire grants a stay of execution, Henry Greathead explains to Culprit Clutch later in his cell at the municipal jail. —The word on the street is they won't stay you anything.

　—I would be more concerned if the lock on the cell door wasn't busted.

　—Where are your jailers?

　—Ain't seen them since they brought me here.

　—You can walk? What's your plan?

　—To stay put. It's safe in here.

It's a game they play. Henry takes on the air of a State Department official and Culprit replies in turn. Neither will break character until the other blinks.

—It would be so easy for me to say that Culprit Clutch must die while his government turns its back . . .

—Or holds its nose.

— . . . because the Dulles goon squad doesn't know what secrets he carries. They would rather see him hang than come back to haunt them, but that is simply not the case.

—What is the case then?

—I could come to you and say it's true, Culprit Clutch holds suspicions about the U.S. Government, which have since been affirmed. It's easy to say that Culprit Clutch has unknowingly consorted with known Communists, and is guilty by association. True, it might also be the case that Culprit Clutch has knowingly consorted with Communists unknown even to themselves, and while this might never be proved in a court of law, when the opportunity presents itself to eliminate Culprit Clutch, you take it. For all anyone knows, Culprit Clutch might wake up one morning transformed into a cockroach himself, a Communist cockroach.

—The spirit of a dead Red living inside him comes and goes at will.

—But the real reason Culprit Clutch must die is to save the U.S. State Department from embarrassment after investing so profoundly in psychological research. The reason why the U.S. Government will not order a stay of execution is because it was believed Culprit Clutch was a homosexual. The pregnancy of the student nurse shows he is not.

—How many Useless Bums do you suppose to be homosexual?

—I wonder about the playwright Mislove.

—All of them were specially screened before they were sent here, they were given a loaded version of the Foreign Service Exam designed to root out homosexuals. All of them failed the test with flying colors.

—Failed because they didn't know the correct answers?

—Failed because they are queer as the day is long.

—You mean all of them are homosexuals? All they do is chase skirts.

—Yes, but that doesn't mean they are not homosexuals.

—What's the barometer?

—A contraption that tells you when it's going to rain.

—That's not what I mean.

—The beauty of your kind of homosexual is you don't know you're a homosexual, and the Useless Bums, they chase skirts because society has conditioned them to chase skirts. For them, there is no existence other than chasing skirts, even if they have no idea what they would do if they caught one.

—Culprit Clutch knew what to do, Culprit says, speaking of himself.

—By and large, it works best for the U.S. State Department if Culprit Clutch is no more. He'll die one day as it is. Sooner than later works best for his country. The government won't have to admit it was wrong and can keep on getting it wrong, which is easier than getting it right. But even more important, they don't want the Russians to learn about their failing. Pavlov was a Russian, and the Soviets have a ten year jump on psychological research.

—That is just the way of the world. Bast loses his mind and unwittingly carries out the government's dirty work.

Abbot Jaffe, with ever-present sweat stains in his armpits, struts along the road to Le Cap with Lafferty and McKenna in tow. Scales-McCabe, Lyle M. Mislove, and Neil the Feel are picking up the rear. They encounter a young woman and aging man. It's the girl they approach.

—You're one of the students, but we haven't met, Abbot Jaffe says, shaking her hand.

—I'm not a student here, she says.

Doctor Zampf steps front and center, —Let me introduce my daughter, Valerie. We're vacationers.

—Oh, more Americans. How marvelous.

—I'm traveling with my father, because I thought he said we were going to Tahiti, which is so much more like Hawaii than this place. I had no idea Haiti would be so different.

—A vacation is still a vacation. You should be able to enjoy yourself, her father says.

—Have you met the other doctors?

—I am not that kind of doctor. I'm an anthropologist, and while this is our vacation, I was hoping to do a little exploring and learn more about voudoun, maybe make a day trip out to the town the zombis built.

—Interested in voudoun, I see.

—Very much so.

—Just follow the drums and smoke in the air, and you'll find voudoun rituals wherever you look.

—We're staying at the Le Roi Christophe, Valerie adds, changing subjects.

—That's a swanky hotel. It's where the American doctors are staying.

—Where do you stay?

—We don't stay anywhere. We live in a Dynaflow capsule in the mountains. It's quite primitive, actually. Sheila's on the crew but doesn't stay with us. She stays at a pension, because her family's loaded.

—Valerie, have you ever thought of going into the spy racket?

—I don't think so.

—I know an operation and have you in mind.

—Me?

—There is someone staying at your hotel with contemptible motives, a Doctor Boldieu Bast. He's the acting provost of the American nursing school, and he's condemned our film director, a Guggenheim Fellow, to death by hanging. Quite melodramatic, if you ask me.

—You make it sound like no big deal.

—If that were the case, I wouldn't mention it.

—What business does a doctor have, condemning a man to death?

—You can find out by helping us spy on him.

—What do you mean?

—We need information. We need to know if he's serious.

—Since you stay at the same hotel, you could eavesdrop on his dinner conversations, or if you would be so bold, you could engage him in conversation.

Her father puts his arm on her shoulder. —Valerie, it sounds like while I am off on my little adventure, you'll have an adventure of your own.

—I haven't agreed to anything. I might say no.

—A man's life hangs in the balance, Abbot Jaffe reminds her.

—I'm not sure you've got the right girl.

Two afternoons later at the swanky Hotel le Christophe, Doctor Bast walks across the veranda onto the pool deck. He's wearing an ascot and smoking jacket, and he's accompanied by two henchmen in Seabee sailor shirts with brightly colored stripes and barrel chests, sternum fuzz poking out from beneath the crew neck collars.

Bast sees Valerie in a bathing suit in a chair beside the pool, though it's the buffet table that attracts his attention.

She stops him with a statement he was not expecting to hear, —Doctor Bast, you must let Culprit Clutch go.

He pauses, turns to her, and replies, —Give me one good reason why I would do that.

—Because holding him is unjust.

He allows himself to compose his thoughts, then replies, —I am so sick and tired of watching morality flush down the toilet. It is my responsibility to protect those girls from moral turpitude while they are under the charge of the Department of State. No sooner does a Culprit Clutch come prancing around than one of the girls turns up pregnant. As the moral authority, I need to send a message.

—I agree with you that he behaved poorly. Death is too severe a punishment.

—You think it's all right to fornicate like rabbits and not bear any consequence?

—My concern is the severity of the punishment.

—Who are you to talk to me like that?

Unseen by Valerie and Doctor Bast, Bayard Pumphrey Huffy, back in the disguise of a traveling pool salesman, and his protégé, Patrick Fitzpatrick, hide behind a tall potted plant.

—Mr. Huffy, this is getting out of hand. Now is the time for you to take charge.

—Shhhh.

—Mr. Huffy.

—You know damn well they stripped my authority to intervene.

—Doesn't mean you can't confront him without authority.

—Let's wait and see how all this plays out. I'm carefully weighing my next move.

—Spoken like a true agent of American diplomacy. All talk and no action.

—Shhhh.

The Useless Bums have strung a phone cord out to the camp and their Dynaflow capsule, winding it around trees, burying it under brush, all in hopes that no one trips over it. Along with an assortment of Nightingales, they stare at the phone, waiting, then startle when it rings.

—Shhh, it's Valerie with a report.

—I was hoping to see her again in person.

—Last thing we need is you turning sweet on the anthroplogist's daughter.

Moments later, —What did she have to say?

—She said she argued with Doctor Bast on whether it was criminal that Culprit and Josie were screwing, pardon my French. He said that if she believes so strongly that he should spare Culprit's life. . .

—It's 1955. I can't believe we are talking this way.

— . . . She could prove it to him that he . . .

—Good grief! He asked her to go to bed with him?! He hardly knows her!

—We hardly know her.

—He's old enough to be her father.

—She says she's waiting until she's married, and even then, come on, it's Doctor Bast!

—The man is not with it.

—That's not exactly how it happened, but she did follow Bast up to his hotel room.

—Where is her father?

—Packing for his trip to the town built by zombis. Abbot Jaffe is with him.

—I can't listen to this. I'm breaking out in hives.

—Strange that Jaffe's planning to leave. He was making passes at Valerie from the start.

—Fewer suitors works out better for you, huh?

—It turns out Doctor Bast is quite the shutterbug. He said he wanted to show her some photographs in his room, so what was she expecting? Pictures of colonial Haitian architecture? For God knows how long, he's been sneaking onto the school-grounds late at night.

—God, I can't listen.

—And he was taking photographs of us girls while we slept.

—Pervert! Swine!

—He got us all.

—From the window? How could he see in?

—He has a key. He was right over us.

—I'm going to be sick.

—I'll kill him.

—Now it all makes sense. I've been waking up to flashing lights. I thought it was a headache coming on.

—Doctor Bast's proposition to Valerie just now wasn't that she sleep with him but that she pose for pictures.

—Dirty pictures?

—Sleeping pictures, photographs of her sleeping.

—He wants her to fall asleep so he can take pictures of her. It would be easier just to sleep with him.

—I hardly think sparing Culprit Clutch's filthy soul is worth posing for dirty pictures.

—Did she tell him she'd do it?

—She told me there is no way she'd do it. She told me she's done with it.

—So what can we do?

—Cast someone else in the role of Valerie.

—It would be easier to talk her into it.

—She's done enough. We don't need to drag her any farther.

—She's leaving right now with her dad and Abbot Jaffe to chase zombis.

—Oh, brother, Jaffe was playing his cards all along. Some friend.

—Does anybody else have any bright ideas?

—Cast someone else in the role of Valerie. Think about it. It's the role of a lifetime.

—What if it's specifically Valerie he wants? The heart works that way.

—It's an ordeal no one should have to suffer.

—We need a dame who doesn't mind falling asleep for photos.

—Belinda Ballard would. She poses nude in paintings.

—Too tall. Doctor Bast would know right away she's a fake.

—I seriously doubt you'll find any Nightingale willing.

—Can anyone tell me why that swimming pool salesman is still hanging around?

—Maybe he still thinks we're potential pool buyers.

—I think he heard you, he's walking away.

—What a laugh to think I'll buy a pool. Once my walking papers come through, I'm on the first banana boat out of here.

—That wasn't a swimming pool salesman. That was Bayard Pumphrey Huffy. In disguise.

—No kidding. Now that you say that, I can see it.

—That explains why the man in fancy green pants is always near.

—Why the get up?

—I'm not sure. I think Huffy wants to play the role of spy.

—The least we can do is play along. Mum's the word that he's lost his cover.

In the mountainous interior of the Nord Department, Doctor Zampf is leading an expedition. The way he talks about the town zombis built makes it sound legendary. Although it goes unsaid among them, the hope is to find a live one.

ABBOT JAFFE

I've been asking the locals about zombis the entire time I've been here. It seems everyone knows someone who's seen one, but no one will admit to a personal encounter. The more I ask around, the less the math makes sense.

DOCTOR ZAMPF

Zombis are like unicorns, like the Abominable Snowman, like little green men from Mars. That doesn't mean we won't see one. We're off on a spark of lively adventure!

ABBOT JAFFE

We are an odd quartet traveling in the jeep Doctor Zampf rented. I'm behind the wheel, and the professor is riding shotgun. In back, it's Valerie, Zampf's daughter, who most likely would have preferred to skip this adventure and take in the sights of Cap Haitien. Before all the ugly Bast business, that is. Beside the girl is Pascale, Pascale the Rascal, the face of the place because he's everywhere. Pascale is an interesting character. He's Josie's friend, and when the Nightingales ask her how they spend their time together, Josie says she is teaching him English, although it's apparent now they were also rehearsing their magic act. The English lessons must have worked, because Doctor Zampf invited him on the expedition as our translator.

My past conversations with Pascale have gone like this. I explain something to him in plain English, and he looks like he's pretending to understand what I'm saying. He's polite enough not to interrupt, and when I'm finished, I'm certain he didn't catch a single word. Then he begins his reply and shows not only did he understand, he has more to offer. He's much more on the ball than we've given him credit for.

Our destination is a place called Pilate, and it's in the Plaisance River Valley. It's not on the map, not that maps help much in Haiti. Maps show where the Haitian government would like roads to go, not where they are already. You can build a road as rock solid as any road back in the United States, and Haiti will find a way to swallow it whole. Vines and grasses will cover the blacktop, and the surface will crack open under the blazing tropical sun. Later, heavy rains will open a sinkhole. You can build a road and come back three years later not only to find the road gone but also no trace that human beings ever passed through that way. If you find human evidence, it might just be the remnants of a fire or voudoun symbols drawn on the ground with flour.

Lucky for us, the first hundred miles of our journey are across one of the best roads in Haiti, Road 100, the connector between the north and Gonaives on the western coast. It looks like it's going to rain, so we pull the canvas cover over the top of the jeep. When the deluge begins, the canvas doesn't keep the rain from seeping through and soaking the four of us to the bone. Lucky for us, the rain is bathwater warm.

We are lost already since we started off not knowing where we are going. We see a family along the side of the road in the heavy rain. The father and son are in short-sleeved shirts and the mother and daughter in cotton dresses. We stop so Pascale can ask them if they know the way to Pilate. The poor souls thought we were stopping to offer them a ride. They point us in a north and westerly direction. Pascale explains that we would take them with us but as they can see the jeep is full already.

Once the pavement runs out, the jeep rattles as we drive over jagged rocks, and the fillings in my teeth shake loose.

We arrive at crossroads. A hand-painted sign planted by the side of the road shows an arrow pointed straight ahead with the word GONAIVES printed on it. There's also the name PLAISANCE with an arrow pointed to the right. This is where we turn to travel the next fifty miles across a donkey-trail of a road. The daylight is fading. There's a small pension on the other side of the road. We'll buy two rooms for the night. Doctor Zampf and his daughter will stay in one, Pascale and I in the other.

Before parting ways for the night, —Pascale, what can you tell us about what crossroads mean to the Haitian? Doctor Zampf asks our interpreter.

—Not much.

—In my observations, Haitians build crossroads in places where there are no roads, where the roads end a short distance from the crossing. In Haiti, no roads mean no crossroads. Then again, it might signify that no roads means everything is a road, and if that is the case, there is nothing other than crossroads. Some say crossroads split the world in two. You stand on one side or the other, in this world or that. One side is the material world, the other the realm of the Invisibles, and Haiti is one of those rare places on earth where mortals such as ourselves are always crossing over.

—I don't know about that.

—The Invisibles, think of them like radio waves. They're in the air, you don't see them, they flow through you. They have their own personality.

—Like Jack Benny, says Pascale.

PASCALE

They think of me as their universal Haitian, believing I should know all things about my country. I grew up in the city and my father was a government worker. What happens out here in the sticks is as mysterious to me as it is to them.

VALERIE
(WRITING IN THE NOTEBOOK WHERE SHE KEEPS HER POEMS)

The sun goes to its death at the apex of the evening, swallowed by the mountains on the horizon. They are the same mountains that swallow roads whole, the same land that swallows you whole when the grave comes calling. If we were watching the sunset from the mountain peaks instead of here, we would see the sun sink into the sea. It's the sea that swallows the sun, extinguishes her flame and sends back night and darkness. Life steps back from the water as does the night.

ABBOT JAFFE

The next morning, we are off in the jeep, and although the trail is thin in places, we squeeze through. We're traveling no faster than walking, but in the sweltering heat, it's far more comfortable to ride. Pascale rides sections of the road on the hood of the jeep, signaling me when he sees dangerous rocks. We follow the hand-painted signs that direct us toward

Plaisance until we reach crossroads and a sign labeled PILATE. We are not lost after all. The angels are at our backs.

We are near, but not so fast. There's a shallow river to cross. I want to say it's the Grand-Rivière-du-Nord, but I haven't seen a map, so I can't be certain. Two weeks ago, before the rains started, this river would have been dry as a bone. Cranes are standing one-legged on rocks emerging above the river's surface.

On my insistence, we attempt to drive through it. Midway across, the water is deeper than it looks. Water gushes in from beneath the doors of the jeep. Wet spark plugs stop us in our tracks.

Doctor Zampf is fuming, while Valerie and Pascale remain silent. It's my suggestion that we wait for the spark plugs to dry out, then try to start the motor and keep driving to the other side.

While we wait, two men in hip boots wade through the water pushing a broad floating contraption. A sign on their mini-barge says LES FRÈRES LAFONTAINE FERRY SERVICE. The two of them are in business helping cars cross the river during times of high water. Their ferry looks like it consists of the flat section of a dock that had broken away from where it was built, with a number of truck tire inner tubes roped to the bottom to increase the ragtag contraption's buoyancy. It looks more experimental than practical.

Their idea is to push us back onto the bank, load us onto the ferry, and walk us across. If we are going to push the jeep, it seems like a simpler idea just to push the jeep across to the side where we're heading. The brothers insist that the mud is too thick, that we would get stuck, and there would be nothing they could do to help us.

So the brothers, Fido and Lido, help us push the jeep backward toward the bank. The five of us men are wearing trousers so the mud merely cakes our britches. Valerie is pushing right along beside us in a denim skirt, a layer of muck covering the skin on her ankles and calves right up to her knees. I want to make a comment on how it would have been easier on her to stay in Le Cap and pose for Doctor Bast's dirty pictures, but I keep it to myself.

It turns out Fido and Lido know what they are doing after all. They roll the jeep onto their ferry, tug it by hand across the river, delivering it safely to the other side, while we tramp along behind them. We pay and thank them, and they are on their way, promising to come back and help us again when we are ready to return to Le Cap.

The jeep is in tiptop shape, not that we can use it. The road is too muddy to forge onward, and the wilderness too untameable to drive farther. With machetes, we hack our way through the thicket. On the other side is our village, Pilate, the town that zombis built.

The zombis didn't do a bad job. The buildings were constructed from an array of available materials, though not quite in the style of Frank Lloyd Wright. They appear strong and well built. If the people of the village are zombis, they have us fooled. Night is falling, clouds are moving in. The village residents close windows and pull down shutters.

The downpour begins and rain slides in sheets off of the buildings' iron roofs.

In one home where the shade is not drawn, we see through a window a bare lightbulb hanging from the ceiling. Through another window, the sound of a man in the habit of clearing his throat. The smell of coffee roasting blends with that of hearth smoke. Drenched, we walk along the narrow, winding cobblestone lanes with rainwater flowing across the top of our shoes, passing by crowded concrete houses, looking for where we can take rooms for the night. The rain has turned Pilate into a ghost town, so we follow our path back to the leaky jeep, where we will settle until the rain subsides.

Maybe it's the legend, maybe it's the rain, I can feel there is something wrong with this place. The river muck, the pounding rain, this is a place that doesn't want us here. We came looking for the town the zombis built, but a town is still just a town. A live zombi is what we were after, and now we're here, zombis are nowhere to be found. All I am left with is a strange feeling that something is not right.

After an uncomfortable, sleepless night sitting upright in the jeep, the rain stops and we are wandering down by the river, waiting for Fido and Lido to ferry the jeep back across so we can return to Le Cap. The brothers seem to have forgotten us, and we have no idea where to look for them. We climb to higher ground to perch ourselves so that we might see where they are.

Doctor Zampf, dirty, his clothing in tatters, climbs up to tell me something.

—There you go, he says.

It's all he says. He's sidestepping down the hillside, catching himself, trying to keep from stumbling. He's not acting frightened so much as he's uninterested, as if now that he's found a live one, the search has become tedious.

As for myself, I'm not sure I'm frightened. I admit to feeling more comfortable with Doctor Zampf nearby than walking away. If I don't take my eyes off him, I will never see the zombi, if it's not too late already.

—Your zombi is right there, Pascale says.

—Then how come I don't see him?

—Your zombi is right there.

It's a rocky landscape, too inhospitable for vegetation, and with the river two hundred feet below, it's surprising to see a rowboat nested away among the large rocks above us. It rained hard last night and I can't even imagine the floodwaters it would take to float that boat away from its perch. But looking around at that jagged, uneven terrain, I know one thing in the world right now and it's that I don't see a zombi.

I follow Pascale's steps toward the rowboat, and there he is, inside the boat. The zombi is lying on his back, stretched out inside, and Pascale is already climbing back down. —I'm going to get the camera, Pascale says.

It's the most extraordinary sight I've seen in my life, a body rekindled. It's like Frankenstein's monster, though not a body patched together from other bodies. Not to mention that Frankenstein's monster was the product of an author's imagination, unlike this fellow lying down in a rowboat, dead though breathing. I touch his neck, and it's warm to the touch.

Here are the characteristics. He's seven feet tall, a giant of a man. Such height is not a trait specific to zombis. He must have been this tall when he was alive. Moreover, his skin is white and hair straight. I suppose there is a possibility that death could rob the skin of its color and straighten the hair's curl, but I suspect in this case that the man wasn't Haitian, but rather a husky, towering Scandinavian. When awake, he's soulless, capable of simple mechanical tasks, like spinning rope or digging ditches, but not much else.

The amateur anthropologist in me is reveling at this moment, but the side of me that's just plain Abbot Jaffe is filled with terror and wishing I had never come here.

Pascale returns not with a camera but with a blacksmith's bellows. —The doctor would like to drag the boat behind the jeep and bring the mister back with us.

—That will make one hell of a bumpy ride for this fellow.

—Use this to blow air on his face, Pascale says, handing Jaffe the bellows. —The air will keep him sleeping while we prepare to move him.

What seems like an hour passes without sight of Doctor Zampf, Pascale, or Valerie, and Jaffe is tiring from the constant accordion motion of feeding the zombi air.

Heavy raindrops fall, and the zombi winces. He doesn't like the water on his face.

Jaffe stops pumping the bellows so he can look for a canvas to cover him. He takes his eyes off the zombi for an instant but when he looks again the zombi is gone, vanished, poof, nowhere in sight, and all Jaffe can think is, —I lost our zombi.

He looks in every direction.

—I lost our zombi.

Where are the others?

—I lost our zombi, he repeats to himself as if it were a Buddhist mantra.

He climbs down from the perch and descends to where he finds Pascale, Valerie, and Doctor Zampf at the jeep snuffing an engine fire.

—Don't worry, Doctor Zampf says. —We'll be on the road as soon as it's put out.

—I lost our zombi, Jaffe says.

—That's all right. He'll find work in the orchards or the city.

—A city? He would stand out like a sore thumb.

—A city is where he will blend right in. Zombis are antisocial creatures strangely drawn to social settings. Think of Manhattan. Think about the mad commute on foot across downtown sidewalks. It can carry you right along without slowing down, as if you weigh nothing. That's the dynamic force of zombis. Think of all the nameless, faceless people who never share a word with you, who ignore you when you stop to ask them for directions. People who are experiencing life as nothing more than a body in a crowd. They aren't just on the street. They're in cars and taxis. Think about all the cars on the street not heading any place in particular. Think about the riders on the subway who never get off. Stop worrying about our zombi. He'll find work, do good work, never complain, he'll carry us along for the ride, and the rest of us in the crowd will be none the wiser.

Halfway down the staircase at St. Marc's, Lafferty begins speaking to the others waiting on sofas in the room below: —Get this, I went back and told them the idea, that we were looking for a girl to play Valerie so that Doctor Bast could take photographs of her while she sleeps, and they looked at me like I lost my mind. They gave me an earful on how untoward it is.

—It is untoward, Nora says.

—Then I mentioned there will be a motion picture camera in the closet and they jumped on the idea.

—That's how bad they want to be in pictures.

—How do we decide who gets to play Valerie?

—We hold auditions.

—Splendid!

—Good grief, Nora says. —Don't the girls know what they're getting themselves into?

—What do you mean?

—Sleeping with Doctor Bast.

—This has nothing to do with sleeping *with* Doctor Bast. It's about sleeping *for* Doctor Bast, just long enough for him to snap some pictures.

—I won't do it, never in a million years. Besides, he'll know it's not her.

—If he's half the pervert they say he is, he won't be looking at your face.

—I would do it in a wig so no one would recognize me, says Samantha Sound.

—Nora, please tell me you'll think about auditioning.

—I am doing everything I can to stop thinking about it.

—I'll do it, says Curly Batson, —I volunteer.

Lafferty sizes up the child: Your frame is slight, you hardly have any skin on your bones, you might be able to pull this off. We'll have to make sure you stay dressed or the good doctor is in for one big surprise. Let's see if you can fit into one of Valerie's nightgowns. There's the problem of skin color. I wonder how much we can do with makeup.

—You can't be serious, Nora says.

—Sorry, C.B., maybe next time.

—Are we holding auditions or not? Mislove asks.

—We are, and we need to get ready. Mislove, I want you to write me a scene in three pages.

—I'll need more guidance than that.

—'Enter Bast and Valerie. Bast asks Valerie to pose for sleeping photographs.' That's your prompt. Now get husky!

In the evening, the same Curly Batson who offered to pose as Valerie arrives at the guardless municipal jail in Le Cap centrale dressed in the style of clothing worn by Culprit Clutch: a powder-blue Arrow shirt and chinos.

—I'm here to trade places, C.B. says as he joins Culprit inside the unlocked cell.

—That's a nice gesture, kid. Are you out of your mind?

—The Haitians think we all look alike, and your jailers are Haitians.

—Kid, you look more like them than me. Do you see any Haitian jailers? Do you see any jailers period? I'm all alone here. The cell's unlocked. I can walk anytime.

—The others are calling for you.

—Gives me all the more reason to stay put.

—The reason you're still here, says another voice, —is that you're waiting for me.

Henry Greathead enters, dressed in black with a flowing black cape, the air of a cat burglar.

—A woman, a wigmaker, and a wild horse are not to be trusted, he proclaims.

—I'm not playing that game. Henry, you look ridiculous.

—I brought dynamite to blast you out, just in case they locked you in. Who's your friend?

—I don't know. Who are you?

—My name is Curly Batson. They call me C.B. I'm with the movie crew.

—He looks like me and dresses like you, Henry Greathead whispers to Culprit.

—Care for a glass of wine?

—No, thank you, C.B. says.

—So tell me, Henry, what do you know about voudoun?

—Is it because I'm black you think I have voudoun figured out?

—Of course not.

—Is that so?

—No, though I do wonder what you make of it.

—Voudoun is too much for me to figure out.

—What do the poles mean?

—What do you mean?

—The way I understand it, the poles divide the world in two. You stand on one side, and you're in your world. The other side is the invisible world. The problem is when you step onto the other side, it's the same side where you started. God knows how many times I've switched sides and not gone anywhere.

—If you weren't cooped up, I'd say the sun was getting to you.

—I'm not cooped up. I've had time to think.

—There's something I'm meaning to ask.

—Yes?

—What kind of example are you setting for our young friend?

—What do mean?

—An exemplary young man is before us, who is as curious as I am why you are still here.

—I'm under arrest . . .

— . . . Says the Voice of Anti-Authority.

—I like the people.

—You are all by yourself.

—I like the meals.

—They don't feed you.

—I like the view from my window.

—It's a putrid swamp.

—You got me. I don't know why I'm still here. Kid, how'd that surfing film turn out?

Henry whispers into Culprit's ear, —It's been a tough time. She won't leave her bed.

—They are complaining that the beach has no waves, C.B. says.

Henry Greathead and Culprit Clutch take that as a cue. They slip into a comic improvisation, the spirit that overtakes them when they are together. One of them starts it, making a ridiculous statement in the voice of someone else. The other catches on and plays along.

Henry Greathead begins, —The word out of the Nord Department is that they will not send us their surfing film for reasons beyond their control. Apparently, there are no waves.

—Then let's make waves, Culprit drawls.

— There's a reef that blocks the waves, C.B. says in his own voice.

—Damn reef, holding back our waves, so that the breakers crash a mile out to sea.

—They roll to the shore as nothing.

—The answer seems simple to me. We extend the beach out to the point where the waves break. That's what bulldozers are for.

—Brilliant. What do we do in the meantime?

—We can use stock footage of Hawaii and say it's Haiti. They both start with an *H* and end in *i*.

—Don't forget Tahiti.

—*Tahiti* starts with a *T*.

—It makes no matter what letter it starts with. It's easier to confuse *Haiti* with *Tahiti* than *Haiti* with *Hawaii*, from a purely linguistic perspective.

—Except for the *T*.

—No one gives a shit about the *T*. But that's a short-term solution. We don't want to disappoint the tourists who will go home and tell their friends Haiti is a bore.

—What would you like me to tell the film crew? C.B. asks, still himself, either playing along or fooled by the ruse.

—How many pregnant nurses have we had so far?

—Just that one.

—We must get busy before they get busy.

—Here's a plan. How about we send Navy subs to torpedo the bastard reef, blowing holes in it like so many chunks of Swiss cheese.

—Even better, we use the hydrogen bomb to blow the reef to oblivion in one fell swoop.

—You go back there right away and tell those kids there will be surfing in Haiti after all.

—The best part, Henry says, stepping outside of character, —is that back home they can't hear a word we say.

In unison, the three turn and and look across the room and see the telephone receiver lying across the table, a phone left off the hook.

—Oh, no, what if someone on the other end just happened to be listening? C.B. asks.

Henry and Culprit take that as a cue. They lift their middle fingers and aim their gesture in the direction of the telephone.

—Back so soon and you have pages for me, bravo, says Lafferty in the role of director replete with a beret and ascot.

Mislove hands his typewritten pages over.

Lafferty doesn't have a bullhorn so he uses his best stage voice not only to get the others' attention but also to create the impression of extensive experience in the theatre.

—All right, we only have one set of pages, so we'll block the scene tight as you read. Mr. Scales-McCabe will play the role of Doctor Bast during our tryout, though Doctor Bast will play Doctor Bast when we open tomorrow night. Valerie is the role we are casting. Keith Clone, how are the preparations for rolling film?

—Boss, I'm all set. I will hide the camera in the closet and muffle the sound with a blanket.

—While you're at it, try arranging the lights in the room for the best possible illumination.

—What if Doctor Bast turns them off?

—Then compensate by opening the shutter all the way, use high-speed film, figure it out.

—Thank you, sir.

—You, Keith Clone, are a good man who knows what you're doing. Now, we drew straws earlier to see who goes first. Lydia, will you please take the stage beside Mr. Scales-McCabe?

—Glad to!

She spits her gum out into her hand and steps onto the makeshift stage next to Scales-McCabe, who is holding the script.

—Let's run through notes before we begin. Lydia, you are a little bit older than Valerie, a tad thinner than Valerie, and about your curly hair, do we have a wig that will work? I want to hear you read, and if we can overcome a lack of physical resemblance, you'll have a better chance of getting the part. It might also help you get a feel for the role.

Two Nightingales whisk onto the set with a straight blond wig freshly powdered. Lydia crouches while they tuck her curls underneath the wig so that it looks almost natural. Scales-McCabes waves the air in front of his face, afraid the powder will make him sneeze.

Lafferty calls places and the reading begins:

SCALES-MCCABE (AS BAST): What brings you back?

LYDIA (AS VALERIE): I'm just a sweet little thing, and there is no way I could let Culprit Clutch go dying on account of me.

—Let's put it this way, sweetheart. An arrangement can be made, just between you and me.

—Tee hee.

—Cut! Lafferty yells.

Mislove whispers as an aside, —We don't use the word cut in the theatre.

—I'm putting an end to this scene. It's ridiculous. People don't talk like that.

—It's not intended to play as a real conversation, Mislove complains.

—It's art.

—Shouldn't it sound at least a tad like the way real people talk?

—That's at the discretion of the artist, namely *moi*, and my answer is no.

—What I think is that you don't have an ear for writing dialogue for dames.

—Mister, you can take a long walk off a short dock.

—You want to know what they say about you, Mislove? They say M. Lyle Mislove, he sure knows how to write, but you'd never know it from reading his work. They say M. Lyle Mislove, he's destined for obscurity in perpetuity.

—You're not a theatre critic. You're a son of a bitch.

—When it comes to writing theatre, Jill chimes in, —you can make your plots and characters as outlandish as you like, but you want the characters' emotional states to seem familiar and true and for people to sound natural when they talk.

—Come on! I wasn't trying to be Shakespeare here. I was just writing a stupid scene for these stupid auditions. I threw it together on a lark. If you don't like it, fire me.

—We didn't ask for Shakespeare, says Lafferty. —What we need is a scene so real that when we send in the actress playing the role of Valerie, never for a moment will Doctor Bast suspect it's merely theatre.

—Fine, if you're all so smug, go ahead and write your own dialogue.

—You're our playwright, Mislove, I will give you a second chance.

—Fine, Mislove says. He removes a portable typewriter from its hard plastic case, feeds it a sheet of paper, places it on his lap, and begins to type a revised scene.

Jill makes small talk to pass the time while waiting for Mislove to finish, —McKenna, you have a captivating sense of humor. Do you put much down on paper?

—Not a word. No one can read my handwriting, and I don't type.

—If you want to write, you can dictate to me, Jill says, —and I'll type what you say.

—That would make it your writing.

—They're your words. It's your writing.

—It makes no matter, McKenna says. —I'm against writing. For me, no scripts; it's all improvisation.

—Oh, really? asks Jill.

—Yes.

—What you're saying is an actor never gets to the core of his part reciting lines written by someone else?

—That's a way of looking at it.

—That's a nice philosophy, but doesn't it lead to chaos on the stage?

—Chaos doesn't scare me. It's appealing.

—McKenna might not write much, but I know his style, Lafferty adds. —He'd open the scene with the girl cracking a coconut over the doctor's head then stealing his keys.

—That's not bad.

—What about you, Keith Clone, write much?

—Nope. I'm just here to operate the camera. Art's not for me.

—Don't let this kid fool you, Mislove says, looking up from the typewriter. —His eye is the best I've seen.

—Thank you.

Mislove turns contemplative. —Maybe that says it all. I studied art history at Columbia, studied under Willem de Kooning, and I turned out not much of an artist, and certainly not a motion picture photographer with an eye as keen as that of our own Keith Clone.

—Thank you.

—I'm more of a name dropper than an artist. I fell into playwriting when nothing else panned out.

—Clone, what did you study in school?

—All's I know are television cameras. I've always been good with gadgets.

—My art is in working with people, I suppose, says Mislove, —How I suffer for my art.

—How's the sunburn, Clone?

—It never was as bad as it looked.

—Tell us something else about yourself, Keith Clone.

—I don't know, I've been behind the camera so long I forget the naked eye doesn't have a zoom lens.

—Bravo! See, everyone, Keith Clone does have a poetic imagination after all. Here are your new pages.

—Where's Lydia?

—She went to powder her nose.

—We can't waste any more time. Who's our next Valerie?

Jill steps forward, takes the page Lafferty is handing her, and steps onto the stage beside Scales-McCabe.

—Before we begin, McCabe, I think you should be smoking in this scene.

—Doctor Bast doesn't smoke.

—I know, but you don't know what to do with your hands, and your fidgeting makes me nervous.

Without a word, Scales-McCabe walks away.

—What's eating him?

—McCabe has a thin skin.

—You'd think that all those years in the joint would toughen him up a little.

—McCabe was in the joint?

—McKenna, will you please do us all a favor and play the damn part?

—Sure, boss!

—Places, action!

—We don't yell the word *action* in the theatre. Lord, what idiots.

JILL (AS VALERIE): I will do this, but first I want you to hear me out. You never lay a finger on me while I'm sleeping, you got that?

MCKENNA (AS BAST): Only the light touches you, and the light is what I unpeel from you by the invisible reach of the camera, which holds the light's memory inside it. Think of the camera as my heart.

—This guy ain't following the script, Mislove complains. —It's the best script I ever wrote for you guys. Swell it up!

—McKenna, your rendition of Doctor Bast makes him sound like a lunatic.

—How could he ask what he's asking if he wasn't one?

—What do you say, Jill? How does it feel?

—I like it.

—We'll try it again. By the way, Jill, you have the part. As Valerie, you're spot on in a Joan of Arc type of way. Is that what you are going for?

—I was just trying to say the line right.

—There was a moment when you turned into Valerie before our eyes.

—I was trying hard not to try too hard.

—Seeing you play the role makes Valerie all the more real.

—Valerie is real.

—We've made her into a fictional character.

—Jill's made the fictional character real.

—Is that even possible?

—Only when the character is well written, Mislove chimes in.

—Valerie's part is not well written. What Jill adds to the role is not on the page.

—I don't get it.

—Poorly written characters can still win you over. A consummate actor will fill in the gaps left by the writer with her own heart and soul. That's what we're seeing in Jill's portrayal.

—All I did was stand there and read lines.

—Did you learn anything, Jill?

—Playing Valerie is less about mistaken identities than self-sacrifice.

—I don't know, have you ever read *The Fountainhead*?

—There is no sacrifice we are asking our actress to make, there's just a feeling of danger. We will station three gorillas right outside the room while you're in there with Bast. You can trust your safety with me.

—Where are you going to get three gorillas?

—Lafferty waves listlessly in the direction of McKenna, Mislove, and Neil the Feel.

—I'm supposed to feel better knowing that ragtag goon squad is looking out for me?

—Wait, we have one last Valerie to audition.

—Svevo!

—This has become a farce.

—Svevo, I don't know what disappoints me more, the idea that you want this part or that you don't look half bad as a woman.

—Come over here and plant a kiss on me, handsome, says Svevo the Obligatory Swede.

—Let's put an end to the fun and games. There's work to do. We open tomorrow!

The next evening, in a balloon borrowed from the Dynaflow Institute, McKenna and the now-returned-from-the-town-the-zombis-built Abbot Jaffe hover near the hotel, the two with binoculars directed toward the window of Doctor Bast's room. But what if he should draw the shades? Samantha Sound posed as a hotel maid and removed the curtains from the room, explaining to

Doctor Bast that she was taking them away for cleaning, and that she would return them within an hour. Jaffe clicks the tape machine on and holds the microphone for McKenna to begin their narration.

—Here's our Valerie, she's entered Bast's room.

—She's keeping her head down, she doesn't have confidence she can fool Doctor Bast.

—No, shyness is part of the role.

—He's giving her a drink with a straw.

—She takes it, sips.

—He downs his drink.

—She's still sipping hers.

—He's saying something, I can't read lips.

—He doesn't seem to notice she's not Valerie.

—He shows her his camera. He's leading her to his freshly made bed.

—She lingers, doesn't want to get too close.

—Who could blame her?

—She's staggering back and forth across the room.

—He poisoned her drink. That man is low.

—Sleeping pills are my guess.

—She reaches the sofa, slumps over, out cold.

—Let's make sure she's not faking.

—It wasn't written into her part. She was told to stay on script.

They watch speechlessly as Doctor Bast drags her limp body to the bed. He positions her and begins taking pictures with flashes bursting out the window.

—So that's it, he really does want photos of girls sleeping. I suspected worse.

—He's covering her with flower petals.

—He's making her into a goddamn corpse. He's a doctor infatuated with death.

—It kills me to do this, but we have to put plan B into effect, the plan of last resort.

McKenna fires a flare into the sky, a signal to the others on the ground. The Useless Bums' supply truck is parked near the hotel. Its back door swings open and out pours a small army of rifle-toting Nightingale commandos in nurse uniforms led by Luckie. The Nightingales enter the hotel through the service entrance. Hotel guests see them and toss their wallets and jewelry on the floor. The Nightingales are not here to ransack. They quickstep up the stairs to the fourth floor. They knock on Doctor Bast's door, less a come-open-the-door knock than a signal to stand back. On the count of three, a half dozen Nightingales slam their bodies against the door. The lock bursts, hinges uncouple from the frame, and the door falls flat. The Nightingales funnel into the room, every rifle aimed at Doctor Bast.

Stunned, he drops his camera and raises his hands.

Jill remains lifeless.

—You killed her, you creep!

—She's only sleeping.

—I'll be sorely disappointed if we don't get to kill you, says Upstart Annette.

—What is this about? Doctor Bast asks.

—We should be the ones asking you that, Luckie says.

—I have the whole story right here, Nora says holding up an album of illicit photos from St. Marc's.

—The St. Marc school falls under my authority. I committed no crime.

—This isn't about the law, Luckie says, —as much as decency.

—You kill me in cold blood, and it's murder, pleads Doctor Bast.

—You've sentenced Culprit Clutch to hang.

A smile crosses Doctor Bast's face. It's a poker game, and he just learned his hand.

—Bust me, strangle me, blow me away, you can't make this right. Unless the order comes from me, the hanging goes on as planned. I have a wire from Washington that instructs me to reject Bayard Huffy's authority, and there is nothing anyone can do.

C.B. whispers into Luckie's ear.

—The boy here tells me, Luckie says, —that ol' Cuplrit Clutch isn't even locked up.

—The lock on his cell is broken, C.B. adds. —He hasn't seen his jailers in days.

—What's he still doing there?

—Drinking wine with Henry Greathead.

—This is your day, Doctor, Luckie says, unclicking the safety on her Colt 45 and placing it against the villain's temple. —Here is how this plays out. We will take the photographs and film in your camera and burn them. If you ever set foot on the grounds of the St. Marc school, you will die. The Useless Bums will walk to the jail and sober up Culprit Clutch enough to get him out of there. He will be out of your custody, and there won't be a hanging. What happens between you and Culprit Clutch is between you and him. I don't owe Culprit Clutch any favors, and I've already given you yours. Let's go, girls, we're done here.

JILL

What a great disappointment to see the inside of the hotel: After all my fantasies, to find their swimming pool is filthy and covered in green scum. All this time we thought the American doctors were living in high style.

C.B.

I have a memory of Doctor Bast from what's ahead. He's on the highways, the superhighways, the long roads where you never have to stop except to fill up the tank. Trucks the size of train cars barrel down them day and night. Their horns are loud and headlights bright. Doctor Bast will be driving one, and he will call himself Rolling Thunder, the Big Dog of Love. I remember this because I was traveling south along a road called the 75 on foot, and he gave me a ride.

Funny is Never Forever (1955, -53)

All the commotion that night turns the St. Marc American School for Nurses into a ghost town. Tipsy Henry Greathead strolls through the empty corridors, peeking into rooms, making sure everything is as it should be. Even Josie's room in the infirmary wing seems more quiet than usual from the outside.

He slowly opens the door to her room and finds her fully clothed and making the bed.

—She's doing fine, if you were wondering, Josie says, speaking of herself as if she were someone else.

—Glad to hear it, Henry replies.

—She's not going to have a child after all.

Henry's face falls. —You lost your baby?

—There never was a baby. It was all a mistake.

—A hysterical pregnancy? Jill asks.

—That's how it sounds, Nora replies.

—She fakes the headaches, too. It's all a play for attention.

—Her headaches are real. I've touched her forehead and felt electricity.

—She fakes that, too.

—She was not the one who said she was pregnant. Doctor Bast was.

—It was Doctor Bast's hysterical pregnancy then.

—I should have known. She hasn't gained an ounce. She's been sick, but she's always sick.

—She's not the one who's sick, it's Doctor Bast who's sick, sick in the mind.

•

That night, Jill is drawn to the window. The demon Doctor Bast has been expelled, Culprit saved, Josie is neither having a baby nor another one of her crippling headaches, and all is right in the world. All is not right in the world. Jill knows it, they all sense it. The others think it's their imagination. Jill knows the truth. All she can do is look out the window to see if she can see it.

JILL

It wouldn't shock me to see a skeleton sitting beneath a tree in a birdcage or a black stroller full of baby pigs in bonnets. A thought crosses my mind, not a thought of my own, but rather a thought cast through the air. I should go check on Josie who's alone in her room. It becomes an obsession, and I just know I won't be able to fall asleep until I check.

In the infirmary wing, there are so many rooms with so many beds and no one to sleep in them, it's such a shame. No one sleeps there but Josie when she has a headache, and Culprit the time he was here after his fall. You can always tell which room is Josie's, as it has tinfoil taped across all of the windows blocking the sunlight, moonlight, starlight, firefly light. Nightingales are always taking the foil down, because if there is one thing we know about the upkeep of a sick room it's that it should be kept bright and airy. When Josie feels a headache coming on, she puts the foil back up.

I slowly open Josie's door. It is too dark to see whether she's awake, but I can hear her breathing. I sense that someone else is also in the room standing in the corner near the doorjamb and moving toward me.

The phantom's skin is so pale that he broadcasts light

even where there is none. He's bald as a stone, a bald old man with a broken nose, and he puts his hand on my mouth to close it, not that it needs closing. I couldn't have screamed if I wanted. I turn to run, and he pulls me by the arm. I grab a pillow with my free hand and strike.

When I awaken, it is light. I am back in my own bed. Yet there is evidence that it wasn't a nightmare. There are spots on my scalp where hair is missing and a heavy claw-shaped mark on my forehead. While the claw shape might be my imagination playing tricks on me, the mark is not. The girls are going to ask about it. How will I ever be able to explain? I put on a scarf and hope that no one notices.

When the day ends, night falls, and the girls sleep, it takes all of my willpower to keep myself from paying Josie's room another visit to see if the bald phantom has returned. These obsessive compulsions, I spent a year in psychoanalysis working to beat them. Forcing myself to stay in bed means a long, restless night of staring at the ceiling fan.

Past midnight, the snoring Nightingales fill the dormitory hall with an even hum. My eyes closed in pretend sleep, I feel a body hovering over me, feel someone's hot breath on my chest. The fear strikes, and I cannot move except my eyelids, which won't stay closed. The bald phantom kisses my hair, my eyes, the palms of my hands. I pull my hands back and try to push the old man away. One hand lands on what feels like a breast while the other falls upon a cavity in the chest where a breast should be.

The phantom is a woman. She turns and whisks away.

Emboldened, I follow her. She seems to know but doesn't mind. She leads me to the head nurse's bedroom where the glow of candlelight seeps through the crack below the shut door.

The door open, I take my first good look at Miss Phantom and see that it's Luckie, Luckie without hair, Luckie in a nightgown that reveals the presence of just one breast.

She sits down on her bed and pats the covers, gesturing me to come and sit beside her. Beside the candles and the pistols on her dresser is a faceless foam bust wearing Luckie's two long-braided ponytails.

—You will forget this bald foolishness, Luckie tells me, her voice coarse, hissing no louder than a whisper, her Wild West accent abandoning her. —If you ever tell what you've seen, I'll kill you.

It is different between us the nights after that. Nothing frightens me. She comes to get me when she wants company. It is easier for us to talk. We talk about how neither one of us can ever get to sleep. She likes that someone knows her secret. She lets me feel her bald head; it is cold as marble. She tells me how her left breast had been amputated, and in the light, I look at what is still there. It is like a soft doorknob or a fleshy mushroom on her chest, the part that is growing back.

—It's nothing anyone should ever see, she tells me. —It's nothing I should see myself, except in a mirror, and when I see it in the mirror, I say to myself it isn't mine.

We both know the breast is not supposed to grow back, but it's nothing we say.

I ask if she's scared.

—As soon as fear possesses and controls your mind, you are a moral and physical coward, and a coward has no place and is of no use on this earth.

I sit on her bed for moments without end, staring at the candles, pistols, and faceless foam bust wearing her hair. Above is her mirror, and I stare at my face glowing bright in the candlelight, and over my shoulder, her face in the shadows. Her mirror image isn't her, and mine isn't me. My mirror image shows a left-handed person, a trickster who can pass herself off as my double, an inhabitant of another world trying to fool me every time I look in a mirror. As much as she looks like me, she's as different as a twin. Once you become familiar enough with twins, it's easy to tell them apart. I can tell us apart.

While Luckie spends her sleepless nights roaming around the grounds making sure all's well, I gaze out the window and see her, her hairless, straight body shining under the waving branches of the tall trees, and all is well. As I fall into sleep, a thought casting through the air plants inside my mind. 'With no left breast, what keeps your heart from spilling out your chest?'

It's a shanty harborside in northern Haiti, Le Cap's most international quarter, replete with buildings whose wood plank foundations are washed by the constant rising and falling splash of salt tides. The wood is rotting away, and one day sooner rather than later, this building, a fish processing plant, will collapse into the water.

PORTUGUESE FISH PLANT OWNERS

Fish processing plants run best when boats can nest up beside them, and if the sea eats the building away, so what? We were never so thrilled about the business in the first place. What are we to do? Paint the wood? Is there ever a time when the wood's dry enough to hold paint?

The swells off the harbor make for unsteady footing on the dock that leads to the plant and assorted other buildings. Culprit steadies himself, walking across the floating railroad ties drilled through and threaded with heavy steel cable. He's looking for his secret meeting, which is perhaps too secret because he doesn't know where to go. It's the one place in Haiti where you can't hear the eternal drums in the distance. Here, the sound has been replaced by the ringing of a bell, its purpose not known.

The smell of creosote mixed in with the salt air seeps from below. Gaslights flicker as the wind rocks them about from the hooks where they hang.

The people milling about are sailors from the world over. The lollygaggers will sleep tonight on their boats, if they sleep. There is carousing to be had, and nowhere else to go than back to sea. While on dry land, they might as well make light.

Go to that bookstore a block or two on, the well lighted one, the one with the words BLACK SWAN embossed on the window glass, and a smaller sign that reads, 'ONE SPEAKS ENGLISH HERE.' No one speaks English there, but patrons will find there are so many old volumes on wood shelves, a section devoted entirely to theatre with titles in English, Italian, German, and French. Culprit finds wood crates piled with used editions of Samuel French paperbound play scripts. They are not in order, and he finds a worn copy of *Long Day's Journey into Night* in a stack with Tyrone Sr.'s lines underlined in red ballpoint pen. He had been meaning to read O'Neill, and it costs him 15 cents American to purchase.

Before venturing outside, he puts on his peacoat and fisherman's cap and steps outside where the pouring rain sounds like paper tearing.

The lodge next door looks as if it might collapse. Its bricks have deep gaps between them, as if the stone masons were running low on mortar and hoped no one would notice. It has the air of a salty saloon, and an obnoxious dog outside completes the scene. He's wearing no collar, no leash, and the rain has made him mean. Culprit is just outside the lodge's bat-wing door when a man is upon him, telling him that he has to meet the talking dog. Culprit knows it's a sucker play for the money in his wallet, the money he needs to keep for later, because otherwise he won't be getting drunk. He's not going to lose it for a talking dog to tell him that the creaking, leaking wood slabs on the top of the building make up what is called a roof. Or that the best ballplayer ever was Ruth, because what a fool that dog must be not knowing it's DiMaggio.

Culprit pushes past and steps to the bar, throws back a shot of rye, and his companions join him, one at each side. They are the Meneer Bros., Norm and Mike, and their business cards give no phone number or street address and nothing more than their names and a general location, Washington, D.C. It's code, meaning they are diplomats for hire, though most often they are called for dirty work.

—The so-called surfing footage, one brother says (Culprit can never tell the difference), —it's pathetic.

—We knew the prospects of surfing here were dim, though we advocated strongly for it.

—Our objective was for the crew to fail, so we could step in.

—I don't like the sound of this, Culprit says. He signals the bartender to bring another.

—You already know about our pet project. We've talked about this before.

—We want to turn the Hiroshima Filmstrip into a talkie.

The Hiroshima Filmstrip is as harrowing a filmstrip as ever has been created. After a milquetoast introduction, each ring of the bell advances the strip to progressively more gruesome images of badly burned bodies, charred bones poking out through tears in the skin. It would have been bad enough if the photos showed corpses, but these victims were alive after those two days in August already ten years ago.

—It's caused schoolchildren to vomit, Mike Meneer says proudly.

—It teaches them everything they need to know about atomic war.

1953. Norm and Mike Meneer are neither doctors nor professors. Nor are they physicists, although they broke their teeth with the RAND Corporation. The last time they were in Haiti, they came to deliver a lecture series to the Nightingales centered upon the Hiroshima Filmstrip, which they had just finished. One brother pulls down the roll-up movie screen hanging in front of the chalkboard, while the other draws the curtains closed. —Hold onto your hats! World War III will begin momentarily, they announce before starting the presentation.

—As you can see, the burns shown in this image are from Nagasaki, says one Meneer.

—That's Hiroshima, says the other.

—What's the difference? It's the burns we're looking at.

—What you see are burns that look like tar patches on the skin.

—The victims' expressions are half lifeless, but I assure you, these folks are alive.

—The way the victims describe it, these burns keep burning long after the blast.

—Don't look away when we show you the next slide.

—We need every last one of you not to act shocked when this really happens.

—In a city like Atlanta.

—Hey, take that back, mister, my sister lives in Atlanta!

—You need to stare at these images long and hard to desensitize yourself. When this happens in America, others will run away in horror. You, on the other hand, will embrace the opportunity and expedite yourselves to the areas hardest hit to provide comfort and light medical treatment. Here's the slide we want you to see.

The image causes an uproar. One student turns on the lights in the dark classroom and another steps outside to knock over the electricity generator, which kills the power for the projector. The Meneers carry on as if nothing happened.

—Any questions?

—We're supposed to prepare ourselves to treat burns like that? Nora complains loudly. —The toughest lesson we've learned so far is how to fluff a pillow.

—I don't have the stomach for this. I might as well go home right now, Dinah says.

—Good luck, you're stuck here just like the rest of us, Jill says.

—The purpose of the strip, a Meneer interjects, trying to win his audience back, —is to prepare you for this eventuality.

—If World War III breaks out, Jill adds, —I don't want to be a hard-luck survivor, and I don't want to be one of the nurses sent in to help. I want to be among the instant dead.

1955. The Hiroshima Filmstrip put the Meneer Bros. on the map, and every new revision of the filmstrip is more sensational than the last. The Meneers are reviled, but there is never a shortage of audiences to view the strip.

Culprit swallows his third shot and feels it.

One Meneer carries on, —You won't get more technical assistance than you did with the surfing film.

—I didn't make the surfing film. I never showed up.

The other Meneer, —Our push to get the surfing film funded worked too well. The Powers that Be still want it. They just haven't figured out a way to make waves, which is why this is all so hush-hush.

—We'll change their minds with our Hiroshima talkie.

—We want you to make the film quickly, before UNESCO gets its act together.

—Are you writing this down? Listen closely; I'll narrate your production script.

—Shoot your movie out of doors. We want your film to look as if it were made in the good ol' U.S. of A. You can hide the mountains, but you won't be able to hide the palm trees, so let's say maybe your setting is Miami Beach. The reason for this is we want your film to show the before and after of a nuclear attack.

—The point is first to show all the pretty girls giving flowers to sailors down by the sea, then follow that with widespread destruction and charred yet living bodies.

—There are plenty of locations in and around Cap Haitien that look like they might have been hit by the Bomb. They are still crawling out of the mess of the 1842 earthquake.

—You'll want to take advantage of these locations.

—The first act shows daily life and stars the student nurses. Pick the pretty ones.

—You'll want to show how white their teeth are, and their pale complexions.

—Let's pick out the blondes.

—Pick out the ones made of pure white light.

—Then KABOOM! The Bomb falls. We don't have the funding to show the obliteration of all your film sets, although it wouldn't make a difference to how the location already looks.

—You can create the effect of the Bomb's detonation by opening the camera's shutter all the way for a moment so that the screen whites out. Then follows several seconds of images shown in negative.

—You'll want to show negative footage for no more than a few seconds, because if you don't you'll lose your shock value. We're not trying to send the message that a nuclear blast turns the world into a negative image permanently.

—When you return to positive images, you'll march out your victims.

—You're in Haiti. You use Haitians.

Culprit, who has listened patiently to this spiel, taking notes for a time before stopping, asks a question, —You're trying to tell me that after the Bomb strikes, everyone looks Haitian.

—Why not?

—They are the darkest people I've ever seen, as dark as the Nightingales are light.

—It seems insulting to the Haitian people, Culprit says.

—It's not our fault the Haitians are how they are.

—It's an ugly business.

Culprit stands and turns to walk away.

—You might get the Useless Bums to make your film. Count me out.

—Don't think there isn't something in it for you.

—I'm not interested.

—Listen, Culprit. This is about taking grains of rice and making Rice Krispies.

—That makes no sense. I'm leaving.

—Don't walk away from the future. There's a future for you, Culprit, in Indochina.

—Yeah, it's what Indochina needs most right now, breakfast cereal.

—We're getting out of the biz the moment the Hiroshima talkie is in the can.

—Ever hear of Viet Nam?

—No, Culprit says.

—It's the jewel of Southeast Asia. It's French occupied, but they're looking to get out.

—We're looking to get in and open a restaurant.

—It's our way of spreading the American Way while pursuing our true passion.

—It's our prediction that in the next ten years Americans will be flocking to Viet Nam. It's our intention to provide them a place to eat that reminds them of home.

—We want to cut you in on the deal, Culprit.

—How does that sound?

Culprit walks away quickly without looking back.

Pandemonium breaks out at the movie theatre that night. There are air raid sirens, and no one has heard them here before. It's because the Meneers have come to town, and it's a test. It's the type of thing they do, break the sleepy silence of a Friday night in Le Cap centrale in the name of preparing the citizenry for what to do when the Big One drops, if any foreign government should ever decide to drop the Big One here.

It is an American movie showing, an Abbott and Costello feature, and most of the audience is American: Nightingales, Useless Bums, tourists. When they hear the siren, their first thought is it's World War III, the end of the world. They push toward the exits, crawling on top of one another, shouting hullabaloo.

In one case, the choice is to hightail it out of there or stay and kiss the boy she's been dying to kiss all night. To get away from the mob, they climb the stage. The film flickers over them. Their mouths devour each other. Their faces become one. Who could have seen a kiss like this coming?

ABBOT JAFFE

I wish I had brought the camera. A scene like this would be tough to renact. Nothing we could stage will ever seem so real.

The scene inside the movie theatre quiets after the panic-stricken have fled and the sirens cease. The stragglers who remain don't know what will happen next. The kissing pair is not waiting to find out.

Lyle Mislove approaches the lovebirds and tugs on the young man's jacket sleeve and hands him a slip of paper.

—What's this?

—I wrote you dialogue, Mislove explains to the lovebirds.

—Why?

—Because, as a playwright, that's what I do.

—You read it, the young man says, handing the paper back to Lyle.

Lyle clears his throat and reads,

'**SHE**: My lips just won't stay on.'
'**HE**: They stay on me just fine.'

Lyle hands the strip of paper back to the young man. —Your turn.

The young man laughs and crumples up the paper, tosses it on the floor.

—Now where was I? he asks.

—Right here, she replies, and off they go again.

—Did you see what just happened? Lafferty asks.

—How could I have missed it? Mislove replies.

—They just wrote their own dialogue, McKenna says.

Mislove offers his thoughts, —He says to her, 'Now where was I?' She comes back with 'Right here,' and they kiss. It's banal, it's cliché. I love it, it's perfect. Damn it, I wish I could write dialogue like that.

—You could always steal it for your plays.

—That's just it. I could do that and all the critics would write how banal and cliché the dialogue is and pin it on me. I have a reputation to live up to.

They look around, still waiting while nothing happens.

—It's a movie theatre now but you can tell it was built for vaudeville, says Mislove.

—Haitian vaudeville, that I would like to see.

—I do miss the theatre, the stage lights and the heat beneath them. The smell of the gels burning so slightly, and always the show must go on, just not all night, or we would burn this place down.

—The Meneer Bros. just pulled up outside, says Dinah.

—Who are they?

—A couple of government tramps.

—They aren't official G-men. They're hired guns.

—You should see their car, a topless Mercedes 600SL.

—I'm in the wrong line of work.

—You know what Mr. Bayard Huffy would say if he were here. There will come a day not far off when just such a car will be parked outside every thatch-rook shanty shack in the Nord Department, and Haiti will have the finest highway system in the world.

The gum, the same gum, her tongue pushes the gum into his mouth. He opens his eyes and sees her eyes laughing back at him, playful girl. He chews the gum, it's not disgusting. It tastes just like gum he might have been chewing himself. He kisses it back into her mouth. She doesn't find this strange. Maybe she's done it before. It makes no matter.

A rendezvous between Henry and Culprit takes on a serious tone.

—You must have been thrilled to learn Josie's not pregnant.

—I already knew.

—It was news to everyone else, Josie included.

—Pregnancy is rare when there was no sexual involvement.

—Then why was she convinced?

—She took it on the doctor's authority. Some doctor.

—He pressed the stethoscope to her belly and heard a heartbeat not hers.

—It could have been his wristwatch.

—You never thought she was pregnant?

—No.

—Now I know you're lying. Who'd you think was the father?

—It didn't cross my mind.

—Pascale the Rascal. That fool should have stepped forward. To think you were going to hang.

—Pascale had no reason to think he was the father. He and Josie were not involved, either.

—Then who was the father?

—There is no child. There was no father.

—Now it's all becoming clear to me.

—What is?

—The reason you stayed in jail with the door unlocked.

—I'm listening.

—You would rather hang than raise a black man's child.

—That's absurd. There is no kid. The point's moot.

—Had there been a baby, not yours, would you have stuck around?

—No.

—You would rather hang than raise a black man's child.

—I wasn't sticking around if the kid was mine.

Henry raises an eyebrow and doesn't say a word.

—I'm kidding, Culprit says. —You know when I'm kidding.

—Go on, kid about it, kid about it, kid about dropping the atomic bomb to blow the reef to smithereens, kid about the gall of coming here and asserting wrongheaded values on people who do just fine without them, kid about Uncle Sam, the good ol' U.S. of A., a nation that's supposed to stand up for every one of us, and somehow the two of us are always left out.

—In my case, it was because of the dead Communist nestled in my psyche.

—In my case, it's because I am a French-Canadian.

—It's because you're black.

—Not always.

—All too often.

—What are we looking at?

—An empty bottle of wine.

—That's not what I mean. You're the star, and I'm the side player, a character role.

—This isn't a show.

—You are always the star, and I am always the side player.

—I don't know what you mean.

—You are complacent and ridiculous.

—You got me. I don't know what you mean.

—You are the Powers that Be.

—I am just the opposite. I'm a born social catalyst, dissenter, going against the times.

—You are the Powers that Be.

—If that's the case, I quit.

—You quit what?

—This.

—You can't quit this.

—Why not?

—You don't call the shots.

—Tell whomever it is who calls the shots that I quit.

—That's not how this works.

There's an unsettling pause.

—Oh, no, Culprit Clutch, you're not going to get away with silence. It's not that easy.

After another lengthy pause, —I quit, Culprit says.

HENRY GREATHEAD

You have no idea how insulting that is. You can disappear, slam the door closed, and then come right back when you get the itch, the door is unlocked. That's your privilege. You know damn well there are others who cannot come and go as we please. When I go, I'm gone. For me, it's not a choice, because there is no choice. I suppose that's a joke to you, too.

The Useless Bums are restless. They have nothing to do but make a surfing film and no way to make the film unless there are waves. Since they can't make waves, the best they can do is pay a visit to the undersea ridge north of Haiti where they'll find the source of Haiti's wavelessness.

—We can ask to use the Dynaflow Institute's submarine.

—They don't have a submarine.

—They do, it's a one-seater, for research.

—We have a better shot at the Russians lending us one of theirs.

—We could always hire the man with the glass-bottom boat.

—Josie's coming along.

—She's up for it?

—Maybe she's ready to be a full-fledged Nightingale once and for all.

—Culprit Clutch will be there, too.

—Are they getting along?

—We'll see.

—They went through so much, even if it turned out to be nothing. I don't blame them for not speaking.

His name is Lafcadio, and a group of sixteen finds him on the pier near the casino. Every morning, he tows a glass-bottom barge filled with tourists out near the reef. To avoid the tugboat motor scaring off the fish, swimmers dive into the water and drag the barge over the reef by their own power so that the the passengers can witness the spectacle through the window on the floor.

The adventuresome among the passengers put on a snorkel and take a swim.

When it comes to swimming, the Nightingales become shy. The only bathing suits they have are the skimpy bikini bathing suits from the State Department. They change quickly behind a curtain and jump into the warm water before putting on flippers and masks. They stay together, treading water a safe distance from the barge, their heads bobbling along the surface with their gleaming hair tied at the back. Jill breaks from the bunch and swims back to the boat. The Useless Bums don't have bathing suits; they wear old pairs of trousers they had cut off at the knee. Aboard, they find an unlocked chest filled with frogman gear, wetsuits, and scuba diving tanks. Lafcadio catches them in the act and wags his finger at them. Lafcadio shows them another trunk filled with snorkels, masks, and flippers. This is the gear they will use. Jill suits up, too, puts on her bathing cap with its white feather-like flaps that keep the salt water off her hair.

It takes a few tries to get the tight-fitting mask to go on in a way so that it doesn't fill with water the instant they go under. They submerge themselves and find the sea bottom not far below the surface. The water is clean, the cleanest they've seen since coming to Haiti, and there are patches of white sand glimmering under the light of the sun.

The swimmers attract colorful tropical fish and dive to the bottom to feed sea urchins. It all looks unreal: the coral fans, rainbow fish, conch shells, the faraway blue-green depths. There are so many electric colors, there is so much light, so much sun underneath the water. It's overwhelming.

Lafcadio blows his whistle, calling for the swimmers to return to the barge. The tug is on its way to tow them back to land. The American passengers are seasick, the swimmers tired. They've experienced all they can in a day. It is time to go back.

—The reef is fantastic.

—You can see why surfing makes no matter here.

—You'll never find anything like this in the American Midwest.

—Of course not.

—I'm from Topeka.

—It shakes you free of everything you know.

—How true.

—How can anyone take into account anything as beautiful as this?

The wind picks up and whisks the sound away from their ears. They talk, but cannot hear each other. They look around. They stare out to sea. They lean on each other's shoulders and catch a snooze. The boat's motor leaves a powerful white wake.

She's not here, after all. A headache at the last minute kept Josie on shore. It makes no matter. Culprit sees her as if he's watching a loop of silent 8 mm film in color. He sees her the way he last saw her, leaving in a car with her Haitian crew in her sunglasses, a blue scarf covering her hair. It was hot, the air still. He sees her again, the car, the sunglasses, the scarf. It was hot, the air still. It repeats until he too falls asleep.

She stays in bed through the day, and no one comes to check on her. There is no reason to come back and check on her. She is a grown woman and can take care of herself, even if she is sick.

When Luckie comes around, Josie is white as a sheet, but her skin is always light. She also isn't breathing. Luckie's first impulse is to revive her. Josie is cold to the touch. She might have been dead for several hours, for all Luckie knows. Her next step is to take a chair across the room, have a seat, and wait. It is Haiti, after all, and the dead seem to revive here more often than in other parts of the world, and certainly, they all thought she was pregnant, and she never was. After several minutes, she realizes that it's a ridiculous idea. She covers Josie's face with a sheet and goes to the phone to call Bayard Pumphrey Huffy.

One of their party dies, the door to the spirit world opens, and spirits are passing through, right in front of their eyes. They think it's because they're crazy, because death makes you crazy. That night Jill will lie in bed, she's supposed to be asleep, and spirits are flowing beneath her bed like a river. She peeks off the edge and sees them; they are made of light. She won't say anything because no one will believe her, and she cannot even convince herself. She is supposed to be asleep, and she might be dreaming.

—It's the conduit of spirits traveling between Europe and North America.

—Don't be a moron. It's Africa. Spirits flow between America and Africa.

There's a history there. It's a route well traveled, though often not willingly, and there comes time for souls to go home, and they flow, of all places, beneath the bed.

It's the spirit commerce. It's like the Friday evening commute. It's the Staten Island Ferry overflowing with passengers. It's walking along sidewalks downtown with hundreds, no, thousands of souls flowing through beneath you, underground.

There is no subway system in Cap Haitien and its environs. That doesn't mean there is any less soul traffic flowing underfoot. There is no more or less soul traffic in northern Haiti than anywhere else in the world. Just here, in the City of Ghosts, it doesn't seem out of place.

—Was she one of ours? Huffy asks when he arrives at St. Marc's. He already knew she was, and was asking that just to be formal. It's a fine thing to say, but they just look at him. Of course, she was one of ours. Whose else would she be?

Later that night, Culprit fools himself into thinking he's sleeping, and then, over there in the corner of his eye, he sees him. Turn your head and he's gone, Baron Samedi. The Top Hat Man outside the cemetery.

He steers clear of your tears, and by morning, he's long gone. He lives in the crust you wipe out of your eyes after a restless sleep.

Mornings later, they clean the floors down to the wood. Miss Penny finds a long strand of hair on the beech floor, and she puzzles over it. The room has a high ceiling and ceiling fan. The sheets are freshly bleached and pressed.

The air is sticky and will not move.

—That Josie, she was one of a kind.

—I didn't always get along with her, and while I never disliked her, all I can say for certain was that yes, she was one of a kind.

—If you die in Haiti, can you still get into heaven?

—That sounds like a line from an M. Lyle Mislove play.

—What are you asking? Is this consecrated ground?

—Is the soil Catholic enough? I am not sure what kind of place this is. Looking around, I would swear it's Africa. You know how I know it's not? Africa has a soft floor, you can dig Africa with your hand, but here the ground is rock hard.

—I don't know. Africa is a big continent. It's not all soft.

—Africa has lions on the loose, and only Tarzan the Ape Man can save you.

—Headaches don't kill people, especially not someone so young.

—Maybe it was the morphine, did her in.

—There hasn't been a drop of morphine here for two years.

—Her Haitian friends were bringing it to her. That's why they were friends.

—I don't think so. She genuinely enjoyed the company of Pascale and the others.

—They had a magic act.

—She liked them better than us.

—I don't blame her, Jill says. —We weren't always nice to her.

—She was always sick.

—I thought she was pretending to be sick to get attention.

—She was sick enough that she died. I hope that answers your question.

—I wonder if she had a brain tumor.

—I've seen brain cancer patients, Luckie says, —and they were sick in a different way.

—We can always cut her head open to see if there's a tumor.

—Let's respect her memory enough not to do that.

—We are women of science. Don't you want to get to the bottom of it?

—I am happy to think it was nothing that killed her, that her spirit left her and decided against a return.

—Are they notifying her kin?

—I don't know that she had any. She never spoke of anyone.

—They have no record on her.

—How could she not have a record?

—It has less to do with her and more to do with them. I asked, and they don't have a record on me, either.

—But you receive letters. I would know to look for your letters to find your family.

—Josie once told me she was from Wilkes-Barre, Pennsylvania.

—She told me Jupiter, Florida.

—She told me she lived all over.

All the walls Jill has built around herself, her very Citadelle nature, come crashing down when sleep comes for her. The real world puts itself to bed, and the Invisibles come out to play.

—I suppose we can wait until someone writes looking for her.
—With any luck, we'll all be gone by then.

When the world deals a crashing blow, a crashing below, Jill is thrown off the boat, she's thrown under the air. Still smarting, she regains footing in a world where everything has changed, except for her.

It is now, after someone dies, and dying is on her mind. Waking up is how she knows she's alive, and it feels like hell.

All that brings her pleasure is decay, and decay is just something else she dislikes. The trashcan knocked over, she leaves it that way. She watches to see what happens, and nothing happens. The seagulls pick it over. Then comes the rain, then a coating of dust. She crawls along the ground under the blazing sun with insects biting her on the back of the neck. She wants to see what is underneath it, careful not to touch it, careful not to disturb it, careful not to set loose what is living there.

JILL
We'll drop her body into the sea, and I wish it was me.

How the Sun
Gives Life to the Sea

CULPRIT CLUTCH

I'm as puzzled as the oyster. All the time I've spent sailing, I
have never given thought to what's beneath the hull. There's
water, it's dark, it's deep, and if you go down far enough
you'll reach solid ground. You won't find civilization. You
might find evidence of civilization, Spanish shipwrecks, a tin
beer can, discharged torpedo shells, a treasure chest, sunken
German submarines, a bottle that sank with a note inside.

HENRY GREATHEAD

The United States goes about it all wrong with its elegant design
of running cables across Haiti for telephone communication.
The telephone wires connect back to Washington through a
thick cable they are running along the bottom of the ocean
from Cap Haitien along the arc of the Bahamas to Miami and
then overland up the Eastern Seaboard of the United States. I
hope Ma Bell can swim.

—We said goodbye to her dead body and tossed her overboard in a makeshift
coffin.

—The United States is playing with fire.

—The salt water and sharks will get to her soon enough.

—The U.S. doesn't want to mess with invisible pipelines and the flow
of spirits.

—I will never again find that same piece of water where we left her, nor
dive deep enough to bring her back.

—Spirits are not as airy as they are fluid.

—I was snorkeling once off the Keys and dove down and touched the hand of Jesus.

—The underwater channel runs straight from Africa into Haiti.

—It wasn't really Jesus.

—From Haiti, it shoots off the back of Cuba and makes a straight shot toward New Orleans.

—It was a marble statue of Jesus fifteen feet below the surface.

—Millions of Christians pray in the wrong direction. Heaven isn't in the sky; it's under water.

—The spirit flow is most vivid on the night when someone near and dear is dead.

—We dropped Josie's body in the water.

—The devil is the voice in your head that says you imagined it.

—Henry?

—You know what you saw.

—I think I'm going out of my head.

HENRY GREATHEAD

Telephones transport the human voice. The ghostly pipelines transport soul traffic. Now you tell me which is more powerful. The danger is in losing sight of the movement of the soul. The danger is in getting our signals crossed.

The wind from the north brings a chill on the morning they take Josie's body out. They wrap her body in burlap and place it in a wood crate left over from the shipment of surfing boards. They add heavy stones so it won't float.

After they drop the crate overboard, a handful of them go down the stairs to the boat's glass bottom for one last look at her as she drops deep into the Atlantic. They might be driven by morbid curiosity to see if the current wrests the body free from the crate. In deeper water, there's less to see below the boat. All they see is the darkness of the water. She is gone already.

Culprit remains on the deck as the boat circles the spot before turning back to the island. Later, when he remembers the moment, he will see it as if from different camera angles. He can see himself from high above and the circle of white ocean water the boat leaves in its wake. He can see himself from the side, his ear, his knit cap, his face red from the wind, his collar turned up and jaw clenched because that's what it does in the cold.

He hears just one voice. Henry Greathead is standing beside him, shouting in his ear over the rush of the wind. —She was a soft-spoken girl with pouting tendencies, wholesome with undercurrents of mystery. That's the way I will remember her.

That's not what Culprit hears Henry yelling. What Culprit hears is that he will remember her straight out of a Picasso painting. It's funny, even if Henry never said it. Culprit even asks Henry later after they return to the harbor, and Henry denies that the thought of Josie and Picasso had ever occurred to him. Yet for Culprit, surreal images from Picasso paintings and Josie are becoming intertwined in his mind, figures on the beach.

Rain beats down on the water, and strong currents sweep the crate containing Josie back toward the surface before gravity takes hold and drags her down to the ocean floor where the crate splits open, and the currents sweep her body free.

The thrills of P.F.C. Roper-Melo are those of loneliness. He watches the shore. He throws human relations to the wind, preferring solitude. He lives in his shack built from driftwood on the secret beach just above where the high tide reaches. Instead of neighbors, he lives among driftwood, broken seashells, shards of glass, clumps of seaweed, broken coral, spars, loose barnacles, pebbles, clamshells, horseshoe crabs, goldeneye, oceanic debris. The American flag hanging outside his shanty has turned white. The sun and sea have robbed its color. He bears the brunt of the same tropical storms that weathered the flag. Though when it's fair, his is an easy life as he breathes in the sweet salt air and has a front-row seat to watch the great ships sail across the edge of the horizon and the fishing boats with their brightly colored sails. He builds a fire at night, and the passage of the stars across the night sky is his entertainment.

Rain beats down on the beach when the P.F.C. spots Josie's body in the distance at low tide. From a hook on the wall inside the shack, he takes down his green fishing rubbers. They are what he will wear himself. For her, he brings a wool blanket. It will soak through but give her cover from the hard raindrops.

He lopes out into the wind to where she's walking slowly in ankle-deep water toward the shore. He wraps the blanket around her. The urge for him is to carry her back to his shack where she can dry off and eat. She resists letting him lift her, so instead he steadies her by the shoulders as she leads him toward the path away from the beach. She leads him along the road into Cap Haitien where the streets are empty; the heavy rain has chased everyone away. She leads him to the Pension Palacial where Culrpit Clutch has a room, into the lobby and up the stairs to Number 247, Culprit's room. When Culprit opens the door, P.F.C. Roper-Melo nods to him, drops his arms from Josie's shoulders and walks away.

The Pension Palacial is a stucco building that stands back from the street with a small garden, alongside a row of other homes. In the lower gallery, there are two large rooms used for dining where you can find a pitcher of hot water and make a cup of sweetened Haitian coffee. The individualized sleeping rooms are sparsely furnished with a high ceiling. The owner, Mme. Letoy, keeps them scrupulously clean. The linens are embroidered in the same colorful pattern as the napkins covering the bread basket in the dining room. The sleeping rooms are surprisingly cool, even when the heat outdoors is stifling.

Culprit occupies a corner room in one of the large upper galleries. From his window, he can see the comings and goings on the street and glimpse the sea. The bathroom downstairs off a rear court is a nuisance, but at least you can lock yourself inside, which is handy.

He forgets to lock the bathroom door while drawing a bath for Josie who had come back wrapped in a blanket though otherwise naked with soupy seaweed in her hair. She is cold to the touch and silent, though alive. A bath will warm and freshen her.

Belinda Ballard, Sheila's frequent visitor, flies down the stairs and flings the bathroom door open without thinking that it is occupied. Culprit Clutch is shampooing the hair of a naked and living though listless Josie.

BELINDA BALLARD

I am spending much of my time in Sheila's room away from St. Marc's, posing for her paintings, then peering deeply into them, the nude bodies based on my own and forced into abstract expression. My good news is I've discovered art is my calling. My bad news is I don't have a flair for it, though I'm learning. When I catch sight of Culprit Clutch bathing a sickly girl who was supposed to be dead, it seems more natural than shocking. Even though I've given up on becoming a nurse, my education has given me certain instincts. I want to comfort them.

The strange carnival ride is coming to an end. The Nightingales and Useless Bums have been riding in circles for what seems like an eternity, but then something changes in the music, in the air, and they sense that it's almost over. They slow down to the point they are not turning, and it's time to step off the ride.

A heavy-footed man in a black shirt and black trousers walks back and forth on the bluff overlooking the Useless Bums' camp. He carries an immense book and collection of papers under his arm. He appears to be looking for a way down to the Godless Bohemian Congregation. They are drinking the last of the St. Marc's wine.

—Who do you suppose that is?

—A Bible man.

—A Jehovah's Witness missionary.

—That doesn't explain what he's doing up there.

—Proselytizing.

—In that case, I hope he stays up there.

—I've only been to church one time since coming here, and all I remember is the kid doing magic tricks.

Finding no other way down, the heavyset man shimmies down the slope kicking loose rocks that find their way down before he does. He hands the men and women envelopes with their names on them. Inside are steamer tickets to take them home and mimeographed thank you letters from Secretary of State John Foster Dulles.

He had already stopped by St. Marc's and given the envelopes to the Nightingales he found there.

—I have two left, he says. —Anyone know where I might find Belinda Ballard and Culprit Clutch?

ABBOT JAFFE

It's always been an unsettling aspect of Haiti, the lack of seasons. It rains for months, the rest of the time it's hot. The falling leaves and scraps from trees are a sign of an eternal autumn that never fully arrives. The leaves disintegrate into a dust that looks like all other dust. It only makes sense the way that dreams make sense, but what it means is that goodbyes are on your mind.

JILL

We're not supposed to be friends, nor are we friends.

We came together on a mission without a mission, and we didn't grow together as much as we made it through these humdrum times together. It was a great time. It's moments when you say goodbye that you feel the invisible tethers that tie you to others. We'll go home, and there will be an invisible thread that binds us all.

STUART SCALES-MCCABE

Ever hear of Viet Nam? They say it's the Jewel of Southeast Asia. They're sending me out there as an advisor, the State Department is, not that I plan to stay a State Department stooge one day longer than I must. Once I'm there, I'm quitting this racket once and for all. The Meneer Bros. are quitting, too, and opening a restaurant in Saigon. They just love Americans there. The Meneers say they need a chef, and I've done some kitchen work. So Indochina, ready or not, here I am.

Bayard Pumphrey Huffy calls a last meeting with his protégé.

—I had a private conversation with our cabinet officer from the White House, and what he said is quite illuminating. Apparently, the President is appreciative of the work we are doing in a theatre as sensitive as Haiti, and is confident that Haiti operations will soon be under wraps, though not without a bang. In the future, the White House would like us to look at Mesopotamia.

—I've heard of it.

—The cradle of western civilization, between the Tigris and Euphrates rivers. It's the place the Limeys are are now calling Iraq. Right next to Iran.

—I wonder if the citizens of Iraq and Iran ever get their mail crossed.

—Mind your *n*'s and *q*'s.

—What's the purpose of Mesopotamian operations?

—It only makes sense if you understand the purpose of Haitian operations.

—I never realized there was a purpose.

—To stop this African infection from becoming pandemic at home.

—That makes sense. Mesopotamian operations are about control over natural resources, the petroleum deposits?

—That's what the United States wants people to believe.

—What is it, then?

—Without spilling too much of what's in the classified file, Mesopotamia has secrets buried underground.

—Fascinating.

—We need to make sure that what's underground there stays lost forever. If our subtle operations don't work, the military plans to bomb the ground so hard they'll never dig out. These things take time.

Late that night, Belinda Ballard opens the door to Culprit's room where Josie is sleeping in his bed while he's curled on the floor by the window. Josie's return remains their secret, and since Josie's been back, all's she's done is sleep.

—You've been kissed, I can tell from your neck, the waking Culprit says to Belinda.

—There's nothing wrong with that, she replies.

—How is Sheila?

—She's leaving tomorrow. They are all leaving tomorrow.

—I am not ready to go back.

—Are you positive it's Josie? Maybe she had a twin.

—There was only one Josie.

—There's that kid who does the magic tricks.

—This isn't a magic trick.

—Does he know?

—Without her, I don't know how to find him.

—I think you do.

—I don't.

—Do you think she's dead?

—The dead don't snore like that.

—What do you suppose you'll do?

—I don't know. Stay put until I know what to do.

—You don't want to go back with everyone?

—No.

—I'll help you change your mind.

They fall asleep on the mahogany floor with a small blanket between them. It's uncomfortable, and the heat breaks and the cold air causes them to play a game of sleeping tug-of-war over the blanket. Then Culprit rolls slightly toward Belinda, and Belinda rolls slightly toward Culprit, so that now they are both under cover. The floor is hard, but it's not as bad when they slide their arms into each other and embrace.

BELINDA BALLARD

I can read your mind, but I have no idea what you're thinking.

CULPRIT CLUTCH

I like you with your hair pulled back tight, and you look like another woman altogether.

In the morning, it's all blue sky along the horizon with scattering puffy clouds. The clouds become darker the higher they go and the darkest are directly on top of them. On the dock, Nora sets down her suitcase and performs a cartwheel.

—That was my first cartwheel since I was a little girl, she says, winded, —but when I think back on this place, I'll always remember that I did a cartwheel on my way out.

—I will always remember today because of your cartwheel, says Jill.

Stuart Scales-McCabe will remember today because as Nora flew hands under head he caught a glimpse of her white cotton underwear, which she hadn't intended for him to see. Yet the moment is enough to seal itself deep within his memory.

Final boarding is called, and the steamer shoves off.

Haiti vanishes beneath the sun.

The jeep driver seems to be lost. He keeps climbing when he should be descending. Finally, they reach the edge of a sea cliff. Belinda and Culprit get out and look over the edge and see where they're supposed to be. The ship is blasting its horn, calling for final boarding, and they are nowhere close.

They had managed to awaken Josie and get her on her feet. She could walk, though not on her own power. As soon as she had taken her seat in the jeep, she fell asleep again.

—We missed the boat, where else can we go?

—I don't know. The beach.

Now that the ship has sailed, the driver seems to know where he's going. He drops them off where the road ends near the entrance to the waveless beach. Josie shows more life the closer she is to water. Along the beach, Culprit and Belinda don't need to help her walk.

Josie makes her way across the beach, her bare feet atop jagged rocks. She steps into the dirty surf and keeps walking into the tide, out past the point where a conscious person would stop walking and start swimming. She's in water up to her shoulders.

Culprit races after her, but not before Belinda catches his arm. Her grip is not enough to hold him back, but he stops.

This is how it's supposed to happen. Josie goes. Culprit stays. Belinda is along for the ride.

She's walked far enough, they can see only the top of her head. She walks farther, and past the point they can't see her.

Culprit won't break his gaze. He'll wait for the Atlantic Ocean to flinch first.

The sea will not flinch. It does, however, turn orange for an instant. Along the horizon's razor edge there appears a mushroom cloud that lingers in the air, then falls flat. Once the water is back to normal, they can't be sure they saw anything, but Culprit holds his gaze. The world is different now than it was.

Then he and Belinda see them in the distance. They trace them from the horizon until the point they break, which is coming nearer and nearer. They break hard before they reach the shore and send a sheet of water that runs through their ankles before changing directions and pulling back.

Here come the waves.

A Race Is a Chase
(1971, -50, -68)

There used to be this car race down the length of Mexico, back when the Pan-American Highway was new, 1950. The race was on a road that stretched from Ciudad Juarez on the United States border to Guatemala, pushed through mountain curves, jungle lowlands, and desert straights, through old mission towns and modern metropolises. The idea was to open Mexico up. Connect her top to bottom. She wasn't going to rest there like a lump anymore. The pavement was so black and new that scarcely a car had driven across the surface and none at top speed. The stockcar drivers beat the hell out of that new road. If you ask me, the road loved them for it. Five stages in five days. The race was such a hit that after the first year, it was placed on the International Sports Calendar as a World Championship Course. There are two things you need to know about this race. One: It took place on public roadways. Two: These roadways were uncharted waters.

—Why'd they stop running it?

—The body count, the dead drivers, dead spectators, dead livestock. In Mexico, the road isn't as much for cars as pariah dogs and coyotes, mules and burros, and a place for cattle to lie down and take a nap. While the race was on, children would wander across the road to get a better look at the racing cars. They just couldn't secure the course. The faster the cars, the more casualties piled up. Don't get me wrong, the road was good, but it was full of switchback turns. There were unforeseen hazards such as low-flying birds of the buzzard variety. Lawsuits were piling up, vendettas were piling up, ghosts were piling up, so the race organizers pulled the plug. They ran the race north to south, then south to north, but nothing worked, so they quit.

—High speed, high danger. I see the attraction. Win or die trying.

—I've been on that road. To see that race and hear it, it must have been something else.

—With most grand spectacles, seeing is believing. With this race, it was the sound that did the trick.

—The louder the roar, the more the speed.

—It was so loud in those canyons that some of the racers lost their hearing and never got it back.

1950. The Nash Motor Co. motion picture team from Los Angeles, California, made a deal with a Mexican child. They got him to stand on an old railroad abutment and signal at the first sight of cars racing toward Durango.

It didn't matter.

First, you feel a vibration in your feet coming from the ground, and then the rumble of the motors. The tremor is strong enough that you brace yourself to keep your footing. The heavy buzz grows louder. In the high mountain desert, the sun's heat bends the air above the blacktop.

Then you see them coming, not the cars, but two great clouds of dust.

By the time the cars are on top of you, racing neck and neck, the sound is deafening, loud enough to rip the mountains apart. The lead car weaves between the lanes, trying to keep the car behind him from gaining position. They're going so fast that one mistake, and it's curtains.

The 16 mm motion picture camera is perched on a ledge a safe distance from the cars, but the photographer flinches as the cars zoom by. He's not accustomed to this. If only he could get closer. He would like to be standing just outside the painted yellow line on the pavement. If he doesn't feel the wind in the racers' wake after they pass, there is no way he got his shot.

With his head still under the camera's black hood and eye focused in the viewfinder, he feels a tug at his shirttail. It's the Mexican kid, trying to coax him backward, down from the perch, pointing up. On the cliffs high above, the roar of the motors has loosened the rocks. It starts as a trickle of pebbles down the mountain. Then it grows into a rockslide almost as loud and heavy as the racecar motors. The cameraman, an American teenager with no idea what he's doing, catches it all on film and thanks his lucky stars he didn't decide to go down there.

The two racers out front are long gone, and boulders now block the wave of cars behind them. The race committee will have to decide whether they want to stop the clock for the backed-up racers or disqualify all of them for not finishing the leg in the time set in the rule book. At the tail end of the pack are two ambulances of the U.S. Army type. Those two leaders better hope that if they crash they die instantly, because there's no way help is getting to them. Not with these mammoth stones blocking the road.

1971. The effect of the roaring motors was not something the race organizers could have foreseen. Don't blame this one on the road builders. Everyone always wants to blame the builders. The Pan-Am Highway was an engineering marvel. It measured up to the highest standards for grades and curves. They built the road not just for the public at large. They built it for top speed, and the road showed itself to perform just as it was designed. The problem that the engineers hadn't accounted for was the rumble of the motors breaking the earth. Now you go ahead and build a high-speed expressway through some of the most rugged mountains in the Americas, and see how you do. Before the road was built, this region was impenetrable. You couldn't get here, even on horseback, and you expect the road to roll out without hidden dangers? Not a chance, man.

—Culprit Clutch was a driver in that race.

—Oh, no, no, the skinny kid was the driver, and they weren't racing. Nash Motors sent Culprit to take photographs.

—Motion pictures.

—That's where Culprit Clutch cut his teeth in movies.

—His race footage is legendary. Did you see the rockslide?

—It's how he won the Guggenheim.

—Not that anyone on the award committee saw Culprit's film.

—Cars weren't the only racers down there in Mexico.

—If you count children riding bicycles.

—No, I'm talking about coyotes running so fast their rotating feet become a blur of motion.

—Oh, brother, you're thinking of Warner Bros. cartoon shorts.

—One of the thrills of the Sonoran Desert is seeing the devilish coyote chasing the elusive roadrunner across the cactus landscape at top speed. Beep-beep!

—Baloney.

—If you waste your time watching kiddie shows on the boob tube, you'll think it's true.

—If you spend enough time in the desert, you'll know it's not. I just finished narration for a TV documentary on the true story of the coyote and roadrunner. I even have a few feet of edited film I can run through the Moviola to show you characters.

—So this is what it's come to, you make nature films.

—You bet. It beats the nine to five. It beats not working in film, even if Mutual of Omaha signs my paychecks.

—I remember the first time I worked in film was like not working in film. It was all just waiting around for ocean waves. It was supposed to be a surfing film. The waves didn't come until we were sailing back to New York.

Lafferty cranks the arm of the Moviola so the film flows through the machine, while reading from the script held in his other hand:

'Mexico and the American Southwest make home to the chapparal cock, known more commonly as the roadrunner. The impression that most Americans have of the roadrunner comes from popular motion-picture cartoons. These cartoons have led legions to believe that the coyote, also known as the singing dog, has forgone the act of howling, giving it over to an obsession to chase the roadrunner.

'Yet scientists have proven there exists no history of a chase involving the coyote and the roadrunner. There are simply no credible reports of such a chase taking place.

'In a laboratory setting, we observe the behavior of the coyote when placed in close proximity to the roadrunner. See how the coyote appears uninterested, almost embarrassed by the situation. He quivers nervously and shows desire neither to outwit nor to eat the bird.'

—Why does this happen, then? What's the basis for cartoons, if not real life?

—Hollywood knows how ticklish it is getting fooled.

—Getting tickled makes you laugh but doesn't mean you like it.

—It keeps the crowds coming.

—Just because I never heard a dog say *bow-wow* doesn't mean *bow-wow* isn't what a dog says.

—Nah, the scientists, they got it all wrong. The coyote does chase the bird. I've seen it with my own eyes. If you spend enough time in the desert, you'll see for yourself.

—No way.

—Spend enough time in the desert, all you'll see is a mirage.

—There's that old saying, 'There is no such thing as a mirage.'

—Of course, there is no such thing as a mirage. That's what a mirage is.

—Something you don't see, because it was never there.

—That's right.

—I'm going to show you fellows. We'll see who gets the last laugh. I am going to the desert and taking my 8 mm movie camera with me. I will shoot the chase myself and then come back here and show you meatballs a thing or three.

—I wouldn't go out in the desert alone if I were you. The sun sets, the wind picks up. The sand can only hold the heat for so long before giving way to the mountain's chill. It's dark when you're out there by yourself. The only people you meet are strangers, and the next stranger you meet might be a killer.

—I speak Spanish, I can talk myself out of anything.

—Your Spanish will get you nowhere. The killers you'll run across in the desert at night in Mexico are North Americans, bloodthirsty enough to make the Manson family blush, and the last thing they want to do is talk.

1950. Culprit Clutch in dark sunglasses walks into the business office of Nash Motors off Ventura Boulevard in Los Angeles, California, U.S.A., asks for a job, and is hired on the spot. The Director of National Advertising takes an instant liking to him.

—Do you know much about what's under the hood? the director asks.

—Nothing.

—Shell or Super Shell?

—Don't know the difference.

—Do you care whether or not I hire you?

Culprit shrugs. He is without credentials and enthusiasm. All he has is a slack-jaw sense of cool and an attitude similar to other boys his age who never went to war.

—What makes you tick, Culprit Clutch?

—Dunno.

—Talking to you is like talking to a wall. You are a new breed of animal, proof of Darwin's theory thrown into reverse. Kids like you are evolving in reverse, back to ape. I just insulted you to your face, what do you have to say about that?

Culprit shrugs.

—You are exactly the type of kid I need to figure out. If you don't care about making purchases, what kinds of products will men like me sell to the likes of you? You'll be a wage earner one day, you know. What will you purchase?

—Dunno.

—How to make a generation of nonplussed youngsters give a rip, that's the $24,000 question. The difference between you and a juvenile delinquent is a JD just pretends not to care, while at heart what motivates the JD is anger toward authority figures, whether it's his father, the parish priest, the math teacher, the truancy officer, the neighborhood flatfoot, the drill sergeant. Kids like you don't care enough to harbor animosity toward anyone.

—Not really.

—You just don't give a damn. I will give you a job, by God, that will make you care.

—All right.

—The Mexican road race starts on May 5, and we want you to cover the Nash team with this 16 mm movie camera, the director explains to Culprit. — You'll learn to care, damn it, you'll care about your paycheck, you'll care about the film you're making, you'll care enough to stay out of the way of the race cars if you value your life the way I think you might. You might even find a senorita down there who turns your head.

The director's secretary, Mildred, lifts Culprit by the arm. Before he can say anything, she jabs a long hypodermic needle in his arm.

—That's the smallpox vaccine, the director explains. —Disease is still quite common in Mexico. You never know what you'll pick up in tropical country. Oh, Mildred, did you see these?

He shows the secretary three round patches of scarred skin triangulating on Culprit's other arm.

—He's already had this vaccine and then some, from the looks of it, the director says.

—A little extra of a good thing can't hurt ya! Mildred says, rubbing peroxide-soaked gauze over Culprit's fresh wound.

Parked outside is a cherry-red Nash with a tapered rear end straight off the factory floor that looks like a streaking comet and is nearly as long as one. The lettering on the side of the car reads: CARRERA PANAMERICANA NASH MOTION PICTURE UNIT.

—The paint's fresh, don't smudge it, the director says, dangling the keys before Culprit.

—No stripes?

—You're not racing, the director says. —Stripes, you have to earn.

The company had filled the trunk with jugs of water; a camper stove; percolator; pots and pans; flashlight; air mattresses; Army blankets; mismatched silverware; a package of styrofoam cups and plates; matchbooks; enough cans of soup, beans, and coffee to feed a small army; and a tin box filled with emergency cash.

—The cameras and film are in the back seat where they will come in handy.

As Culprit reaches for the keys, the director tosses them to a lanky kid standing there without Culprit noticing.

—Paul Panama will be your driver, Culprit, the director says. —He's a new hire who has shown a propensity for mechanics much the same way you have shown such a flair for the arts. You're the man in charge, and he's the man with the keys. Go ahead and figure that one out, and while you're at it, get a move on.

Paul Panama is a kid so skinny his bones knock together, and his high voice makes you wonder whether his balls are just pretend. On the desert highway east from Los Angeles, Panama drives open throttle. His body contracts when shifting gears, his shoulder nearly flying out of its socket. The landscape blurs beyond recognition, road signs and mile markers pass too quickly to read. His driving will leave Culprit shell-shocked long after the finish of the race.

—Ease up on the gas, kid.

Culprit's comment has no effect on the way Paul Panama drives.

—They sure missed a golden opportunity sending you down there as a chauffeur while I make home movies, Culprit says. —They should have entered you in the race.

—Shut up!

1968. Owing to bizarre circumstances, Culprit's race film was never widely seen, though he had a funny way of bumping into the handful of people in the world who knew. There was the woman who called herself a magazine writer and racing fan who insisted on buying Culprit drinks at the bar near Washington Square in June.

—You filmed the action at the start and finish lines with only one camera?

—I couldn't help that the kid liked to drive fast.

—You also shot the crack-ups in the middle of the race.

—We weren't there sightseeing.

—Your footage included a series of churches and pueblos.

—That was to use up the leftover film on my way home.

—That film was a remarkable feat, a masterwork.

—I would have liked to have recorded sound. I didn't know what I was doing. It felt like we were everywhere at once. We were so fast, they called us cheaters. We weren't even entered in the race.

—Did you take shortcuts?

—There are no shortcuts. The new highway was the shortcut.

—After the fellow who was with you, Paul Panama, cracked your telephoto lens, how did you manage to get all those tight shots?

—I had to bring the camera in close on the subject.

—Your subjects were racing cars!

—A safer bet than atomic missiles.

—What do you remember most from the race?

—The velocity was staggering. Cars go faster now, though back then they felt faster. There was more physical stress on the vehicle, I suppose. The Nash was awfully stiff. The conditions of the road, the tight turns without guardrails, the last 100 miles of the race over gravel, made it seem faster than it was.

—So Culprit, what are you like? Tell me everything about you.

—Everything I know about me I learned from my FBI file, he says half joking.

She looks at him sadly. She knows it's true.

—Now why would you have an FBI file? she asks.

—That's a good question. The answer is not in the file.

—Do you suppose that happens often? The FBI keeps an open file on a soul after forgetting why it started one in the first place?

—Sure.

—I have an FBI file on me this thick, she says.

—Why do you suppose that is?

—I'm an attractive woman and not unintelligent. I'm a foreigner, and I've known many interesting people.

—If I were the FBI, I would be suspicious of you. God knows of what.

—Culprit, let me buy you another drink.

—I keep thinking what a coincidence this is, that you know so much about me and have all these burning questions about Mexico. The problem, the way I see it, is that I don't believe in coincidences.

—Oh, Culprit, when did you become such a nonbeliever?

—When was I ever a believer, or is that something else you know about me that I don't? You know so much, it's almost like you were there at the race.

—I've seen your film. It's like I was.

1950. Panama and Culprit arrive at the starting line to set up the camera minutes before the first leg is set to begin. Racing enthusiasts from a panorama of national origins crowd the scene. The nearest Panama will be able to find a place to park the Nash is a quarter mile away. He drops Culprit off and peels out to park in the hinterland.

The crowd is pushing and shoving to get a look at the contest vehicles and their occupants. Culprit unfolds the tripod and mounts his camera, but race fans rush in front of him every time he's ready to roll film. Soldiers use their rifles as handheld barricades to push people back, forcing Culprit to move his gear time and again. He looks up and sees a building with an unoccupied fire escape. Using the tripod as a makeshift hook, he pulls down the ladder and climbs to a perch where he can set up his shot of the colorful mosaic of stockcars revving and ready to go.

Panama is nowhere to be found. Then Culprit hears a blaring car horn and sees a parting in the crowd. Here comes the Nash driving right up to where the racers await the grand marshall's waving of the green flag. There is no place else for him to park other than behind the racers at the starting line. The nerve of that kid! He's choosing to make a race of it, up against the best drivers in the world with their black leather racing gloves, and all they gave Panama was a stock model straight off the factory floor and a glove compartment with no gloves.

—*Quarto, tres, dos, uno, ARRANCA!*

There is a cheer from the crowd with church bells ringing in the plaza as the roar of race cars rips through the air, and in one-minute successions, the racers shoot with thunderous speed off the starting line.

Once the last car lumbers out of the gate, Culprit jumps down from the fire escape with the camera and tripod in his grip and climbs into the Nash through the passenger seat window just as Panama steps on the gas in pursuit of the racers.

After the start, a solid mass of people, autos, and dogs stretching for ten miles bottlenecks down the middle of the road. Panama weaves through the crowd, honking, making them get out of his way.

The first stretch of the race is tough going. There are hairpin curves, unbanked switchbacks, and washboard washouts barely visible until the driver is roaring into them. Blind spots and rises in the road hide tight curves and treacherous railroad crossings. To make conditions even worse, a thick fog rolls in.

Right out of the chute, cars spin out of control. The wrecks of the early leaders clog the center of the lane. Driver Starling's 1949 Lincoln careens over an embankment, rolling six times, leaving him shaken but unhurt. He walks in circles, saying, 'Why me, why me?' He raises his hand to block the lens of Culprit's camera, not wanting anyone to see his emotion and embarrassment after losing the race so early.

Back on the road at full speed, nothing else matters to Paul Panama.

—Goddamn if I don't have to pee.

Despite the perils of this stretch of road, steep curves without guardrails and cliffs that drop thousands of feet, Panama steps on the gas and soon catches the pack of racers from behind.

Ahead, cars are stopped in an endless pileup. The drivers lay on the horns as the cherry red Nash sneaky petes past them along the treacherous shoulder. The honking is the drivers' way of telling him not to pass, that it's not safe just now, that you'll get yourself DQ'd, that you're a son of a bitch for trying that, but the Nash doesn't have a number and isn't entered in the race.

Culprit opens his passenger-side window just enough to poke out the camera lens without getting hit by the objects thrown by irate drivers. He captures footage of smashed cars, black sedans with dying horses under the hood, their bumpers bent and radiators blowing steam plumes into the air. There's more honking, not all aimed at the Nash. It's the way the racers stuck behind the wheel of unmoving autos vent their frustration.

There are bodies strewn, some facedown in the middle of the road and others thrown into the shoulder. The pools of blood surrounding those who were bleeding have dried already, leaving the new asphalt stained. While Panama jiggers his left leg nervously, Culprit climbs halfway out his window, bending at the torso, taking in the sight, not thinking, depressing the camera's trigger until he runs out of film.

Away from the pileup, Panama stops the car, bursts out, jumps into a culvert to relieve himself, while Culprit stays in his seat, methodically placing the camera and a fresh film magazine into a lightproof black velvet pouch, inserting his hands into gloves sewn into the bag, and changing the film without seeing what he's doing. It is nothing for a rank amateur, but Culprit doesn't feel like an amateur. He doesn't know what he feels like.

The rest of the day's course is smooth and uneventful. The Nash cruises along at a high rate of speed, but it feels like they are hardly moving. The driving becomes so easy that Panama makes small talk.

—What separates Arizona and Guatemala?

—I don't know, what?

—This is not a joke. It's a real question. The answer is Mexico.

—I already knew that.

On the fifth and final day of the race, the sprint from Tuxtla Gutierrez to El Ocotal on the Mexico-Guatemala border is run over a gravel surface through more mountainous country and proves to be the slowest and most treacherous of the race. Two hundred and fifty-one cars started the race, and only forty-seven remain in the field. An American named Pete Fontana holds the lead until the final unpaved leg of the race. On the gravel course, the Lincoln driven by Argentinean Dagobert Runes holds up better than Fontana's car, and Runes beats the American by thirteen seconds.

The vibrations from chasing Fontana and Runes over the gravel highway are murder on Culprit Clutch. He knows he won't stop shaking hours after the race is over. He knows most of the day's footage will be too shaky to watch.

The vibrations are not even the strangest physical sensation he's experienced in the last five days. There's a quality of speed that racers don't like to talk about. It's known, it's experienced, it's never discussed. Here's the thing: You go fast enough, and the human body gets ahead of itself. The soul bobs in the drag behind the car. After the checkered flag, the driver slows it down, and the soul still traveling at top speed slingshots several hundred feet ahead. Then it snaps back like a rubber band. It hurts. The rider's first steps outside the car are wobbly. His bruised body and soul still feel like they are going 110 miles an hour, although it's good to have the both of them back.

In the winner's circle, the race organizers and dignitaries deliver the prizes to the accompaniment of countless flashbulbs, which leave Culprit blind. The drone of the motor over ten days has already left him deaf. The race nearly pulls the life right out of poor Culprit Clutch. Midway through the race, he promised himself never to do anything like this ever again. His only remaining responsibility is to return the car and exposed film to L.A. safe and sound. It should be a quiet trip, and he will drive alone since Paul Panama took off on a horse on the second to last day of the race.

1971. The story of Culprit's film is as strange as the race itself. Afterward, he turned over the cans of exposed stock to the Nash Motor Co. It floored them. It was not what they expected. Sure, they could cut out snips and make promos for the Nash car line. The film was more than that. It was extraordinary, a film in its own right. The rockslide was just the beginning.

They would show it after hours at private parties, lodge meetings. They would run the film again as soon as it ended. The footage was mesmerizing. It was pretty much exactly what Culprit saw through his viewfinder when he pulled the camera's trigger.

—Law enforcement caught wind of it. Thought it was a Mexican stag film or cockfight.

—Word traveled fast, reaching the office of none other than J. Edgar Hoover, at the Federal Bureau of Investigation, who decided that it was in the country's interest to quarantine the film.

—Boy howdy, I have to see it.

—Did they confiscate it?

—They stole it, sent Cubans to take it. Nash had the negative and two 16 mm prints. The Cubans took everything.

—Bastards.

—Whatever the agency's intent, it had the opposite effect. The legend of the film continues to grow. For me, it became an obsession. I met Culprit Clutch many years back, which is how I learned of the film, and I took it on myself to make things happen. I broke into the FBI building and stole the film back.

—That took some derring-do.

—It's extraordinary the places you can go disguised as a janitor.

—Why put yourself through the trouble?

—It's what you do when you realize that for all your passion to create art, you'll never be anything more than a hack, so you switch gears and apply all that creative zeal to someone else's art, as a fan, and in my case, as a fan of a movie I had never seen. I don't know what came over me, I didn't know what the hell I was doing. I was obsessed. I got the film.

—Bravo.

—I also took a folder, Culprit Clutch's FBI file. The idea was to send him his movie and the file. Instead, I bought a projector and viewed the film alone in my apartment and read the file. I decided I would keep the movie and send him the file in an anonymous envelope. He needed to know what his government thought about him.

—What's the film like?

—Let's just say that it cuts to the heart of that race. It's unlike anything I've ever seen. It was like Culprit knew what was going to happen before it happened and started the camera just in time to catch it. He is in control of all the elements within the shot. It seems staged, rehearsed, but you know it's not. It was all improvised, done without a script, in one take. It makes you wonder about the person holding the camera and making the film. You see his shadow once in a while but you never see him.

—Do you still have the film?

—Nah, sold the negative and original prints.

—Sold it?

—I needed the bread.

—Who paid you for it?

—An acid rock band from England. They caught wind of the legend and had this idea they wanted to compose a musical soundtrack for it and put it out in theatres. It'll be one of those types of movies that kids go see when they're high on LSD, like *2001* or *Willy Wonka and the Chocolate Factory*.

—Which band? The Soft Machine?

—Never heard of them.

—How about the Pretty Things?

—Not them, either, and not the Who. Ever hear of the Pink Floyd?

—I think so.

—The Pink Floyd bought the film.

—I have to see the movie. Now I'm the one who's obsessed.

—I did make a secret print that I kept.

—Where are you stashing it? God, I can't see it fast enough.

1950. You come unspeakably close to death with every mountain curve. Losing control means giving it all away. Losing control means going over the side.

Was it really all that bad? Travel has a mind-clearing effect, though there's nothing quite like racing. You can't trace your finger along the route on the map fast enough to keep up. The melting scenery whizzes by. Mountains in the distance roll toward you. Once top speed is reached, your mind lets itself go. The tether that holds the soul to the body becomes stretched to the fullest. Your soul will catch up when it's caught up, fifteen minutes after the body's arrival.

On the return trip back north, the road looks different. There is so much that Culprit hadn't noticed, it was as if it wasn't the same road.

In Tuxtla Gutierrez, where the rivers run wide and shallow, Culprit pulls out the camera to capture the motion of a flock of tropical birds turning the sky into a colorful mosaic. In Oaxaca, he marvels at the green-hued stones. He keeps the camera rolling through many stops in the Tehuantepec Zone, one of the most vibrant and colorful in Mexico.

They say angels guided the Spanish to the site of Puebla, a town with four volcanoes watching over her: Popocatépetl, Iztaccíhuatl, Matlalcueitl, Orizaba. Culprit sleeps that night spread out in the backseat of the car and wakes early to explore Puebla's cathedral, filled strangely with Flemish tapestries.

He picks up a map of Mexico City at a Pemex filling station, then parks the car to tour the central metropolis on foot. The height of modernity, the business district is filled with more hustle and bustle than he's seen elsewhere in Mexico: the serious looks and hurried gait of people dead set on making money. The cosmopolitan night clubs and cinemas are dark until nightfall, by which time Culprit will be back on the road. He's in no hurry to return to the states but is compelled to keep moving.

His next stop, Toluca, offers many sights and sounds: a Friday market of Indian crafts and goods, women carrying baskets of colorful fruit on their heads, carts selling varieties of flowers, herbs, and beans. He sleeps in Querétaro and awakens to chruch bells. He photographs the view of the famous aqueduct from a hilltop convent, studies stone fountains flowing with water turned green from algae, films a pair of tzentzontle birds singing on a shady veranda, while knowing his footage will never be complete since the camera can't capture the birds' song. By midday, he arrives at Tlaquepaque where the streets are filled with the gay sound of trumpet and guitar music. In Guadalajara, it is warm and dry, with houses built around tiled patios, as the people here prefer to spend their afternoons outdoors in the shade. León is a city of parks and orchards, and in Durango, he sees a sign leading down a branch road to Mazatlán, the port city on the Pacific. An excursion to the ocean is tempting, but Culprit keeps his northern course. He passes into Chihuahua, a modern city of easygoing people and blazing hot temperatures. As the town ends, the landscape turns into cattle-raising country and looks like Texas.

He pulls over to sleep for a few hours. Tomorrow, he's back in the U.S.

Thousands of racing fans line the parkway in Durango cheering the racers on. Led by a procession of army motorcycle officers with their sirens wailing and flashing red lights, the day's leaders cross the finish line of the third stage of the race, while Culprit grinds out foot after foot of film, long shots, close-ups, running here and there to capture human interest material and keeping his exposed film in sealed metal canisters. A tropical climate is murder on exposed film. Culprit carries the canisters in his gadget bag and never lets it off his person.

He returns to the parked Nash to get a can of soup to heat up, but when he opens the trunk, he finds none of the provisions. Instead he sees a thin layer of ice cubes concealing a payload of Mexican beer. To Culprit, Panama doesn't seem like the type who could polish off all these cans by himself. To Culprit, Panama is the type who sails three sheets to the wind after a sip or two. It's a ploy, a scheme to make a few extra bucks on the race circuit's black market.

After a day like today, a cold can of beer sure looks good to Culprit. Yet Panama manages to outwit him. When the skinny boy cleaned out the provisions, he also took the can opener. It's a game of chess, and Panama best not underestimate the resourcefulness of Culprit Clutch. The can is cracked open just as members of the press corps are strolling by in search of the action.

—Hey, what are you birds looking at? Culprit says. —Ain't you ever seen a man open a beer with a tire iron before?

—No, but I wouldn't mind trying that out myself, says Stanley Kline, a hotshot reporter from the *Los Angeles Times*.

Before long, all the gentlemen of the press are opening Panama's beers with the tire iron, laughing at unfunny jokes, throwing their arms around each other in a rugged embrace, and Paul Panama is nowhere to be found.

The racers' village sport center is replete with Quonset huts and signs hanging over them, DINING PAVILION and RACER DORMITORY. In the pavilion, soft drinks and hot dogs are for sale, and the dormitory building funnels sleepy racers into a circus tent with 300 cots set up with blankets placed in neat lines for the drivers, crew, and race officials.

—Driving all day is a sedentary activity, but boy, a man can build an appetite.

—Drivers eat like lumberjacks.

—It's exhausting, too. Tonight the drivers will sleep like angels.

—Hey you apes, get husky in the dishes department or you'll be making your own eggs and coffee in the morning!

The impound area is a blur of activity. The race committee promised to lock down the fenced area where all the autos were parked by 9 p.m. to prevent the crews from rebuilding their cars overnight. Mechanics with Army flashlights and lanterns rush to change tires, brake pads, and oil and beat the curfew, while the drivers hover nearby.

—See the scars on the fender? They're from tire treads slapping off blowouts at 90 miles an hour.

—I was talking to one of the Americans, the driver of Car 12, who said he made up for not knowing the road by judging the rubber the cars ahead of him had put down ahead of curves. He reads skid marks like a fortune teller reads palms.

—Whose car is this?

—Driver 52 is taking a leak.

—When Driver 52 gets back, tell Driver 52 his motor has unusually high compression.

—It's high but within factory specifications.

—I'm not complaining. The guy has a one-in-a-million motor under the hood.

—Nah, it could blow tomorrow like anyone else's.

—The course ain't as hard on the engine as it is on brakes and tires. All you need is to change the oil twice a day to keep the motor happy. Tires and brakes are another story.

—Blow a tire on a switchback mountain curve without guardrails, and your wreck will never be found.

Silver-maned Tartuffi comes around, followed by the beery and lingering racing magazine stringers, with a story about his countryman: —Antonio Pagnoli, racing flat out in his Ferrari on a hundred-mile straight, his right-side rear tire blows, coupe leaves the road, hits the bank, and flies 160 feet through the air.

—Dead?

—Not dead. He's walking with crutches under each arm.

—There was a driver killed on the first day of the race. With all this speed and frantic braking, more are bound for injury or death. The car spun out into a lamppost. Unfortunate Señor Xochipilli was killed instantly.

—I heard he didn't buy the extra insurance. All his widow in Mexico City will get is his wrecked Lincoln delivered to her door. Such a shame, they have a boy and another kid on the way.

—The short stages tempt you to treat each leg as a flat-out sprint. Crack-ups are part of the game.

—The news angle is how many mistakes they made in planning the race. The planning committee must be real imbeciles. For instance, there aren't enough filling stations along the route. The faster you race, the more quickly you run out of gas. If you run out of gas, slower cars pass you by. Who ever heard of a racing strategy that requires drivers to conserve fuel?

—It's the name of the game in road racing.

—If you play it just right, you can coast the last 100 meters into the service station on fumes without losing time.

—You hear about the highway into Guatemala? It's unfinished. All gravel. Someone could have said something. Someone could have said that the course is not ready. Maybe they thought this day would never come. Maybe they just wanted to see what would happen. All they told you was to expect rough road. Gravel is the same as no road.

—The unpaved section of the highway is strictly for donkeys.

—Hee-haw, hee-haw!

— Aw, if I wasn't half drunk, I would keep my mouth shut.

—One beer does this to you?

—One can of beer and four shots of rye.

—It was a drunkard who said, 'A race is a chase, equal parts tragedy and comedy.' It can twist on a pin.

—A race is a chase for survival. It's on you to decide to be the stalker or the prey.

—Which is better?

—The stalker always has the advantage.

—Not when the prey streaks across the finish line first.

—Ah, that's bunk!

—Did you fellows see the German team filtering the fuel through chamois skin?

—I wonder what they know that we don't.

—They don't like the Mexican gasoline.

—Mercedes sent a team from Munich out here last October to plot the course, map out the variables. They brought tire specialists from Continental, Bosch engineers, the works.

—Do you know who the German racers are?

—They act like hotshots, like they think they're Italians.

—They sent their two most famous drivers to share a car.

—Hans Freleng is Mercedes' most experienced road racer. Karl DePatie was one of the greatest pre-war Grand Prix aces, and he's the co-driver.

—I don't know anything about European racing but I've heard the names DePatie and Freleng.

—You're thinking of a couple bigwigs from kiddie cartoons. Same names, different gentlemen.

—I dunno, says one of the drivers, trying to get a word in edgewise with the fast-talking magazine writers. —I'll take my Lincoln any day over one of those European coupes. This American-made, high-strung bucket of nuts and bolts was built for speed.

A reporter for *Road and Track* from Waco, Texas, Adrian Barnes, holds an unfolded map of the country and has this to say, —I've been covering every leg of the race so far and following the radio broadcasts, and this is what I've figured out. When the American drivers want to pass the Europeans on a flat course, they pour on the gas, and it's a piece of cake. Yet when the track turns into curves, that's when the foreign road racers show their skill and catch the Americans from behind. What this race will amount to is how many miles of the course are straight versus how many are curved. Do any of you fellows know?

—The Germans know.

—Nah, the winner is driving the jalopy that holds together on the last day's gravel.

—Speaking of the Germans, says Stanley Kline, the *Los Angeles Times* reporter, tilting his head in the direction of the last car entering the impound area. It's a Mercedes with front and rear windshields blown.

The lone driver climbs out of the coupe. Covered in blood and feathers, he shakes glass shards off his pant legs.

—What happened to that car? Barnes asks.

—You don't know the story, and you call yourself a reporter? Kline says. —They hit a buzzard.

—I'm a good reporter, but I don't have your nose for news.

—I heard it on the radio broadcast. He says it sounded like a gunshot.

—How fast were they going?

—He says they were purring along at 135 miles an hour.

One of the reporters releases an admiring whistle, then says, —To think my parents rode in a horse and buggy.

—My cousin, Mickey Davis, topped 200 miles an hour on the Utah Salt Flat in a special he built himself, Bobbin says.

—Did I mention my mother-in-law is the Queen of England?

—Where is his co-driver, Herr DePatie?

—In the medic's tent.

—Is he all right?

—Sure, just rattled, says Kline. He opens his notebook and reads to the others:

'At the last tire change before the collision, DePatie didn't fasten his helmet strap. When the buzzard came barreling through the windshield, it knocked his helmet off and his neck flung back. He lost consciousness and was bleeding from the head. Like the true champion he is, Herr Freleng never stopped the car. Rather he poured a cup of warm tea from his thermos and tipped the cup back into his mate's mouth, reviving him. The car then returned to top speed.'

Freleng himself staggers over to where the writers are talking about him.

—How are you holding out, my good man, Hayward says. —We are glad it wasn't worse.

—He doesn't speak English, Tarnovsky says.

Yet Freleng replies in English, answering, —I have glass in my ass.

—Don't squirm, and it won't cut you!

To Freleng, the words of caution evoke the same physical response as squirming. It begins with giggling and turns into a roar of laughter. The shards embedded in his groin and buttocks dig in all the more.

—Leave it to a German to find this funny when it happens to him.

—Might be the first time I've seen laughter wipe the smile off a man's face.

—Someone, please go fetch this man a pair of tweezers.

—Where's the buzzard now? The Mercedes team might want to have it stuffed.

—Why would they do that?

—As a trophy, as a souvenir from Mexico.

Kline returns to his notebook, reading:

'The increased air pressure in the car's interior following the collision blew out the rear window, which shattered on the pavement. With the back now open, the drivers tossed the carcass out of the car behind them and cheered as it bounced on the highway floor.'

—You didn't stop to clear the glass from the road? Or the carcass?

—That was the next driver's problem, says Freleng, steadying himself.

—They said on the radio that the jeep control car swept it up, though not before several cars had blowouts.

—It's not like those tires weren't going flat one of these days, Freleng says, making himself laugh again, which brings on another wave of deep pain and causes him to bowl over and begin staggering away in the direction of the medic's tent.

—Herr Freleng, there is good news. A Chevrolet team lost control on the first leg and flipped in a field.

—This is good news?

—The crew bought a windshield from a local dealer and stuck it on with masking tape. The car won the next leg.

No sooner is that said than six members of the Mercedes crew appear carrying a factory windshield for Freleng's car, as well as a sealant strip and a pair of steel bars to bolt across the face of the windshield.

—Buzzard bars, Kline says. —Just in case lightning strikes twice.

—Drivers, you should be getting some sleep. The race starts back at six in the morning.

—I don't think I can sleep with the ringing in my ears.

—The race will make you deaf if it doesn't kill you first.

—You can always quit now and save your ears.

—Not a chance.

—Did you hear? The Mercedes team of 23 is now a team of 22.

—DePatie succumbed?

—He's fine.

—Someone else, then? It must be the drinking water.

—They can get by without the whole crew. Other teams have no one, zilch, just a driver and mechanic.

—They lost Freleng's girlfriend. She hit the road.

—He seemed so cheerful, everything considered.

—He doesn't know yet.

—What tough luck. First, he gets a buzzard through the windshield, and now this.

—Does this mean he's out of the race?

—That's his choice to make. I doubt it.

—It's easy. You've come this far. You keep going. You can always deal with her later.

—For all anyone knows, she's as far gone as Chicago by now.

—I don't remember seeing her.

—She's a child, just old enough to be a runaway.

—Typical of teenagers.

—She's a kraut. Are German teenagers anything like our teenagers? The war wasn't that long ago.

—Don't say another word. I have a picture of her in my head. A tragic overbite and dimple.

—A nose like the Wicked Witch of the West.

—Keep this on the down low, but there's a rumor floating that she switched allegiances, that she's taken up with another driver, an American, and hiding out in the back seat of his car, like contraband.

—That should make her easy to find. All the cars are in the impound area for the night.

—That was the first place they checked. She's still missing.

—Obviously, she only hides in the car when the race is on.

—That's clever on her part. They can't search for her while he's racing.

—Wait until Freleng finds out!

—The rumor is that she's taken up not with a racer but with a member of the Carrera Panamericana entourage.

—A race official?

—Heavens, not one of the reporters. We are all present and accounted for.

—Not unless one of you birds is hiding a girl somewheres.

—I could take offense at that, as I see it as my professional responsibility not to pull wool over people's eyes, but I have nothing to hide, and I have never seen the girl.

—I think it's safe to say she's not hiding out with anyone from the press.

There are no cots reserved for Culprit and Panama. The press is allowed in the dormitory tent, though many drive ahead 100 miles to stay in hotels. As representatives of a car company, Culprit and Panama are not press and have no leg to stand on. They sleep in the Nash.

Last night, Panama never came back for his payload of beer, never came back to sleep in the back seat.

Culprit doesn't give it a second thought until morning, just before the race is set to start at 6:03 sharp. He returns from a trip to the latrine to find Paul Panama under the hood pouring a quart of oil into the engine. The surprise comes when through the glass he sees a girl hiding in the backseat.

—Panama, this isn't the time.

—The time for what?

—For making friends.

—I'll be no trouble, she says, rolling down the window.

—Where did she come from?

—Frieda's Austrian. She was with the Mercedes team. I'm nuts about her.

—The German will kill you if he finds out.

—If he finds out. It makes no matter. We're in love.

—What good will that do when you're dead? He might even kill me to get to you.

—You take your life in your hands every time you ride in a car, Panama says calmly. —There is danger on every switchback, danger every time I push past 100 miles an hour. So don't talk to me about danger. A little extra of a good thing ain't gonna kill you.

Back on the highway, Culprit can't get a grip on what's happening. It starts with a feeling of well-being followed by a sense of foreboding that leads to a fear that they are failing their assignment.

—Panama, we need to stop so I can shoot footage. The pack will be coming through.

—The movie can go to hell, says the young driver whose mood has soured. He steps on it.

Miles later, Panama slams on the brakes, puts the car in reverse, and backs off the road where it is concealed by a billboard advertising Coca-Cola.

—We can hide here and shoot racers as they whiz by, Panama says, shutting the motor off.

—You are outfoxing the foxes, the girl says.

—That's the thing about Germans, Culprit says as he removes the camera from its case. —Every time you beat them they come back next time stronger. It's a historical fact.

The pack passes without incident. There is no sign of Freleng's car. Culprit packs up, and they are back on the road.

Nearing the end of the fourth stage of the race, there are fewer cars left in the field. There aren't as many country people residing near the track who know there's a race. The highway is a ghost town. There are no signs of other human beings until they are outside Tuxtla and reach an agricultural checkpoint where all cars must stop for a hoof and mouth disease inspection.

—Don't they know there's a race on? Don't they know we're not smuggling livestock?

Frieda answers with a question of her own, —Are you sure we are going the right way?

—We're wasting time. The Germans are catching up, Culprit says. —They will want the girl back.

—Shut up, they can't have her.

After the inspectors have looked the car over, they drag over a pressure tank and spray the chassis of the car with a strong-smelling disinfectant.

A Mercedes pulls up behind the Nash, the German racers.

—Don't look now.

Panama pulls the girl's head down in the backseat so they won't see her.

—They are the top car in the field, Culprit says. —They're lagging only because they're looking for her.

—Of all the dumb luck.

—Do they know I am with you? Frieda asks.

—I'm not waiting long enough to find out, Panama says.

He lunges from the Nash and grabs the hose from the station agent who backs away from the maniac American. Panama sprays the green disinfectant in the direction of Freleng and DePatie who were outside their car genially walking toward him. He moves the spray around, dousing the Germans as they stagger back toward their auto while clutching their eyes from the stinging.

Panama jumps back into the Nash and hammers the throttle.

—We were skating by just fine, Culprit says. Now they'll come after us tonight at the racer's village.

—There won't be a racers' village.

—How's that?

—They can kill me, Panama replies, —But I won't let them lay a finger on you or you.

The car becomes claustrophobic. Frieda is crying in the back.

—If you want, we can turn off and hide. After they pass, we can head back toward Mexico City.

—I didn't come all this way not to finish the race.

—We're not in the race.

—Listen, there's a land bridge near Tehuantepec that connects Mexico and Central America. We might be able to veer off course and find our way to the finish line ahead of the others. It's a shortcut.

The car shoots across the broad valley and low mountain ranges south of Oaxaca before yielding to a long flat straight and an hour of easy, open-throttle driving before reaching the Pacific edge of the Isthmus of Tehuantepec.

—This is where we change course, Panama says.

The highway stops. At its end is a T in the road and a twenty-foot cement bank, brand spanking new, an engineering marvel considering the rough terrain. Panama makes a screeching, ninety-degree right turn onto a new road and then a left in between two high cement walls. There are no other cars. The highway is not yet open to the public, and the racers are supposed to go the other way.

They pass a sign with the words SLOW, DANGER in Spanish. When Culprit thinks of it later, he remembers the sign but not the Spanish. He remembers the sign but not the curve. The long-body Nash is unable to make it and plunges over the precipice, landing in the mud beside the river.

Panama guns the motor but the auto won't budge.

Since the crash took place at the entrance to the village of Tehuantepec, citizens and officials rush down the bank to see what help they can give.

Away from the car, Panama checks himself to make sure he's in one piece. He focuses his eyes on the precipice above, the area where the Nash had left the road. Then he looks for the girl.

Culprit pulls the camera from the case to shoot the accident's aftermath.

Then they hear it. The roar of a racing car slashing through the river valley. The ground shakes and the people hold their hands over their ears. The sound has a way of surrounding them so no one can tell from which direction the car is coming, but since they are off the road there isn't the need to get out of the way.

Only Panama seems to know where to see the car, and when he sees it, it makes the same mistake he had made, drives off the same precipice, soaring through the air and down toward the river bank. When Panama crashed, there were no people down there. Now there are dozens. The Mercedes lands on top of the crowd before crashing into the rear end of the Nash. The second accident kills the two German racers and four people on the ground including a soldier, a policeman, a bureaucrat, and a news reporter. It also frees the Nash so that it can be driven away from the accident site.

The scene is in pandemonium, as family members weep for their dead loved ones, and police pull the dead race car drivers from their wreck.

Frieda is unhurt, a safe distance from the crash scene, comforted by a Mexican motorcyclist. He is attaching her bag to the back of his bike. When she sees Panama coming toward her, she grabs the motorcyclist by the arm.

He lets her bag fall to the ground, mounts his bike and she climbs on behind him. The two of them speed away leaving her bag behind as Panama feebly makes chase on foot, throwing his fist in the air. Not about to let himself come undone, he shakes an old man off his horse, climbs the horse, and rides off in the direction of the motorcycle.

Culprit catches it all on film.

Through a detective who speaks English, the Mexican authorities will question Culprit extensively and conclude that there were no obvious reasons for either accident other than that the drivers were momentarily blinded by the sun and that sometimes lightning strikes twice.

When it's over, Culprit will drive away in the Nash by himself.

One more leg tomorrow, and this race is history.

The Physic and the Psychic (1968, NYC)

Jill was the last one you'd ever imagine under arrest. She steps outside of the theatre and looks both ways for a phone booth. Two New York City police officers are standing there, waiting. She adopts an air of nonchalance, and likewise, they pretend they don't see her. She turns her back, which is their cue to approach. Sensing they are making a move, she begins to lope away.

—Hold it, lady, one says, grabbing her arm from behind. —Let's see what you have in your purse.

He reaches into it and pulls out a small paper bag.

—Now where did you get your hands on these?

Her heart races. There is no way around it. They won't give her the bag back. She is under arrest. Every impulse tells her to run. They know what she's thinking. They pull her arms behind her back and handcuff her.

It is happening to Neil the Feel, too. A trip to the back room of an East Village bookstore had yielded a briefcase full of smut, which he accidentally left on the train. When he goes to the lost and found counter to pick it up, constables are waiting for him. Riding downtown to get booked, he wonders, did he want to be caught? Is it easier this way?

Curly Batson also is under arrest, but his is a case of mistaken identity. Police are after a purse snatcher who matches C.B.'s description.

—Where did you hide the tommy gun? the officer keeps asking.

—Tommy gun? C.B. had never even heard of a tommy gun before.

They take him downtown, pose him in a lineup with a group of young men who resemble him in age and skin tone, and release him an hour later.

ABBOT JAFFE

Back in Brooklyn with my feet planted on the ground, the tops of buildings are spinning in circles while I am standing still. I'm stuck inside a bottle, and the cap is getting screwed on. Something like that.

I've been bombed many times, from catatonic to comatose, and I've never experienced anything like this, and I didn't even take that much.

It's raining green stamps. It's not part of the trip. A frumpy woman in curlers is beating a rug on the fire escape above me. The carpet must have been covered in green stamps, as they are flying off and into the air and pattering down on me.

I can't feel my mouth.

I'm staggering across the alley, veering toward the brick wall to lean against, stepping over empty tin cans, bundles of newspapers, and wine bottles. I find a paper bag filled with small cardboard boxes. They are calling me to see what's inside. I rip them apart, one by one. Each contains a leather-bound Bible. I'll take them with me, I can sell these. One of the boxes is too light. It can't possibly have a Bible in it. I pull the box apart to find it filled with rolls of tinfoil. I pull apart one of the rolls. It's hashish.

Now the cops are on me. It's like they knew what was in the box and were waiting for me to open it.

—Fuzz, I hear myself saying.

—You're carrying, I hear one of them say.

—It's not mine, I try explaining. (If it were mine, it would be ingested already, is what I don't say.)

—Tell it to the D.A.

My wrists are drawn behind my back. —What's a little hashish, anyway?

Did I say that?

—If you mean, 'What is hashish?' it's like jazz.

Did the fuzz say that? Who said that?

In my jail cell, the stuff is wearing off, or maybe it's passing into another phase where I don't feel its hold on me. Then a bonafide miracle takes place. I see Jesus Christ standing in the corner beside the sink. He's robed, bearded, slight, a Jewish nose, made holy by a halo above him. He's trying to tell me something. I ask him what he wants to tell me. He fades away.

I'm in jail, all alone, left to think about everything that happened that led to this and the mystical appearance of Jesus Christ. They bring in others as the night wears on. The hardened thugs and petty thieves in the cell with me, they are in bad shape. Yet they are no worse off than I am. We wound up in the same place at the same time. The difference is I have a lawyer I can call who's going to get me out of here. Does my lawyer like me? Does my lawyer love me? What was Jesus trying to tell me?

On his first night in jail, Jaffe thought he would go home the next morning. His second night in jail, he realized he might be in there for a while. On the third day, he was released. The charges were dropped. He could go home.

At a bar on Lexingon Avenue, he scribbles furiously on a paper napkin:

Jesus Christ, they have a funny way of taking your name in vain. I see God where you would least expect to find God, places like the Factory and Max's. Where people are the most reckless is where you'll find God the most, and you'll find God in recklessness itself. The God I believe in is less concerned with morality than creation, and has there ever been a creative act that didn't carry with it an element of recklessness?

—What are you writing? asks the bartender.

—Just my thoughts after three days in jail.

—I didn't know you wrote much.

—It's only a napkin.

—I can get you scratch paper.

—I already have everything on the napkin, thanks.

—You still didn't say what it is you write.

—It's nothing. But I'm thinking about writing the book for a musical revue on Jesus' teachings.

—Fantastic. Are you thinking of getting it produced?

—The idea just came to me.

—Who's doing the music?

—I don't know. The idea is still pretty new. Know any composers?
The bartender pauses. —Yeah, I know someone.

—It's one of those things. People all say they know someone. I never run into anyone who writes music personally.

—Yeah, this guy I know, he plays piano in the pit in *The Fantasticks* down at the Sullivan Street Playhouse. Writes mostly for television, you know, jingles, but he's looking to move into musical theatre full time. I think he's your guy.

—I might try writing the music myself. I know I must sound like a lunatic, since I don't play an instrument, but I've never written a musical before, either, and I'm not letting that stop me. I just need someone to show me how to play a few Laura Nyro chords on the piano, and I'm off.

—At least you're not tone deaf. Hey, Jaffe, it's last round.

—It's only afternoon.

—Yeah, and today's Easter.

—Easter? I didn't even know today was Sunday.

—That, too. We're closing up.

—In that case, I'll take one more. Do you know anyplace that's staying open? Maybe a Jew bar. I'm not ready to go home and hit the sack.

—I do know of a party, a party for all you bohemian Village heathen types who don't celebrate Easter. It's to celebrate the unveiling of a painting by an artist, Sheila Somebody, not that I know why you'd throw a party just to look at a painting. It's on Sullivan Street near the playhouse.

No sooner does Jaffe arrive at the party than a familiar person bounds into the room, crying out, —Harpoon! McKenna delivers the line with deep feeling, like a consummate actor, wielding a harpoon hoisted above his shoulder as he darts past the members of the crowd careful not to spill their drinks.

The harpoon fazes a handful of partygoers, and everyone clears out of his way. Once McKenna leaves the room, and chances of getting impaled are gone, the scene continues as it had before his intrusion.

Abbot Jaffe says out loud to no one in particular, —I know him. I haven't seen him in years, but I know him.

—You don't want to go around saying that. You don't want anyone knowing that, says Lafferty from across the room. —I know you, too, by the way. I would recognize those sweat-stained armpits anywhere.

Jaffe hasn't seen McKenna or Lafferty since the return trip from Haiti, more than ten years ago, yet it's no surprise to see them here, up to the same old tricks, not missing a beat.

—I don't get it, Jaffe says, joining Lafferty and waving loosely in the direction of McKenna's exit.

—He'll run in again with the harpoon in twenty minutes.

—What's the point? Is this a joke?

—It's not a joke.

—Then I don't get it.

—Don't think of it as a joke, think of it as social experiment.

—How is that possibly a social experiment?

—The first time he bounded in an hour ago, everyone ducked. After the fifth time, the crowd still moved out of the way, but that was more to avoid getting injured should McKenna slip or trip, but no one sounded the alarms. The key is to watch the new arrivals. Take yourself, for instance. When you saw him, rather than panic, you behaved like anyone else in the crowd, calm and levelheaded. The danger is the same, but people are more used to it. Their sense of the danger is deadened.

—How is that possibly a social experiment?

—It shows that false alarms desensitize people to real danger. You can translate this effect to the deterrent capability of the United States arsenal of nuclear weapons. I'm afraid that if the Bomb doesn't get dropped somewhere sometime soon, Americans will forget the danger it poses and leave the nation more vulnerable.

—This gag is more like satire. For a proper experiment, you'd need a control group and a clipboard.

—The United States needs to find a target soon or the complacence at home will be just as bad as a massive surprise attack.

—Next you'll be telling me you're voting for Nixon.

—I am voting for Nixon, unless Goldwater runs again.

—That's bunk. I know you.

—You don't know me.

—Did it occur to you that no one takes the harpoon seriously since we are not underwater?

—Harpoons work fine out of water.

—A harpoon out of water is just a spear.

—Harpoons and spears are equally sharp.

—Oh, yeah, do you know what I think? Jaffe asks. —I think McKenna has a real talent.

—How do you mean?

—When he ran in last time, yelling *harpoon*, he sounded so sincere. It's not easy to yell *harpoon* and sound sincere.

—I know what you mean. He is extraordinary. I lie awake at night trying to yell *harpoon* the way he yells it, with the same emotion, the same depth, and my rendition is as sorry as it gets.

—Your neighbors must adore you.

—Yeah, they're good sports.

McKenna, with the harpoon stowed away in a coat closet, joins them in conversation, shaking hands with Jaffe.

—It's a wonder the two of you are ever invited to parties, Jaffe says.

—No kidding, McKenna replies.

—We're never invited to parties, Lafferty says. —We only go to parties when we're not invited.

—It's either that or never go to parties.

—We used to go to wedding receptions for people we didn't know. McKenna would goad people into singing, then as soon as the singer would reach full voice, he would lob a huge piece of cake into the singer's mouth with a slingshot.

—Why'd you do that?

—He thought it was funny.

—I didn't think it was funny.

—It was a social experiment.

—Now I know you're pulling my leg.

—It was funny.

—A person could have choked. The way I remember it, the two of you were always pulling stunts, like on the *Candid Camera* show.

—*Candid Camera* is only funny because there is a camera, Lafferty says. —The victims of Funt's pranks are only victims because they are on camera. McKenna and me, we never had a camera. Funny to think we used to be on a film crew.

—We need a camera.

—Is the Sheila Fauntleroy whose painting will be shown tonight the same Sheila who was our film editor in Haiti, our film editor with no film to edit?

—You mean the Sheila who hid her paintings of the nude in the bath of her pension and thought it was so clever that she was keeping us from finding them? It's a different Sheila.

—I never knew Sheila's last name. I wonder what became of her.

—She's in Brooklyn. She and her artist's model broke up a year ago.

—Belinda Ballard?

—Belinda moved out to the coast.

—I wonder whatever became of Mislove. Ever hear from him?

—He's still involved in theatre. Fortunately for the theatre, only as a spectator.

—I suppose that's fitting.

—Mislove is the type of person the theatre needs. He has given up on the desire to act, direct, and write. He's the ideal spectator type. He remains quietly in his seat when the scenes are hushed, laughs heartily when the moment presents itself, and applauds raucously at the end of a deserving performance. I figure there need to be at least one hundred people just like Mislove for every working actor or director.

—How about you? Weren't you writing plays about nuns?

—The unions, the gossip, the publicity, the star system, the three-year run. I'm done with that.

—I'm with Stupid, McKenna says, making a voice.

—I'm Stupid, Lafferty says, following suit.

—I am writing a musical, Jaffe says.

—I advise you against it. You shouldn't try your hand at creativity. You should just leave that to professionals.

—I just decided today to write a musical.

—Let me give you advice. Don't shoot for the stars. Shoot for off-Broadway, because that's where it's all happening, and if the show's a smash, Broadway will come find you.

—What type of musical?

—I'm thinking it's a musical revue.

—I just saw *Oh! Calcutta!*

—I can give you the number of a composer.

—Let me give you more advice.

— . . . I don't have a name or song or even a single line of dialogue, just some ideas and a main character, Jesus Christ.

—Let me give you advice. You need investors. Once you have Mr. Deep Pockets in place, the rest is a cinch.

—Why Jesus?

—How I came to it is quite funny actually. For so long, people were offering me good news, and not just the good news but the Good News for Modern Man. Jaffe holds his hand over his mouth in case anyone is reading his lips from across the room. —Then I found out it was secret code meaning marijuana.

Lafferty and McKenna release a sarcastic gasp.

—It's originally an expression from Jesus' teachings, but I didn't know that. Was raised outside of the church. Now that I know it, I have traded in one good news for another. Whatever that high is that comes from marijuana, I can get from Jesus.

—Does that mean you used to smoke marijuana?

—Quite heavily, but don't tell UNESCO. I might ask them for a job if my show flops.

—If the drug-addled and feebleminded are actively seeking out the Good News, there must be something to it.

—Are you high now? Lafferty asks.

—Yes, on Jesus.

—Every time I run into people from the good old days, Lafferty says, —their hair is longer and their perspectives are even more far out, but you take the cake. High on Jesus, that's a first. These days, hair grows too fast for my ability to keep up with all that's happening.

—I saw Sandy Koufax on the street in Brooklyn, Jaffe says. He's smaller than me. If you would look at the two of us side by side, I look stronger. He can throw a baseball. He can really throw a baseball. Our heads are the same size. It's so different what's inside of them. He's a genius when it comes to baseball. What do I know? I know hashish. I know the Good News for Modern Man.

—There is a bigot hiding among you, says McKenna in a booming stage voice with the air of someone engaged in a different conversation. —There is a queer hiding among you. I will shake hands with you but I don't know where your hand has been, and if I think about it, it makes me sick.

Abbot Jaffe, —I'm working on the book, but it's loose. It's all the book I could fit onto a bar napkin.

—You're writing your Jesus musical on a bar napkin. That's priceless.

—It's a musical revue, so I need songs, but many of the lines will be improvised by the actors. All's I'm writing is the scaffold, the situations and where the songs fit in. I am beginning to see it as a rock musical, like *Hair*, though based on the Gospel.

—And you want me to compose the music?

—I didn't know you wrote music.

—It's because you think I'm Jewish. I'm not Jewish. I look Jewish, and my name sounds Jewish, but I'm not Jewish. You know, Jesus was a Jew.

—The name McKenna doesn't sound Jewish.

—Leonard Bernstein is a Jew.

—Leonard Bernstein writes music.

—I was thinking of writing the music myself. It's all very personal to me. I'm looking for help in finding a producer.

—That's where you need a Jew.

—I wrote down an address on the back of this napkin for you, it's for Leonard Bernstein, it's a small apartment where he works. Go there and meet with him, tell him your idea, he'll help you.

—Leonard Bernstein is Jewish. Why would he help me with a musical review about Jesus?

It was a fine idea to call on Leonard Bernstein, whose friends belong to the the literati and the intelligentsia, and who could help Jaffe mount his musical. The Bronx neighborhood where the address scrawled on the napkin led him doesn't seem like the type of place where you would find Leonard Bernstein. The address is a tenement. Jaffe opens the gate, climbs seven flights of stairs and arrives at a door half-open. The force of his knock pushes the door open the rest of the way.

It's a chair-less apartment populated by men seated on the floor. It's not lost on him that all the men are black. Blueprint sheets of machines are spread out in the middle of the floor. Nowhere in the room is Leonard Bernstein. Nowhere in the room is a piano.

—Pardon me, I have the wrong place.

Jaffe turns to leave, but not before one of the men is blocking his path to the stairs. Jaffe recognizes him.

—Henry Greathead.

—The name is Henry 7X.

—You don't remember me, we lived in Haiti back in the summer of '55. Abbot Jaffe.

—I've never seen you before in my life.

—Henry Greathead is your name?

—Henry 7X, the man replies, biting down on the sound of the X.

—Why 7X? Jaffe asks, continuing to engage the man in conversation rather than attempt to leave.

—The X is for my unknown African name, the name that was stolen by slave traders.

—I thought you were French-Canadian, family moved from Eastern Africa to Nova Scotia to spread the Gospel. Moved to Lowell, Massachusetts. Hooked up with the State Department where you posed, of all things, as a butler, but we all knew you were much more than that. I know you.

Henry makes eye contact, a sideways glance, tuning in to the reaction of the others who have gathered behind Abbot Jaffe. With a wave of his hand, the man signals his compatriots to stand down and retreat into the apartment.

—See Henry, I knew you'd remember me.

—I've never seen you before in my life.

—Then how did I know your name is Henry?

—I'm not the only black man named Henry in New York. For instance, there were six Henrys in the Nation of Islam before me. What are you doing here?

—Do you know, is this where I can find Leonard Bernstein?

—Does this look like where you can find Leonard Bernstein?

—He's supposed to help me get backing for my musical.

—Get out of here, Henry 7X says again, articulating every word.

—I was on my way. You don't have to be rude about it, Henry.

—White devil.

—Touchy! Jaffe says, walking around the man and down the hall toward the stairs.

After walking down a few flights, Jaffe hears what sounds like a stampede charging down the stairs. He turns around to see one man after him, Henry 7X.

—Can I help you? Jaffe asks.

—No.

—Why'd you come after me?

—They sent me to kill you.

Jaffe recoils.

—Man, I am pulling your leg, Henry says. —Since when can you not take a joke?

—What is this all about? I can understand why blacks are so angry because of slavery and racism, but Henry, you're French-Canadian.

—I am African. I bear the brunt of slavery's vestiges and never wanted any part of it. I don't have a problem with people, but people sure have a problem with me, which makes it my problem, and if it's going to be my problem, it's going to be everyone's problem.

—You used to say it all the time. Your family never was in slavery.

—It was a different kind of slavery.

—You come from a line of missionaries.

—Christianity is the slavery my family suffered.

—It's probably the wrong time to mention the musical I'm writing is about Jesus Christ.

—I'm not interested.

—Leonard Bernstein is Jewish, I have no idea what I am, you're Muslim. The three of us, we make the perfect team to write a Jesus musical. The Father, Son, and Holy Ghost.

—I suppose that make me the Holy Ghost.

—Damn it, Henry. I'm already getting second thoughts. Maybe I should leave playwriting to the Lyle Misloves of the world. I'm still bothered by Haiti. Do you know what was strange? How the nursing student had a hysterical pregnancy, but then the girl died, and we all knew we were going home, and then we went home, and I had a feeling that the girl didn't really die in the same way she never really was pregnant. It was like we knew what was happening, and we didn't know anything. I didn't understand your role. You were a spy?

—I was no spy.

—You were spying on us?

—That's a delusion.

—You were reporting to the U.S. Department of State, you and Culprit.

—There was nothing to report.

—You were on the take.

—I cashed a paycheck cut by the United States Treasury. What was I supposed to do, frame it?

—They paid you.

—I didn't make out like a bandit.

—You never said much to me or the other Useless Bums, just Culprit.

—You never had much to say to me. Culprit and me, we were on the same wavelength.

—What were those diagrams?

—What diagrams?

—The blueprints on the floor of that room upstairs.

—That was nothing.

—Henry, level with me.

—Sure.

—On one hand, you might all be TV repairmen.

—Sure.

—On the other hand, you and your black nationalist buddies might be building a bomb.

—You don't say.

For an instant, Jaffe begins to flail before restraining himself, —Henry, tell me please it's not an A-bomb.

—Do my brothers and I look like the Rosenbergs?

—Tell me it's not a nuclear bomb.

—What's the difference? Either way, people die.

—You're kidding. You're pulling my leg. Why are people always taking out their punch lines on me?

—You're right, those diagrams are not a bomb.

—Thank you.

—Those diagrams are for an object far more deadly and beautiful than the bombs of your wildest dreams.

—Is it or is it not a bomb?

—It's the Mother Plane.

—I've never heard of it.

—That's because you and me, we don't travel in the same circles, and I doubt you've seen the Mother Plane before unless you've spent time in orbit, which I doubt because freaks like you aren't exactly the astronaut type. The Mother Plane is the largest mechanical object in the sky, it fills the space of one hundred football fields, and it was designed by the finest minds in the history of the human race. Its bombs are constructed from the toughest steel and it can carry the payload of 1,500 bombing planes. It's capable of staying in space for six months at a time, and it will be touching down soon. You better believe I will be there.

—What's the purpose?

—Before 1968 is out, the Mother Plane will bring about your country's doom. The white devils will perish, and our black brothers will join us in the cosmos.

—That sounds like Ray Bradbury. It's all made up.

—You wouldn't know the difference.

—Someone is feeding stories to you.

—You sound like just another white devil.

—You know that mumbo jumbo isn't true.

—You sound like just another white devil, and maybe when the massive destructive force of 10 million megatons is raining down on your head, you'll change your mind.

—I'm terrified of the Soviets, I'm terrified of the Chinese, I'm terrified of Mayor Daley and Richard Nixon and Hubert Humphrey and Fidel Castro and Ho Chi Minh, but I'm not terrified of the Mother Plane. If it exists, it's like an earthquake or a natural disaster. If it comes, there was no preventing it, and until it does, there's no point in worrying.

—The Mother Plane exists. The only uncertainty in my mind is whether it will rain down destruction on all you white devils. You can talk to my brothers in that room upstairs, and they will tell you about that happy day, the happiest day in the history of the human race, but you're not talking to them, you're talking to me, and I will tell you what it means if that day never comes. It doesn't mean the Mother Plane doesn't hold the power, no. It means we won't unleash it, and the reason we won't is because that's what you would do. What makes us who we are is that we are not you. I may be black and treated like a nigger all my life, but at least I am not like you. I would never trade places with you. Now you go and write your play about Jesus Christ, but ask yourself who is Jesus is speaking to. Is he speaking to you? Is he speaking to me? What exactly is Jesus saying? Ask yourself is he any different from me, except I'm not claiming to be God. Ask yourself is it Jesus or me you should be writing your play about.

Later that afternoon on the northern edge of Little Italy, Abbot Jaffe sees another familiar face, Culprit Clutch on the other side of the street, but he quickly disappears. Before Jaffe can cross the street to catch him, pandemonium breaks out. A purse snatcher picks the wrong woman to accost and is getting pummeled in front of a pizza joint. A crowd circles the scene, and the purse snatcher can't get in a lick in against the wiry blonde drag queen.

—I know you from somewhere, Jaffe says to the blonde who is using the purse snatcher as a punching bag.

—That's the oldest line in the book, Charlie, the blonde says in a thick British accent.

—It was Haiti, summer of '55. A passenger plane made an emergency landing. They had a plane hopper. A stowaway was holding onto one of the wings, and they flew like that all the way from New York.

—It wudn't me. You musta been drunk.

—He was a British spy. He offered everyone gum.

The purse snatcher frees himself from the blonde's grip and runs off.

—It wudn't me, the blonde says, dusting himself off, checking his face with the mirror in his compact. —Now buzz off.

Culprit Clutch had drunk himself blotto in a hotel bar and stepped out onto the sidewalk to find his way home. That was when he first saw Josie in New York.

She was across the street, opening the door of a taxi. He stumbled in her direction, off the curb, meandering into the street. His head was bursting into flames. It was the rye whiskey coursing through his bloodstream. He could barely walk but started to run. Tires screeched as fist-waving drivers avoided running him down. By the time he was halfway across the street, her taxi had vanished. It had turned invisible among so many identical taxis. Then he saw her again, a gray blur through the rear-door window glass, and she made eye contact with him. He couldn't follow. This time his legs wouldn't move.

What mattered was he had seen her and will see her again. She is here, and next time, he will be ready. He will find her again in this city of millions and won't stop to consider that when he saw her in the taxi she was on her way out of town.

He can't allow himself to be drunk. He can't allow himself to be slow. His first step will be to improve his physical fitness because seeing her again will inevitably involve a chase. When he chases her next time, it won't be in a car.

He purchases a pair of sneakers and shorts, uses the orange necktie from his only suit as a headband, and sprints in circles around the running track at Columbia. He tires easily and can barely keep his legs beneath him. He will run until it hurts, until his body eats itself and drinks itself from the inside.

Within weeks, his running improves. His legs are rolling beneath him like wheels. His arms keep balance, and by leaning forward, he can go even faster. He will lie in his bed in the moments before falling asleep, staring into the pattern on the ceiling, and sense his body changing out from under him until it doesn't feel like his own body anymore. Next time he sees her, he will keep pace.

It's her, look again, it's not her. See her again from another view: Wait, it is her. Look more closely: It's not her. It's right to think that until you see her again from across the street and make your chase. She climbs into a taxi that races off. He bounces off storefront awnings, across the hoods of idling sedans, and catches up to find it isn't her, just a reasonable facsimile, though the points of similarity are too overwhelming to call it a simple coincidence.

—Next time, he says aloud to no one in particular on the street corner, not thinking whether he sounds crazy.

A man standing a few feet away in Groucho glasses, a fez, and a hospital gown open at the back is talking loudly to himself, —Bastard, bastard, blond wigs, blindfolds, Great Society, Great Society, bullshit, bullshit. His rant gives way to a fit of coughing, while Culprit jogs away peering obsessively through the windows of taxis.

What will he say when it really is her? She will pretend she doesn't recognize him. She will think he's a maniac.

When it happens, her hair looks like she just climbed out of a swimming pool, and she carries a leather bag shaped like a tennis racket. She's taking lessons at the Midtown Club. Funny, she never mentioned an interest in tennis.

—Do you know who I am? he'll ask.

—No.

—Do you know who you are? he'll ask.

—Of course, I do, she'll say, —but I don't know you.

He can't say for sure it's her.

He's running full wind in his necktie headband through Central Park the next time he sees her. This time, she won't get away so easily.

In full aristocratic riding gear, she keeps a brisk pace on a steed along the horse trails. He turns on the speed, but her horse gallops away, nimbly hurdling over steeplechase barriers that are too tall for him to scale. He tries a shortcut through the shrubs and trees and finds chain-link fences.

In a clearing he sees two police horses tied to hitching posts. He's not a rider but it's worth taking a chance. He undoes the tie, takes the bridle, and climbs upon the horse. And away they go, herky-jerky, but in the right direction, and catch up to her just outside the stable.

They don't say anything. The horses move together in a circle while neither Culprit nor the woman breaks eye contact.

Up walks the police officer whose horse Culprit has stolen. He lightly swats Culprit on the leg, signaling him to get off the horse. The officer climbs on and trots away without a word.

Culprit stands there, sweaty in his racing-stripe gym clothes, and knows he can only say the wrong thing, so he says nothing. She feels the same, because she doesn't say anything, either. It's clear to them both that this wasn't supposed to happen, nor can it keep happening, nor can they keep it from happening. She climbs down and leads her horse back to the stable.

He watches her walk away and realizes there is no stage direction, no scene to block, no script to follow.

Yet the play is not over. All there is left to do is improvise.

The Transbay Tube
(1965, -68, -72)

1965. It is not lost on our futurist egghead set that the peace sign resembles a rocket at launch.

The rocket is a fitting symbol for peace.

The Space Race is all part of an effort to stave off future war, and a nuclear war is a war to end all wars because under the worst case scenarios, it will leave no one to quarrel. The ultimate consequence is an everlasting peace for no one to enjoy. Aren't wars ultimately over land? I understand that the Cold War involves an ideology, market economics, and Godlessness, but it's over land where there these beliefs are held.

That's why space is peace.

In space, there is no land to fight over. Space is limitless. Everything belongs to everyone. As far as ideologies go, there is enough room up there for people to think what they want to think. Space is so vast that you can peer into it and see the face of God or not. If you're of the Soviet persuasion, maybe it's the face of Karl Marx.

Space is a boundless source of freedom.

It's not a race to space. Space ends the race.

Get us to space. The sooner the better, I say.

The task at hand is not finding the people with the skills who can get you there, as that barrier has already been broken.

The task at hand is finding people who can make space a place for the human race.

1968. Every child in America wants to grow up and be an astronaut, and a bushel load of grown men do, too. Sometimes you don't want the best and brightest. The best and brightest always have an ulterior motive. They think of space as a stepping-stone to business success or public office rather than an end itself. Sometimes you need a man who's not in it for himself. Rather, all you need is the right man for the job. That's why God gave us Keith Clone.

—What makes Keith Clone special?

—He's an excellent mechanic, but what's more, he's an unfeeling man.

—Aren't we all?

—He's unfeeling in another way. Physical stresses don't get to him. G-forces, extreme variance in temperature, solitude, you name it, he doesn't feel it.

—What planet does he come from?

—He's one of Bayard Pumphrey Huffy's Haiti men from back in the day.

—One of those.

—Bayard Pumphrey Huffy. Now there's a name I haven't heard in a while. I wonder what the old dog is up to.

—More of the same. Floating swimming pools is the last I heard.

—You're pulling my leg.

—The Soviets invented floating swimming pools in the twenties.

—For Pete's sake, that's the dumbest idea I ever heard. Why do you need to float a pool on a body of water?

—Apparently, they're cheap to build and easy on the plumbing.

—I'll say.

—The idea never took off.

—It doesn't surprise me.

—With their floating pools, the Soviets made an interesting discovery for the physical scientists. When a team would swim across the pool, the force would propel the pool in the opposite direction. It's a property of physics called reaction. It's natural that when Americans caught wind of the idea, their first inclination was to swim a pool across the ocean with all the fanfare of Lindberg's flight.

282

—That sounds marvelous. I never heard about it.

—It never happened, got stuck in red tape. The only one still pressing the issue is Bayard Pumphrey Huffy. The idea he's selling is a flotilla of swimming pools filled with Olympic swimmers bound from New York to Haiti.

—Still fixated on Haiti. Some things never change.

—Haiti is a dead horse. These days, the theatre is outer space. Someone should ring Bayard Huffy and let him know.

1972. —I've been reading old files, because there is nothing else to do. Found this one on Keith Clone. His last known whereabouts: Project Magic Island.

—His name resurfaced a few years back. He's now on the crew building the Transbay Tube. Underwater work, frogman gear, welding sections of the steel together.

—Let's bring him aboard the Skylab project. We know him already. They say he's the unfeeling man.

—I'll send someone to make contact.

KEITH CLONE

Once the electric trains start to run between Oakland and San Francisco, you won't get the smog, not that smog would form beneath the bay.

The 30-foot diameter sections of double-barreled tube were constructed in the Bethlehem Steel Yards. If you placed one of the sections on dry ground, it would be bigger than a house. The tube is double-barreled so trains can run simultaneously in opposite directions and flexible enough to withstand the water current and earthquakes.

The crews working above the surface float the sections of tube across the bay, then submerge them under the Bay Bridge. I'm with the diver crew which attaches and welds the sections together underwater.

When the tube is sealed, connected, and complete, I am lucky enough to participate in the first test rides aboard the Brutalist-style cars built by Rohr Industries, a company that made a name for itself in aerospace engineering. Along for the ride are engineers, politicians, and news reporters.

—What are your impressions so far?

—I liked the stiff wind and the smell of the wheel grease as the train entered the station before we boarded.

—It's like being in a train station on the moon.

—I'll bet you ten bucks you can't do it.

—What's he going to do?

—Hold his breath all the way from West Oakland to Embarcadero Station.

—I'll put down ten bucks says he can.

—The Tube might last five minutes.

—If there's anyone who can do it, it's our underwater welding magician, Keith Clone.

—What kind of stunt is this?

—It makes perfect sense to me. If you're underwater, you might as well hold your breath.

—When I was a kid, we always said it was good luck if you could hold your breath all the way through a tunnel.

—He can get his name in the *Guinness Book of World Records* before anyone else has a chance to try.

The train leaves the station and enters the Tube.

—My ears just popped.

—I don't know if we can run with it sounding like that.

—Maybe as the wheels wear, it won't be so loud.

—It could also get worse.

—Anyone on the train who wants to read the paper can forget about it.

—Its sound is eerie.

—It's like the wheels are screaming. It's like human voices, operatic and atonal, a chorus to accompany a nightmare.

—Stone-faced commuters won't care. They will be glad they don't have to park in the city.

—Let's look on the bright side. It's a transit works project that will alter the region.

—They say the Tube is earthquake proof. Underneath the bay is the last place I would want to be during the Big One.

—It'll be safer on one of these trains than on Market Street.

—The Tube is a miracle. No way around it.

—The Tube will take the pressure off the Bay Bridge, which is something we all need.

—The Bay Area has the worst traffic on earth. This will help make it better.

—What good are downtown skyscrapers if workers can't get to them?

—That's what troubles me about this. The poor will live in Oakland and work in San Francisco. It's another way to keep the labor cheap in San Francisco, to force the laborers to live outside the city and ride trains.

—The only people who live in Oakland choose to live in Oakland.

—You can't have 50,000 restaurants in the city without an army of low-wage dishwashers. The dishwashers have to live somewhere, and you can't set up beds for them all up on Nob Hill without riling up the rich people.

—Maybe the Presidio can be converted to low-cost housing when the war's over?

—So they can destroy it? The Presidio is far too valuable a piece of real estate. I would rather have it sit as parkland than let the underclass have their way with it.

—My God, he's turning blue!

—Hang in there, man. We are almost in San Francisco.

—Hey, he could have been sneaking breaths this whole time, and no one would know.

—I've been watching him. He hasn't taken a breath once. He's going to make it. Your ten dollars is as good as mine.

Blow Away
Dandelion (1968)

Superman's not welcome here, dig? Not in the Erogenous Space of Golden Gate Park. These winding garden paths lead in circles, lead you straight into the Phantom Zone. Supe's in league with the pigs, you know. Supe is the shining hope of the white master race. Batman's far out. Batman's in tune with the scene. Batman's in line with the freaks. Batman's like me. Batman likes to get high. The Wild Batman of Love.

—We live under the Golden Gates of America, one new nation under God.

—We celebrate and ring in the new. Shit!

—What's that you say?

—Shit?

—No, Golden Gate Park!

—I can't hear you!

—Golden Gate Park!

—What do *you* see in Golden Gate Park?

—I see Atlantis rising out of the duck pond.

—What do you *see* in Golden Gate Park?

—I see rabbits running across the shaking ground.

—What do you see in Golden Gate *Park*?

—I see faces, I see people, I see freaks.

—What makes Golden Gate Park so beautiful?

—Me!

—Are you beautiful?

—Yeah.

—Tell the beautiful people in London, England, about Golden Gate Park.

—Golden Gate Park is full of eucalyptus trees falling from the sky.

—What about the phonies? The people walking around pretending to be in bands.

—They say they are the Diggers, they say they are the Mime Troupe, they say they are the Family Dog.

—They are not what they say.

—Is your name Joseph?

—Call me Eric Clapton.

—I want a baby, Joseph.

—Only God can make a baby, but we can give it a good old-fashioned try.

—Oh, Golden Gate Park, such a dirty spot for an immaculate conception.

—Mary?

—Yes, Joseph?

—Do you love me in Golden Gate Park?

—I love you in Golden Gate Park, Joseph. Why do you speak in riddles?

—A small package bearing the gifts of the kings will arrive for you shortly.

—What's that sound?

—The Dead.

—The who?

—The Who's in London, England. What's your name?

—Mary.

—My name is Joseph, and we're from San Francisco, California. Tell me what do you like about me?

—Everything.

—Do tell.

—I like your clothes, I like your hair, I like your flowers, I like your fleas, I like you.

—If I was a boy in London, England, I would want to know all about Golden Gate Park.

—I want to know all about the boys in England.

—I want to know about the girls in England, because my name is Joseph, and you are. . .

—Mary.

—What else do you do in Golden Gate Park?

—We ride the rainbow wheels down.

—And?

—We slide with our angel wings on.

—And?

—We bust the animals out of the zoo and call them by their secret names.

—And?

—We do crazy things.

—I saw Jesus Christ walking the paths of Golden Gate Park, and he told me my name is Joseph and yours is Mary.

—He called me Ma and you his old man.

—Ethos.

—Buncos.

—Pathos.

—Eros.

—Heroes.

—Queeros.

—Cheerios.

—Zeroes.

—Lobos.

—The wolves are at the door.

With her Mary Tyler Moore mouth and hair in a bun, Belinda Ballard doesn't look like her bohemian friends, nor does she try. She doesn't care if they think of her as square. She doesn't care if they think of her as thirty. (She just turned.) She's in it for the poetry and not much else. Poetry is her soul's salvation. Her first published poem is in the *Evergreen Review*, hot off the press.

She takes her date's hand and pulls him toward the bookshop, but Mario drags his heels, reluctant to enter, instead making comments about the sign in the door.

—I have always found *entrance* such a curious word, he explains to her. —You can pronounce it with the accent on the second syllable and change its meaning. *Entrance* becomes *En-trance*: You are now in my power and beholden to me. I'll charm you like snakes, and the music playing is of Morocco. It's fitting that shops want to en-trance you before you go in, that's the ol' high and mighty capitalist spirit at work.

Once inside, he wants to drift toward the heart of shop, where the novels are, but she holds him back, near the entrance, where they shelve the literary journals. She wants him to find the one with her poem. She wants him to find it by accident. She wants him to read it and dig it.

—Don't you like poetry? she asks.

—It's not my bag.

—Then you haven't been reading the right poems.

—I've read plenty of poetry, but it's not my scene.

—What is your scene?

—Everything from Shakespeare to Tarzan the Ape Man, except poems.

Off the rack, she picks the *Evergreen Review* with Mexico City on the cover and hands it to him.

He doesn't know what to do with it.

—Read, she instructs.

He skims through the pages, confused about what she expects him to find. Perhaps Shakespeare or Tarzan. He passes by her poem without stopping.

Belinda rips the journal from his hands, throws it on the floor, and bursts through the exit.

Storming away, she gestures as if to tear her hair out. Her arms land in an outstretched position and nearly sock the faces of passersby on the sidewalk. So thick her emotion, she becomes oblivious to the scene: a cat playing guitar, a chick on tambourine, painted faces, wild clothes, a tour bus filled with gawking tourists from the Midwest.

Belinda walks quickly down the sidewalk in the direction of Stanyan, toward the park.

—I am such a lost soul, she says to herself. —I am so lost.

It's becoming her mantra. She says it so often that it becomes true.

Even when it's filled with people, Golden Gate Park is large enough that Belinda can make herself disappear.

Say there's this kid on the corner named Brian who arrived by Trailways from What Cheer, Iowa, and he's already made a family for himself. It's a new kind of family where no one's related and they all share a bed. The bed's not big enough for all of them, so they take turns sleeping. Don't let sleeping fool you. It's not the bed's only purpose, wink-wink. Some members of Brian's new family sleep about as often as they bathe, which is to say hardly ever.

They are hippys.

Martha didn't have to travel far to move in with the rest of them, just up from San Jose. Martha has found her purpose. It came to her the first time she tried LSD. When she came down from her trip, she could no longer remember what her purpose was. She took more trips trying to recover it, and the more she tripped, the farther away her purpose moved from her. Her only comfort was in knowing she had one. Then Kenny explained it, because he knew. Tripping was her purpose, tripping for nothing other than the sake of the trip.

Walter Beechwood was a trip all by himself.

He drove in from Sacramento and showed up looking for his daughter June outside a Family Dog dance at Longshoreman's Hall. There was no way the dance's organizers would let someone so square in the door on a night when the Airplane were playing, so Walter Beechwood tried again a few minutes later in a Prince Valiant wig and costume jewelry love beads. The dance organizers still didn't buy it and wouldn't let him pass. That's when Beechwood found Jimmy, a lanky hippy kid in Levi's jeans and glasses with his hair tied in a small bow in the back. Walter Beechwood had the nerve to pay Jimmy ten dollars to fetch June from the Hall. With her school photo concealed in his palm, Jimmy steps inside and checks out all the girls. June isn't hard to find. He asks her to dance, which is old-fashioned, like people do when they are their parents' age. Jimmy and June dance beside each other, the colors from the Day-Glo light show reflecting off their shiny faces. He asks her if she'd like to step outside and get high.

She falls for the ruse.

Once she's outside, Walter Beechwood pounces, pulling his daughter by the wrists back to his car. She looks over her shoulder, back to Jimmy, giving him the saddest look that kid has ever seen. He knows then that it is love. He stands under the lights outside the Longshoreman's Hall basking in the glow before realizing that if he doesn't go to her now, he may never see her again.

At the Standard station, he steals an idling chopper and makes haste after Walter Beechwood's car now starting up the ramp to the Bay Bridge.

Not so fast, Jimmy! When it comes to the Hell's Angels, the last thing you want to do is mess with their bikes. When they see him racing away on one of their hogs, it can mean one thing: That kid is a dead man. One by one, Hell's Angels race out of the gas station parking lot after that chopper-stealing cocksucker.

Yet no matter how riled up the Angels' emotions, they're no match for a hippy boy in love.

Faster, faster, the Angels can't keep up with Jimmy. The chase slows as Jimmy catches up to Walter Beechwood's station wagon. Then the Angels get it, as if the message were delivered by angels in the heavens, and the Hell's Angels on earth merely catching wind. The kid has his reasons. The kid is chasing someone else. That someone else must be one by-God son of a bitch who deserves to have his head bashed in for that kid to steal a bike like that. In what they believe to be an act of Christian charity, the Angels decide the least they can do is help the kid give chase.

All the while, Walter Beechwood has no idea that the menacing array of discombobulated headlights in his rearview mirror are following him.

Beechwood pulls off the freeway in Vacaville at a diner for a predawn breakfast and cup of coffee. June has become subdued. No sooner are the father and daughter seated than Jimmy sits down at their table. Beechwood is at first confused, what the hell is that kid doing here? Then he feels antagonized. He is about to ask the waitress to call the police when four lumbering Hell's Angels pull up chairs.

–What the heck! Walter Beechwood says. — Please let's talk about this reasonably.

–Can I buy you a cup of coffee? one Angel asks.

–That's gracious of you to offer, Beechwood replies.

–Cream and sugar?

–Just sugar, please.

–One lump or two?

–Three, please. I have a bit of a sweet tooth.

With that the Angel drops three sugar cubes into Beechwood's coffee.

All that's left to do now is wait.

Before long, the Angels have their chopper back and Jimmy and June are driving Walter Beechwood's car back toward San Francisco, while Beechwood spends the dawn lying on his back among tomato crops watching a circling seagull above signal the encroaching dawn and wondering how the ocean got stuck in the sky.

Don't look now, but back in the family house in San Francisco, that's Margorie as she arrives home and goes to bed. She squeezes herself in on the left side, causing the sleeping body on the bed's right edge to fall out onto the floor. It's Brian, and it's time for him to wake up and go find something to eat. It's 4 p.m., and the scene outside is just as he left it, a cat with guitar, a chick on a tambourine, the same painted faces, the same wild clothes, another tour bus filled with yet more square tourists from the Midwest pasting their noses to the glass, because they have never seen anything before quite like the American hippy.

BELINDA BALLARD

The thing about Golden Gate Park is you can hide out but not for long. People are crawling around the park like ants. When you find a place all to yourself, someone else with the same thought will arrive there soon. Hippy Hill is swarming, and no one will leave you alone at the Conservatory of Flowers, so I drift toward the empty stadium. It's the spot in the park that draws the greatest crowds when there's a football game and the most silence when there is not.

The turnstile is unlocked, and I climb several stairs to find the passage leading into the stadium landing where I can have my pick of thousands of empty seats. At the instant I realize how glad I am to have all this space to myself, I see someone else: a woman doing the same thing as me, choosing a seat just on the other side of a railing. She's wearing dark sunglasses and a black leotard top and flowing black pants and sandals with three buckles and straps. Just another San Francisco freak.

She takes off her glasses, our eyes lock, and I know her. Then again, maybe I don't. I thought it was Josie, the girl in Haiti with the hysterical pregnancy who died and came back not herself and then walked away from Culprit Clutch and me into the sea.

I call her name, but she won't turn her head. She stares toward the field below.

—Fine, if you're going to be that way! I yell, then plunk down in my seat and sulk.

I tell myself not to turn my head and look, I tell myself to fix my eyes on the field and ignore her, then I realize that rather than clear my mind, which is why I came here, I'm only thinking about her. Not about her, about everything.

I never think about Haiti; it was so long ago. I still think of the view from the Citadelle and seeing it again through Sheila's eyes in her paintings. I still think of the Hiroshima filmstrip they showed us and the Japanese with burns that turned them black. I still think of Culprit Clutch, which means I still think of Josie.

I look in her direction, I can't help myself. She's gone. That is so like her.

She's down in the park by now. She could have gone in any direction. She could disappear into the crowds lining the sidewalks on Haight Street. She could be walking along the offshoot of a trail in the park. She could have gone inside a museum. She could have caught a bus zooming away from here.

She's not lost. I'm the one who's lost.

I might find her if I have patience.

I don't have patience.

In the Victorian-style flat on Cole Street where Belinda lives with six others, the roommate named Ashby steps in with a frail older man with a long beard.

—Hey, get this, Ashby announces to the room. —I've found us a gentleman who's lived on planet Venus.

—Does this look like Venus to you? McKinney asks the old man.

—Venus is silent, the old man says.

—That affirms what I just said. This isn't Venus.

—Venus is silent, but you will soon discover why.

—That gives me the creeps, man, the way you said that.

—Venus awaits your move.

—You're giving me the creeps, man. I'm ditching you, man. Get Sonny to show him the door.

—Hey, did you hear they are putting in an underwater subway from San Francisco to Oakland?

—Cool.

—I am not sure I would like being in a train under the Bay during an earthquake.

—They say the Tube will be the safest place you can be.

—Of course, they'll say that. If you're going to tell a lie, make it a whopper.

—What is there in Oakland anyway? Just a bunch of blacks. Not that I have anything against black people.

—My church is in Oakland, the People's Temple, says Maryanne.

—I don't want to know about it.

—Oakland is the true spiritual center of the Bay Area.

—Yeah, and my mother-in-law is the queen of England.

—They all say, those San Francisco hippys, they're a bunch of rich white kids from the suburbs. Their spirituality is fake.

—That's what the straight world wants you to believe.

—Theatrical, maybe, but not fake.

—You should try my church, the People's Temple. It's in Oakland.

—You keep on saying that. You won't drag me out to Oakland for church, not even on an underwater subway.

—In ten years, everyone will know the People's Temple.

—Signe, why the concerned look? Did I say something wrong?

—This is how I always look.

—No one can be as concerned as that look on your face.

—It's because my grandmother was a Navajo Indian. The look of concern is from my Indian ancestry.

—Has anyone seen Belinda Ballard?

—Not today.

—There's a freak at the door, says he was her date, says she ditched him at a bookshop, says he wants to talk to her.

—Go tell him if she ditched him, she ditched him. 'Nuff said.

—She's not here anyway.

—Go tell him he's barking up the wrong tree. She's thirty.

—She is?

—That's why she's so square, that's why she can't comprehend the scene.

—I don't mind that she's thirty, with that body all sloppy with curves, the way her sweaters hug her torso, that farewell overbite, her eyes pulled back in a way you might call deep set.

—Spoken like a poet.

—I always thought she looks like Mary Tyler Moore.

—Not a bit.

—Mary Tyler Moore is not that tall.

—Belinda Ballard is the only person I know who doesn't have a real overbite who makes herself look like she has an overbite. She pulls her lower jaw in, like this.

—I'm astonished. That looks just like her. You do a terrific impersonation.

—Have you read any of Belinda Ballard's poems?

—She writes poems?

—It's all she ever talks about.

—I guess I've never been able to stop staring long enough to hear a word she says.

—Let me read you part of her poem. I just found it in the new *Evergreen Review*.

—Good for her.

—I'll read the part someone underlined:

People speaking all at once
We cannot hear a word they say
Above the racket of ourselves.

—Doesn't she know how to rhyme?

—I don't think anyone has written a rhyming poem since 1965.

—That's the most narcissistic poem I ever heard.

—I like poems that give you insight into the person who wrote them.

—There's another poem in here, and every line is underlined.

—Is it by Belinda Ballard?

—No.

—Then let's hear it.

I remember waking up on the beach
naked, sweating

—I like this already.

—Shh.

—Are you sure this is not by Belinda Ballard?

—Yes, I'm sure.

sun pouring hard on our sleeping bag.
I had sand in my crotch and mouth and hair.
You stunk of Gallo, sweat,
and long methedrine days.
The bright waters hurt my eyes
and the ocean's life was too strong for me.

A boy and girl rolled their beach ball by us.
They came after it with curious eyes,
but their mother's frightened call came after them,
and they left the red ball
shining
in the burned black bed
of our night's fire.

She must have seen us like I did—
two rotting, glaze-eyed fish,
flies wanting to eat our heads,
just being dead
and smelling in public

—What's that sound?

—The neighbors upstairs are at it again.

—They mean business when she's banging the pots and pans.

—Shh, I want to hear this. Turn down the hi-fi.

From upstairs, the roommates hear a woman's voice, —You want to know why I stopped digging you? It's the way you live, it's your lifestyle. You're a filthy pig. Don't you ever wonder about hellfire? You screw women right and left, and every other word out of your mouth is the Lord's name said in vain. You don't seem concerned about your soul's salvation. When you die, you'll burn for eternity.

A man replies, —I am acting out a part in God's plan.

The woman, —That's great news. You really made my day. I'm glad everyone seems to have a role in God's plan, except me. Maybe I'm the one marked for eternal damnation. I go to church, I pray, I tithe, I treat others with respect. How can you be so pure in God's eyes when you're such a heavy son of a bitch to me?

The man, —There are plenty of others just like you, who will find themselves at the river with a choice to make. It's an easy choice. Accept Jesus Christ as your lord and savior or never cross to the other side.

After that, it's silence, as if they have nothing more to say, or they caught on that the kids downstairs were listening.

—What do you suppose they are doing now? Ashby asks. —Fucking?

—She should walk out on him, Signe says. —She needs to shed her old life like a snake sheds its skin.

—I can turn my life around just by shaking my head and causing dandruff to fall.

—Can you cut out your sarcasm, just once?

The door opens. Belinda Ballard stands there, pale and worn-out.

—Well, well, what have we here!

—I'm Humphrey Bogart's double, here's looking at you, sweetheart.

—I don't fit in with this, Belinda Ballard complains.

—We love everybody, Belinda Ballard. We love you, Ashby says in a troll-ish, sarcastic voice.

—I need to find somewhere else to go.

—These are the times. This is the life. It doesn't get better than this, baby.

—I am such a lost soul. I am so lost.

—This is the place you want to be. You can go anywhere you want, and there's still a war in Viet Nam, still lynchings in the south, and still groovy sounds coming out of London and L.A. You can go to the end of the earth, and you'll still be here. It makes no matter if you stay or go. This is the place you'll take with you.

—The scene is supposed to be about love, but that's not what I'm feeling.

—Love comes from the shared experience of getting high.

—I've done that and never felt love. When I get high, I feel comfort, I get turned on. Love is something different. Love is someplace else.

—You keep on looking, Belinda Ballard.

—I don't want to end up one of those women on Haight Street stinking of camphor and booze.

The silence and the look on their faces signal to her that they think that's what she is now.

—You are all just horrible.

As Belinda runs upstairs with her mind set on packing her things, Terry walks in and greets the others.

—I have been dead these past three days, he says, — I come before you as a ghost.

—You're tripping, man

—Three days.

—Do you know how I know you're tripping? It's the way your face bends and stretches. You look like you're straight out of of your own trip. Why does anyone else here need to drop acid when all we need to do is take one look at you? Terry, you know the house rules. No tripping in the house, unless everyone's tripping.

—I'm a ghost, man. I walk through walls.

Maryanne climbs the stairs after Belinda Ballard and finds her in the bedroom.

—I heard what you said down there, Maryanne says to her. —I used to feel the same way. I felt like a lost soul.

—You seem so put together. What changed?

—I started going to church. There's a church in Oakland I go to. It's called the People's Temple. Everyone's welcome. There are young people and old people, black people and white people. It's a celebration of life, and it changed my life. Belinda Ballard, would you like to come to church with me?

The Mexico City Olympics (1968)

Last time Culprit was in Mexico, he saw eight people die in seconds, and he could have easily been one of them had he not moved out of the way just in time. Now, the seconds tick off his wristwatch, and nothing happens. The landscape remains unchanged. It's a good sign. He can breathe now.

Last time Culprit was in Mexico was 1950. He and Paul Panama were in pursuit of the Carrera Panamericana racers. Culprit was a motion picture photographer, and while most of his footage showed lumbering American cars swishing by the camera, he also captured many crack-ups and human interest stories. No one saw his film, yet he made a name for himself.

The leg leading into Mexico City had ended by early afternoon, so Culprit suggested to his youthful driver, Paul Panama, that they take in the sights of the metropolis. In the central city, they saw a strange sight up in the air.

—Have you seen the saucer?

The words were on everyone's lips, in Spanish, English, Italian, and German.

—Have you seen the saucer?

They all had seen it.

—Have you seen the *flying* saucer?

It was a construction of wood and tin set high on a platform in Mexico City plaza. A little man in green greasepaint with pipe cleaner antennas attached to his ears was driving a miniature car in circles. It was a promotion for the race and a big hit with the car racing crowd.

When Culprit learned people were only talking about that plaza attraction, he realized he had seen something different. He didn't want to call it a *flying saucer*. He didn't know what else to call it. He was standing outside a church in Zacatecas at dawn when he looked up and saw a hubcap-shaped hunk of metal hovering over the treetops.

Another extraordinary aspect of the phenomenon was that it made no sound.

The saucer, for lack of a better word, hung in the sky, then moved off beyond the line of sight. It didn't move fast. It didn't leave a blaze in its wake. It was the picture of silent motion, almost like a balloon in its grace, though not a balloon.

It was a rare moment during the Mexico car racing trip when he wasn't holding his camera, when he wasn't seeing the world through the viewfinder lens. He would have no permanent record of this occurrence, just his memory to rely on, and moments after the saucer passed over the treetops beyond his line of sight, he wasn't sure what he saw. He wasn't sure he saw anything.

So he doesn't think it strange that during his return to Mexico nearly twenty years later something else would happen. While Culprit walks down a barren road in the middle of nowhere, a man is following him. It is August, not the Day of the Dead, yet the man on Culprit's tail is dressed in black tights head to toe with the form of a skeleton painted in Day-Glo orange over his body. Generally, the man's method of hiding whenever Culprit looks over his shoulder is to hang low to the ground. Even in the bright days of summer, it gets so dark in the shade, so many shadows, and that's where the man hides, and as evening sets in, it's harder to see the man and easier to see the skeleton. He reminds Culprit of P.F.C. B.J. Roper-Melo, and he chalks the incidence up to the idea that everyplace must have a man like that.

On the road ahead, Culprit sees a woman walking in his direction. It won't surprise him that he knows her; it's just that kind of day. Her skirt is long, and her arms are crossed, and there's a chill in the air. A sweater is draped over her shoulder, she's not wearing it, and even if she were, it's not enough to beat this chill.

Culprit looks behind him, and the man in the skeleton costume is nowhere to be seen, though he might be hiding among the soft and steep sand dunes whose shape reminds Culprit of the V-2 rocket. He looks in this direction, he looks in that direction, and he doesn't see anyone else. Just the woman who seems familiar although she is still too far away to see who she is.

CULPRIT CLUTCH

We are the only two human beings within miles of here, not counting the man in the skeleton suit. I know you from before. Not only that, but the two of us used to be close. We woke up beside each other once, and not just once, often enough to rub off on each other some. I slept with my head against your shins, your legs locked at the knees. You are Belinda Ballard after all, and I am Culprit Clutch. We stood once, the two of us, staring north across the Atlantic Ocean, and watched it turn bright orange for an instant.

—I half expected to see you here, Culprit. Had you not shown up, though, I never would have thought twice about it.

—I am here on business, the coffee trade.

—Not planning to get rich are you, selling coffee for a nickel a cup?

—The people I work for aren't planning to charge a nickel a cup.

—Where's your vehicle?

—The bus broke down, thought I'd walk. I'd like to walk over to Mexico City and see the Olympics.

—Don't you read the news?

—Not in Spanish.

—It's horrible what happened, Culprit.

—The Olympics haven't even started.

—There was a protest that ended in massacre. They killed students.

—In America?

—In Mexico City.

—I didn't know Mexico had a student movement.

—Mexican students didn't know there was one, either, until they all got together, and the police fired on them.

—What's the body count?

—That's your reaction? Where is your sense of humanity, wanting to know how many dead rather than the quality of the lives lost? Body counts are obscene. The coffee business is just right for you, because you are full of beans.

—I don't know any students in Mexico.

—You know me, and I was there.

—You're a student in Mexico?

—No, but I was just there.

The conversations stalls, as they each know what the other is thinking but don't know how to discuss it.

—Do you still see her? she asks.

—I think so.

—I may have, too.

They pause again. Enough has been been said about that.

—Culprit, how can you be so callous. People died, young people, with their whole lives in front of them.

—Can you tell me one of the victims' names?

—No.

—Did you see anyone struck down in person?

—No.

—Do you have photographs?

—No.

—I can't just feel it. I need an eyewitness account, a photo, some connection to the victims. With nothing, I can only sympathize by hearing the body count.

—You haven't changed much, Culprit. There is no body count.

—A massacre and no one died. Is what you're telling me.

—The government won't say how many dead bodies they collected on the square when the riot ended. The rumor is that the morgue is so full that corpses are lined up along the hallway floors in the police building.

—My God, I don't know what to make of these times.

—Other protesters disappeared.

—Disappeared.

—They wound up in jail, unable to contact their families. Others slipped away to start new lives with new identities. They joined bandito groups and their parents won't admit it. Their parents don't want the police after their children and believe it's better to think them dead.

—Virginia is for lovers, Mexico is for disappearing.

—I could disappear here. People do that, you know. They go into hiding and come to Mexico.

—Why are you here?

—My church is thinking of building a farm.

—Which church?

—The People's Temple.

—Found Jesus?

—No, I found Jim Jones.

—I have heard of Jesus.

—Jim Jones helps people feel better, he helps the poor.

—How do you feel?

—I don't know. You feel so much you stop feeling.

—A fine pair we make.

—I have been thinking of what this would be like, wondering if seeing you would make me want to kiss you.

—Is that how you feel?

—I feel like we've kissed already, like we've kissed so much we're tired of kisses. It's like the world has ended and we're still here, and we are very much alone and far apart and too worn-out to kiss.

—Are the Olympics still on?

—As long as the world comes to Mexico. As long as people are still making money.

—You're more cynical now than when I knew you.

—See that mountain over there? On the other side, it's the Olympics. It's the fastest and the strongest human beings on the planet. From here, you can't see anything.

—We can go to the games, forget anything ever happened, go home together. My mother left me a piece of land.

—Build a quaint colonial style home with picket fence and kids and cats. It's not for me, Culprit.

The Celestial
and the Extraterrestrial (1975)

They shot Keith Clone into space quietly. His name was listed at the bottom of the press release, a last minute addition to the crew after it was reported that one of the regular astronauts came down with a case of the Hong Kong flu. To those in charge of the mission, Keith Clone didn't fit the image of the American astronaut, even though he was athletic, obeyed the law, didn't smoke, and drank nothing with more kick to it than Tang.

Sending Keith Clone to Skylab was less about perpetuating the astronaut image than about making emergency repairs to fix problems that could send the space station barreling back to earth, repairs that the other NASA astronauts didn't have the constitution to endure. Extreme variations in temperature and pressure didn't seem to bother Keith Clone, nor did long working days or extended periods of solitude. He would never complain. The NASA physicians didn't quite understand why, but there was something wrong with Keith Clone's ability to feel, a short circuit in the receptors that send sensations to the brain. He was just as vulnerable as anyone else when it came to danger; he just never sensed it. For NASA, he was an asset.

—Now if we can only make more astronauts just like him, laughed the Skylab project director.

As soon as it reached orbit, Skylab was a battered old bird. The hull was a stage from a Saturn V rocket refashioned as a space station laboratory and living quarters. One of the two solar wings that generate electricity had broken off at launch. The heat shield that keeps the ship's interior from reaching 300 degrees when in the direct sun had ripped off and replaced with what Ground Control refers to as a parasol, though the astronaut crew calls it a tarp.

Keith Clone's assignment is to repair the malfunctioning gyroscopes that steer and propel the space station. The task will require a series of space walks longer in duration than any human being has ever experienced (unless the Russians are keeping secrets about a Keith Clone of their own).

In a few years, the shuttle fleet will be ready and roaring, and crews can remedy all of Skylab's idiosyncracies. However, if the space station continues to lose altitude at the present rate, it could come barreling toward earth, which would be a PR nightmare for the agency. Not to mention, if it falls into the wrong hands, all her secrets would be compromised, and the Soviets would have a glimpse at the true reason behind America's competitive spirit in the Space Race.

The view of the earth from orbit mesmerizes Keith Clone's crewmates. It's the first thing they see when they awaken in their sleeping bags strapped to the wall. (In zero gravity, there is no up or down, so you might as well sleep on the wall to keep the living space uncluttered.) They stare at the earth for hours, new sights emerging as Skylab moves through its orbit.

The earth three hundred miles below is brightly colored, and the refracting sunlight blankets the orb with a bright blue glow. The clouds look like mountains, and the rivers look like blood vessels. Italy, it turns out, does resemble a boot; Michigan, a mitten. They study solar flares through a telescope that blocks all but the sun's corona. They take hundreds of photos of the comet Kohoutek as its streams across the solar system.

On the twenty-first day of their twenty-eight-day mission, crewmates Pysters and Corsi call in sick. To the chagrin of Ground Control, they turn off Skylab's communication devices in order to give their souls a rest after pushing so hard. The preparations for the mission were intense and they have been working nonstop since arriving in orbit. They need a day to stay in their sleeping bags and stare at the earth looking outside the bay of windows.

Keith Clone doesn't get it, how they can stare at the earth all day without growing bored. If Keith Clone could stay in the sack all day and stare at something all day, it would be Colonel Corsi. He can't do that without giving himself away. It's better to spend his waking hours working on the gyroscopes. All he asks of his mates is that they monitor his oxygen supply, which isn't asking too much, not that he can count on them to help if anything goes wrong.

As soon as he's out of the airlock, his crewmates comment about him.

—He makes us look bad, Pysters says.

—He doesn't care how we look, says Corsi. —He doesn't know anything but work.

—He's an odd fellow. If little green men weren't little and green, you could call him one.

KEITH CLONE

It's only happened once or twice back home, that I thought of a man this way. There is just something about Colonel Corsi. I can't take my eyes off of him. That asshole Pysters doesn't make me feel anything. It would be nice if Pysters were back on the ground.

The worst of it is when floating around the cabin, I bump into Corsi. When my face is near his, I want to kiss him.

Houston is monitoring my vital signs. They haven't said anything, but they must think I have a heart problem, the way it races all the time. I just want it to stop.

In his white spacesuit and helmet that make him look like a man from Mars with his oxygen hose, Keith Clone uses a pair of modified garden shears bought at a hardware store in Florida in an attempt to unjam the broken gyroscope parts. He keeps the earth over his shoulder, it's too overwhelming, it sucks him in; looking at it gives him vertigo.

In the third hour of his space walk, he feels a shadow moving behind his shoulder. Before he has time to turn and see what it is, the thought crosses his mind: God Almighty, this is not possible because all there is out here is space.

To turn his head means he has to turn his body and what he sees is remarkable: A humongous craft in the shape of a wagon wheel with windows along its outer rim. Its approach had been silent, as outer space is silent. Through the windows, he can see the craft's occupants just as clearly as they see him. The silence of space is broken by a thumping beat and bassline. He makes eye contact with one spacecraft occupant, a man in an orange shirt and a gold medallion hanging from his neck, a Black Power Afro. The man next to him wears dark sunglasses and is flashing the peace sign. They have nothing more to communicate with Keith Clone, and even if they had something to say, it's outer space and voices do not carry, just the funky beat. The wheel begins to spin so fast it blurs before Keith Clone's eyes and zooms away to corners of the universe unknown.

Pascale's Letter to President Clinton (1995)

19 May 1995

Dear Mr. President:

I hope my letter finds you in the best spirits, and I mean that quite literally. I am writing in reply to the letter you sent me dated 17 May. You congratulated me on the occasion of my 100th Birthday. Mr. President, I am sixty. I am not a young man, but I am not a hundred. Where did the other forty years go? Nowhere on my Citizenship paperwork does it say that I am a hundred. Perhaps it is that the Haitian life is so short that for me turning sixty counts the same as an American turning a hundred. You're not the only person to make this Mistake. My friends tell me they announced my name on the NBC Network Today Show. I am honored. It is amusing. What has caused the confusion? Maybe you've caught my Magic Act.

Of course, I kid you. Now that I have you, I hope you continue reading my Letter. Please bear with me as I introduce myself. The part you will want to read comes later in this Missive. When I came to the United States in 1960, it was with the desire to perform as a Modern Magical Entertainer. I grew up in Haiti to parents who were Bureaucrats. When people hear I am from Haiti, they first ask about the Voudoun. I was taught to ignore the Voudoun, as it was the Religion of the country people, and we lived in the City. What I know about this Religion from my home is what I read in books by American Authors. You can read the same Books and know as much as me.

When I came to New York City, I found no one wanted to pay to see a Black Magical Entertainer with a French accent. So I put on the dark

Sunglasses. I put on a Top Hat and Tuxedo jacket with a tail. I hissed in a coarse Voice. I made a Sign that said I was from New Orleans. Since I was a Black Magician, I called my tricks Black Magic. The tricks were the same as they were before, only my Personality was changed. I terrified Adults with my act, while children found me amusing. I called myself Professor Elf, and People whispered that my real name was Baron Samedi. I did nothing to correct them. At some point, I no longer had to pose. Baron Samedi had become me. Even without my Costume, people called me the Baron. It was all in fun, as my Soul was still my own.

Mr. President, I want to speak personally with You and please do not take me wrong. If you look deep into the Soul of your Soul of your Soul, you know you are not President. I don't say that because you didn't win most of the Vote. I say it because President is what you made yourself and not what You are. You can fool the People into thinking you are something you are not. It's the same as making myself out as Baron Samedi. There is in the Cosmos a Roaming Spirit of the U.S. President that strikes certain persons on the Back. That Spirit never struck You. You know it, and I know it. There's no need to be ashamed.

The important message I have for You is lower yet in my Letter. Read more first. Because of who You are, You are better able to understand me in ways that other presidents do not.

People in the U.S. think there is just One Voudoun. There are Two. The Rada is the Voudoun of Africa. The Voudoun of the New World, of America, is the Petro. The Rada Drummers play on the beat. The Drummers of the Petro play off the beat. While a child in Cap Haitien, I thought the Drummers weren't very good because they never played on the Beat. I did not know about the Petro. The tradition of the Petro is driven by Rage. It's fitting for the Americas and Haiti and the U.S., because these Places were also founded in Rage against their Colonial Oppressors. Once the Colonists were repelled, Haiti turned its Rage on itself. The U.S. also turned its Rage on itself and after that on Poor Countries like Haiti and those in Africa. What did Haiti and Africa ever do to You?

When I came to the United States in 1960, a Rage caught me up.

Here's an example. To this day I cannot understand how the Blacks in the U.S. don't govern themselves. Don't misunderstand me. I believe truly in the Universalism of Dr. King and his Message that we can look past our Differences and get along. However, Blacks in the U.S. suffer from a Lack of Representation. Why not establish a Sovereign Nation of American Africans? There is no Reason why our two Nations cannot coexist side by side in the same Land and Cities.

How the U.S. is now, there are not enough Voters of my Race to win the Elections. Blacks in the U.S. must trust White Politicians to act in their best Interest, but the White Politicians have done nothing to win the Blacks' Trust. This excludes you, Dear Mr. Wonderful President Clinton. I know you have many Black Friends and Supporters. You must admit the Black Vote only counts in close Elections or when there is uncertainly on which way the Black Vote will lean and when Black People vote together as One.

In New York City, I came to meet with Others who like me believed in a Free Black Nation within the U.S., and I saw firsthand the Rage of American White people tear apart this movement through the Drugs and Murder. This is how the U.S. uses its American Rage. You don't realize the mistakes You make. You make the same mistakes on the World Stage. It's easier to stare down a Viet Nam, an Iran, a Libya, a Nicaragua, a Bosnia, and a Haiti when they are not here. They are here. All of those countries are inside the United States. If You must see them as Enemies, then Your enemies are here, too. Your worst enemy is your American Rage misplaced.

The Americans of the U.S. become aggressive and militant when Justice is denied them. U.S. Citizens are tough in a Fight, more than tough when fighting back. The Danger is when you become bored and don't know when to pick your Fights.

I do not write to preach but to reach. Even though I believe that which I said above, I am a Man who doesn't believe the purpose of the U.S. is to beat up on Smaller Nations. I may be one of the few Haitians who believe that.

The Grave Danger at your doorstep is the Death of the Poetic Imagination of your Nation.

I am not one to praise the Spiritual Power of the Voudoun. Yet there is something to be said. The Loa are not fed anymore. They cannot survive when you put them down at every turn. Suppression destroys all that is good inside the Soul and unleashes Reaction and Rage unchecked. The Spirits can no longer support the Host. The U.S. treats everything as a Battle, and this is a Battle that cannot be won. You create in yourself what you wish to destroy. You lose your National Character and are overcome by the Gluttonous.

Be wary, Mr. Clinton, of those who will try to strip your job from you, who will come to Power after you. They will wreak havoc and not think twice. Be wary of Jerry Brown and Boris Yeltsin or any Politician with Nuclear Weapons who welcomes Possession by Malicious Spirits.

Play Music, Mr. Clinton, and put out the Welcome Mat. Celebrate, and stop the Fear. I may only be the Master of a gamut of Vest Pocket Tricks with cards, coins, and pencils, but I know what I am saying.

Ever your Servant,
Pascale LePlace

Acknowledgments

As the author of a rare contemporary American novel that scarcely mentions family, I'd like to thank my family, Jen, Amelia & Grover, and my parents, Dick & Sandy.

Many thanks go out to early advocates and readers: Autumn Whitefield-Madrano, Matthew Hunte, Frank Webb, Karen Parmelee, Mary Duffy, David Duhr, Jess Miele, Spenser Davis, and Erik T. Burns.

Thank you to the readers of the Red Lemonade community whose input shaped the novel in its early stages: Kathryn Mockler, Brian Joseph Davis, Melissa Chadburn, Tsaurah Litzky, R.V. Branham, M.F. McAuliffe, T.G. Bradshaw, Iain Coggins, Terese Svoboda, Dave Sterner, Mikita Brottman, Henry Williams, Richard Fulco, Lucien Quincy Senna, Matthew Bokovoy, Bill Ectric, and many others.

The gorgeous poem ('I remember waking up on the beach . . .)' that appears late in the book was written by Louann Wakefield Kotulski who graciously let me use it here. Its original title is 'My Best Love Poem, To Michael.'

Thank you also to my agent, Laura Strachan, and to Percival Everett, Monica Drake, and Jonathan Evison for supporting the novel.

Thank you to Nora Nussbaum, for copyediting; Luke Gerwe, for designing the book's interior; and Goodloe Byron, for designing the book's cover and his conception of the puppet lizard.

Much love to Maya Deren, William Gaddis, Ishmael Reed, Marguerite Young, Leon Forrest, Robert Altman, Virginia Woolf, and Cole Porter, whose artistic voices many times have lifted the soul right out of my body.

Most of all, my gratitude goes out to the fearless visionaries behind Red Lemonade, Richard Nash and Mark Warholak, and for his undying enthusiasm for bringing this book to life, Brian McFarland.

About the Author

Richard Melo [1968–] landed in Portland, OR after fleeing San Francisco in the early 1990s. California was too costly for someone like Melo with such complete lack of ambition for anything other than the novels galloping along inside his head. While other young people flourished in San Francisco's dot com boom (producing remarkable achievements like pets.com), Melo ran movie projectors and did AmeriCorps in Portland while scribbling away at his first novel. He has now lived in the beautiful Pacific Northwest long enough to have been caricatured on Portlandia (the episode titled 'Grover'), a pleasure all the city's residents will have had by the time the show reaches the mid-point of its fourth season. He has also published two novels.

About The Process
Of Publishing The Book

This is a Red Lemonade book, available in all reasonably possible formats—trade paperback edition and in all current digital editions, as well as online at the Red Lemonade publishing community at http://redlemona.de

A word about this community. Over my years in publishing, I learned that a publisher is the sum of all its constituent parts: yes and above all the writers, and yes, the staff, but also all the people who read our books, talk about our books, support our authors, and those who want to be one of our authors themselves.

So I started the Red Lemonade publishing community, designed to make these constituent parts fit better together, into a proper community where, finally, we could be greater than the sum of the parts.

For more on how to participate in the Red Lemonade publishing community, including the opportunity to share your thoughts about this book, read what others have to say about it, and share your own manuscripts with fellow writers, readers, and the Red Lemonade editors, go to the Red Lemonade website http://redlemona.de

Regards,
Richard Nash
Publisher